BEACH

SOUL BEACH

Kate Harrison

Indigo

First published in Great Britain in 2011
by Indigo
This edition first published in 2012
by Indigo
a division of the Orion Publishing Group Ltd
Orion House
5 Upper St Martin's Lane
London WC2H 9EA

An Hachette UK company

1 3 5 7 9 10 8 6 4 2

A catalogue record for this book
is available from the British Library.

ISBN 978 1 78062 033 6

Typeset by Input Data Services, Bridgwater, Somerset

Printed and bound by CPI Group (UK) Ltd, Croydon, CR0 4YY

The Orion Publishing Group's policy is to use papers
that are natural, renewable and recyclable products made
from wood grown in sustainable forests. The logging and
manufacturing processes are expected to conform to the
environmental regulations of the country of origin.

www.orionbooks.co.uk

For Mum, Dad and especially Toni –
because sisters are forever ...

The girl is dead, no doubt about it.

That face, the one that launched a billion internet clicks, is flushed, as though she's spent too long in the sun. Somehow, her skin still glows – one of the TV critics called her dewy – but that won't last, of course. After the struggle, her hair was tangled, but now it's combed straight and fanned out against her pillow. Like Sleeping Beauty.

Is she truly beautiful, or just pretty? When she was alive, there was no doubt, because the whole package – the face, the confidence, the walk, and that voice – was irresistible. Now she's still, it's easier to be objective.

Ah, let's be charitable. Let's call her beautiful. The creamy white dress is draped oddly and it looks a little slutty, but it's too much work to change it now. Dead weight is hard to shift.

Her eyes are closed. A few seconds ago, at least ten minutes after she stopped struggling, the lids fluttered several times, as though she were dreaming. Of an eternal spotlight, maybe? Then, when it seemed that she might need to be smothered again, she stopped moving. It must have been a last reflex.

Or maybe that was the exact moment that she went. Where is she now? Lying in a soft meadow, with butterflies and bees dancing around her? Or on a tropical beach, where the sea laps against her body?

It is time to go. But at least whoever finds her won't be haunted by her appearance. For a corpse, she is anything but lifeless.

1

The first email from my sister arrives on the morning of her funeral.

I know. What kind of sick freak checks her email before she goes to see her sister being buried? But sometimes it hurts so much I feel like I've got acid in my veins instead of blood, and that's when I go online.

Online, everything's *normal*. No inquests, no detectives, no TV cameras. Just Facebook updates about who's dating who. And junk emails from African princes offering me a share of their fortunes. Oh, yeah, and emails from dead people. Not *quite* so normal.

I almost miss the message, and as soon as I do see it, I know it can't be real. It's a sick coincidence or someone's hacked her account, the one she used to send me college gossip and drunken photos.

But even though I know it's a hoax, my finger locks onto the mouse and I can't breathe as I wait for the message to load . . .

To: AliceinWonderland@forsterfamily.co.uk
From: Meggie@MeggieForster.net
Date: September 15 2009
Time: 10:05:09
Subject:

[THIS MESSAGE HAS BEEN LEFT BLANK]

To report this message as a phishing attempt, click here.

The white screen makes my eyes hurt, but I don't dare to blink in case the message disappears.

'Alice. What are you doing up there, sweetheart? The car's here.'

I can't speak.

It's got to be a glitch. A ghost in the machine. The email version of those newspaper stories about someone suddenly getting a Christmas card that was posted in 1952 by a long-dead granny.

And surely it's nothing but a fluke that my sister's long lost email appears one hour before her final ... *performance*.

'Alice?'

I jump, even though Mum is still outside my door. 'Nearly ready,' I shout.

But I don't move. I can't. I feel like there's something there. Something I'm not seeing.

Maybe I really have lost it now. 'You're not real,' I hiss at the screen. 'You're not.'

The longer I stare, the more I know I'm missing something.

I stand up. My legs are like lead, and I can't look away from the screen. What is it I'm not seeing?

'Alice? Come on, now.' Mum sounds ratty. I guess today isn't going to go down as the best day of her life, either. I should try harder. *Be a better daughter*, now I'm an only child.

Up. Towards the door. One foot in front of the other. Keep going.

And then I turn back to the screen and I see it. The time.

10:05:09

Either just past ten o'clock on the morning of Meggie's funeral.

Or 10/05/09.

The date of my sixteenth birthday. And the date Meggie was murdered.

4

2

We're supposed to be yesterday's news. Or, more accurately, four months ago's news. The tragic Forster family.

There've been hundreds more murders since Meggie's. Stabbings, shootings, crashes. But then my sister's death would have been headline-grabbing even if she hadn't been a reality TV star. According to my media studies teacher, Mr Bryant, newspapers prefer their murder victims female, pretty and white, even though most kids who die are male, spotty and black.

Though he hasn't given that particular lesson since Meggie died.

As the car pulls away I recognise two of the local TV journos standing outside our house. I used to watch them on the portable telly in my bedroom, as they reported live underneath my window. If I muted the sound, I could hear their voices through the glass.

I close my eyes, to shut everything out. Except it doesn't work, because now I can see *that* screen, and *that* date. It can't be chance, can it?

'I hope no one spots your cufflinks, Glen.'

My father sighs. 'Why?'

'They're too shiny. Too cheerful. Appearances matter today.'

Mum's appearance is spot on, in her brand new grey silk dress. Before Meggie died, she'd have been gutted to be a size fourteen. *Old* Mum did yoga and Pilates and Body Combat. New Mum does Grief Counselling instead. Her body is flabbier but her spirit is honed. Monday night is Group, Wednesday afternoon is One-to-One with her therapist, Olav, Thursday is social, and then at the weekends she's online the whole time, *sharing*. She's a big celebrity on the grief forums.

Dad's gone the other way. He won't join the Group, even though it'd shut Mum up, and he looks like a tramp in his funeral suit, it's so loose. His diet now is peanuts and whisky. He's the strong, silent type, like a cowboy in an ancient Western. Well, a cowboy who moonlights as a solicitor.

I am piggy in the middle. And don't I feel like a piggy today, in shiny tights that are too hot for the Indian summer, a granny-ish black skirt and a puffy-sleeved cream blouse that my mother chose. I sweat between my parents, dressed like a five-year-old on her way to a birthday party, and I have to jam my hands under my legs to stop myself reaching for the door and making a run for it.

As the car pulls up at the church, the size of the crowd is shocking.

Could Meggie's murderer be here?

The first person I recognise is Sahara, because she's so tall. She raises her muscular arm in a half-wave. Sahara lived in the room next to Meggie in halls, and I recognise some of the other girls from my trips to uni alongside her. I scan the faces, looking for guilt. Or evil.

Did one of you kill my sister?

I want to scream the question at them, to see if anyone reacts. But would knowing the truth make any of this any easier for me to stand?

A couple of the girls have been crying already. Sahara's boyfriend is the only guy with them. What's his name? Andrew? Aidan? He's *that* memorable.

There's no Tim, of course. Mum was going to ban him, but Dad pointed out that he wouldn't have come anyway. He's the kind of guy who'd understand that it'd be the wrong thing.

Mum tutted and muttered something like, '*And the kind of guy that murders his girlfriend and gets away with it*'.

But I don't believe for one second that he killed her. And I know that today he'll be thinking of us. Thinking of Meggie.

To the left of Sahara there are more people who could be students, but I don't recognise any of them. So what the hell are they doing here? I clock the glazed eyes and the slack jaws and the way they're staring at me, and then I know. They're the same people who hang out on the net, posting comments after the clips of Meggie on YouTube or on the *Sing for your Supper* fan forums, saying how they miss her and how they loved her and how she was their best friend.

All it took was one series of that crappy reality show for them to believe she was part of their lives, and that they owned a little part of her.

But does that mean one of them killed her?

Dad says they're just harmless nutters, but how did they know to come to this church today? Maybe there's a website for people who get off on death.

Or a website for people who want to impersonate their dead heroes?

I might be looking into the eyes of the person who hacked her account and sent me that email. I feel *sick*.

We get out of the car, and Mum is swallowed up by a huddle of people. Her grief buddies. Five women, and a tall, sandy-haired man with swollen lips, like a supermodel's, and an airbrushed face. I know straight away this must be Olav, the Expert in Loss.

Robbie and Cara are standing by the church entrance. They're always here for me. In a parallel universe, where the only reason to remember 10/05/09 is for my sixteenth birthday, Robbie would still feel like my boyfriend and Cara would feel like my best friend and all three of us would be planning which uni to apply for, and wondering whether our folks will let us go on holiday together. Instead . . .

They hug me, Cara first, then Robbie. Cara looks the same as ever – she's going through a phase of always wearing black, even on the beach – but Robbie, who lives in jeans, looks so much older and more serious in his suit and, well, kind of sexier, I guess. Except I don't know if I feel that way about him any more.

Dad looks lost. There's no one here for him.

It's hot outside after the air conditioned car, and then cold again as we step into the dark church porch. I feel feverish.

Oh, God.

That can't be her, in that coffin ahead of me. We file into the front pew, and I stare at my hands. Anything but look at it. She's with us, but not. And she's certainly, definitely, one hundred per cent not able to send me blank emails at mystically significant times.

The vicar has a booming voice that fills the church space with words about my sister, a girl he never knew, and never will.

'Today is a day for grief, but also for gratitude, for the life of Megan Sophie London Forster. The long wait to put Megan to rest has been taxing for those who loved her, and most of all for her mother, Beatrice, her father, Glen, and her sister, Alice . . .'

Around me, people are singing. Sahara is belting it out, and so are most of the stalkers. But hymns meant nothing to Meggie: even *Amazing Grace*, the song that launched her reality TV career, wasn't *her* choice. She only liked girl solo artistes with voices as powerful as her own. She would have *hated* this.

I think of her under the lid of her coffin. I know she's wearing stilettos and her second favourite dress, the one with big red hand-painted poppies. She couldn't wear her true favourite, the silky white wrap dress that flowed like

8

spring water, because she had it on when she was found. It's *evidence*.

I thought coffins were as sturdy as a Landrover Discovery, to see the passenger safely into the afterlife. But hers is slim and sleek, with chrome handles as flimsy as the straps on her stilettos.

That's when I stop acting brave. And that's when I start crying.

I can't do it. I can't see her buried.

It is the worst thing that could happen to her. She hated the dark, hated cramped spaces, and as for dirt ... my sister never even made sandcastles because she didn't want filthy nails.

Instead, I run home – two miles through the back streets, so I don't bump into anyone I know. All the way, I try to block out images of her under the ground, hands grasping at the heavy earth, lungs gasping for oxygen but filling up with soil with every breath.

Is that how she felt when the killer held a pillow over her face?

My hand is shaking so much that I can hardly get the key in our front door, and my own breath is loud and painful. When I'm back in my room, I peel off my sweaty clothes, but my skin still smells of church, of incense. Of death.

My computer suddenly seems menacing. I power up, half expecting to find that I imagined that email. And half hoping there will be another one.

But when I log on, nothing's changed. The email's still there but nothing more.

I stare at it, in case there's a picture there somewhere, hidden in the pixels, but nothing changes. Not even the time: 10.05.09

Four months and five days since she left us.
I open up my email and begin to write.

From: AliceinWonderland@forsterfamily.co.uk
To: Meggie@MeggieForster.net

My dearest sister,

No. Totally the wrong way to start. I never used to call her soppy names, and even though she's never going to see this, she'd laugh, or think I'd gone properly crazy if I started now.
I delete the first line, and start again.

Megster!

Better. It's one of the thousand or so nicknames I had for her.

Where were you, big sis? You missed it. Your own funeral. And they played the worst ever music, you'll be turning in your grave, eh?

I've never used that phrase before.

I hope you're OK. In your grave. Though that sounds too weird. I'm really sorry I didn't stay to throw in the earth or whatever it is you're supposed to do. I couldn't face it.

Earth. The word makes my breathing go shallow again.

I guess if you're ... here, somehow, still, then you might have seen me in church. I'm sorry for that too. I know you hate cry-babies.

I tried to tell them not to bury you. I said we should scatter your ashes somewhere you loved, like on the beach in Corfu, but then the police said you had to be buried, in case ...

I stop. Would a dead person even care about the fate of their body, or would they have abandoned it like last season's Primark specials?

Well, let's not go into that. But you had a hell of a turnout, Meggie. So many people loved you, although even all their love added together isn't as much as I loved you. You knew that, didn't you? Even though we didn't say it often enough ...

I'm saying it now. I love you lots,

Your baby sister xxxxxxxxxxxxxxxxxxxxxxxxxxxxxxxxxxxxxx

I re-read the email. Maybe I should be telling her everything that's happened since she went: the silences at home, the tribute single, my 'better than expected, given the circumstances' GCSE results, my relapse as a nail-biter.

But if she's watching from heaven, then she knows all that already. What she needs to know instead is the stuff that *really* matters, and I feel lighter now that I've told her. OK, so if that blank email *was* sent by a stupid, sicko fan who hacked her account, then I've given him more than enough drama to make his day. But who cares? If there's a tiny chance she'll hear me – even if it's tinier than me discovering men on Mars or a cure for cancer – then it's worth the risk of some sad loner with a fetish for dead girls knowing how I feel.

I press *send*.

3

My parents are arguing again downstairs. Same old, same old. I thought the funeral might possibly make things better, but a week on, they're still at it. I used to feel smug when my friends moaned about their parents' rows. Not any more.

'Doesn't this matter to you at all?'

'Bea, don't do this, please.'

'No. I want to know if it matters to you.'

I switch my music up, but it doesn't really block out their voices.

'OK. No. No, it doesn't matter to me one bit.'

'Glen, you can't mean that. Megan deserves the right tree. Something beautiful and delicate but strong. Maybe a fruit tree is best. But then would it be strange to eat it? Oh God, you see why I need your help . . .'

'Megan couldn't tell an oak tree from a Swedish pine. She was nineteen, Bea. She didn't give a stuff about gardening.'

'It's not gardening. It's a symbol of her life.'

'Do whatever makes you happy. Water your tree with champagne and feed it caviar, it makes no difference. We can't replace Megan with a tree, or a rose bush or a bloody hanging basket.'

Maybe talk radio will drown them out. I push my headphones into my laptop.

What now? I could call Robbie, but he'll want to talk about the funeral, because he thinks it's the right thing to do. Cara would try to distract me with her latest crush, which I can't face either.

If I'm really desperate, I could do my media studies assignment. I pick up the sheet: *A globalised, centralised media inevitably means an impoverished world view. Discuss, with relevant examples.*

Maybe I'm not that desperate.

I know what I *want* to do. It's been at least ten minutes since I last checked my email, so I want to check again. Since the funeral, nothing's come from Meggie's account. Perhaps the ghost in the machine has floated off to haunt someone else. I've been fighting the temptation to send another email. It might be crazy, but sending that first one made me feel a tiny bit better.

The spam folder shows three emails, none from Meggie's account.

I'm about to delete them and then I see the subject line of the bottom one . . .

4

What the hell? *Soul Beach?*

I go straight onto Google, but nothing shows up. I try going directly to the website: soulbeach.org. My hands are shaking so much that I keep mistyping, but when I finally get it right and hit *go* the browser freezes. Nothing happens. Nothing at all. I feel like screaming at the screen, but I know Mum would hear me. So instead I whisper.

'What does this mean, Meggie? Where the hell are you? Are you even there?'

But of course there's no answer. How could there be? I guess it's two-nil to the sick bastard who must be loving the fact that I was dumb enough to respond to that first email.

There's a rushing in my ears, I'm so angry. I need to get out of here. Dunno where. Anywhere but in front of this bloody screen. I shut down Firefox and then ...

Oh my God.

I stare at the desktop. I've had the same wallpaper forever – since before it all happened, a photo-collage of brilliant days with my mates, my parents, and, of course, my sister. In the centre of the screen is a shot of the two of us on a camping holiday in France, just after we won the fancy dress contest as Alice and the Mad Hatter. (Of course, Meggie got to be Alice, despite it being my name. She just looked the part.)

Except, she's not there any more. None of us are. The collage is gone, and in its place there's a new image.

Of the most beautiful beach I've ever seen.

5

Cara reads the email print out about fifty times before she says anything. Then, finally:

'Sickos.'

She pops another Nicorette gum into her mouth. Her mum's a GP and has been slipping her a pack a week since school reported Cara for smoking before her GCSE Physics exam. What *Mummy* doesn't know is that a) Cara bought her first packet of fags on her thirteenth birthday, and b) the gum doesn't stop her smoking, it just keeps her going at break, as smoking *anywhere* on site now would get her permanently excluded. Two strikes and you're out at Redview School for Girls.

'I mean,' she says, twisting a strand of newly-dyed blue-black hair around her finger, 'what kind of psycho does this kind of thing?'

'You'd be surprised how many weirdoes there were on forums talking about Meggie after she died.'

'You *Googled* her?'

I blush. 'Yeah. Does that make me weird too?'

She chews it over; the gum keeps reappearing, grey as a headstone next to her newly whitened teeth. 'Nah. I'd have done the same if it had been my sister.'

Cara's an only child. We used to say that we were soul sisters, until Meggie died and I realised too late that there's *nothing* like the real thing.

'The Facebook stuff was pretty normal, if sending tonnes of virtual bouquets to someone you've never met counts as normal. But then there were whole forums about her voice, her face, even made-up stories about her life. And everyone posting had some unique theory about who'd killed her, and why.'

Cara gives me a sympathetic look. 'Like it's not obvious.'

I frown. 'He hasn't been charged. If it's that obvious, he'd be in prison, Cara, you know that, whatever the papers say.'

Tim isn't the murderer. I'm not sure about anything else in the world any more, but I know that a guy who used to rescue spiders from the communal kitchen in the student flats, can't be a killer.

But if it's not him, then who?

She gives me that look, the one that says *well, we all know you fancied Tim right from the first time Meggie brought him home with her from college so you can't be expected to see sense.*

It's not even true. I liked him because he was the first one of Meggie's boyfriends to treat me as an interesting person in my own right, but Cara couldn't believe it was that simple, and she used to tease me about him all the time – though she has cut me more slack since my sister died.

She reads the email again. 'So, what's it like?'

'Eh?'

'The site, dummy. What's Soul Beach like? Is every day really *as beautiful as the last?*'

It's my turn to give *her* a look. 'I didn't click on the actual link. It was probably a trap. Anyway, I Googled Soul Beach and it doesn't even exist.'

Cara stares at me, as if she doesn't understand me at all, and then the bell goes and I head off to English and she goes to Law and I don't listen to a word the teacher says because I'm too busy writing my reply to the Soul Beach *psycho* in my head.

6

To: admin@soulbeach.org
From: AliceinWonderland@forsterfamily.co.uk
Date: September 23 2009
Subject: Re: Meggie Forster wants to see you on the Beach

Dear saddest person who ever lived,

How did you get to be so sick?

Well, I really hope you're proud of yourself. Cos it's such a great achievement, isn't it, taking the piss out of someone whose only crime is to miss their sister?

I hope one day someone hurts you like you're trying to hurt me and you realise what a scumbag you are.

Alice Forster

I feel better for about twenty seconds after I press *send*. Then I start to shake, and I hear that rushing in my ears again.

What if the person emailing isn't some random stalker, but someone I know? I don't have many enemies. At school, a few of the girls dislike me because I hang round with Cara and they hate her for her big mouth and her big boobs. But if someone wanted to upset her, they wouldn't do it through me, would they?

Messenger flashes up.

Later? I'd forgotten all about it, even though Robbie is the least forgettable boyfriend in the world. All the girls like him because he has a broad smile like Zac Efron's, and thick golden hair that's too good to be true. We met in Year Ten, when Cara was dating his friend, and though she dumped the friend after a month, Robbie and I have been together ever since. A year and a half. Makes us pretty much married, according to our friends.

Then the news came, and when Robbie turned up at my house, crying almost as much as me, it was like a switch had been turned off inside me. I felt nothing. And I still don't.

Maybe I should finish with him, but I won't feel like this forever, will I?

> ROB'S WORLD: U there?
>
> ALICEINWONDERLAND: Sorry, distracted. Can't wait 2 see u later.
>
> ROB'S WORLD: What time shall I get u?

I shiver. I don't like being alone with him any more.

> ALICEINWONDERLAND: I'll make my own way. Got homework.

I log off Messenger. There's the beach again on my screen. I can't get rid of that picture, whatever I do. It's not even a normal photo. It's too vivid, the colour of the sea too turquoise, and the breakers against the shore so bright white they fizz like sherbet in front of my eyes. It's almost like a 3D image, even though I know you don't see 3D images without those stupid glasses. But whenever I see the picture, it makes me think of the email, and it's driving me mad.

I search for my old photo collage in My Pictures, but when I find it, it won't let me load it as wallpaper. The blood rushes so loudly in my head that it sounds like waves.

'Enough!'

I slam the laptop lid shut. Is this just a phase? Mum told me that when you grieve, you go through these different phases, and anger is one of them. But now I've shut the computer, the rage has gone, like that.

And yet ... I can hear Mum's hairdryer humming next door, and the telly blaring downstairs.

But underneath the routine noises of our house, is the distant but unmistakeable sound of waves crashing against the sand.

7

Robbie, Cara and her new man, Mickey, are in the pub garden already.

'Hello, lovely Alice!' Robbie gets up, kisses me on the lips, and heads for the bar.

Mickey mutters some kind of Neanderthal greeting. He's twenty-two. Cara met him when he served her a Big Mac and Fries. He's cute, in that *bit of rough* way Cara likes these days.

'So have you replied to that email?' she says to me, over Mickey's head.

I nod.

'I knew you would. And?'

'No reply yet.'

'I've been thinking,' she says. 'It's not random, is it? Someone wants to get at you, Ali. Or get your attention.'

'Yeah. But who wants my attention that badly?'

Robbie arrives back with my beer. 'Someone trying to get your attention, Al? Should I know about this?'

I shoot Cara a warning look but she chooses not to see it.

'We're trying to work out who is sending these freaky emails to Alice.'

I see hurt in his eyes. I used to be able to spend hours debating what exact shade of brown they were, chestnut or dark chocolate. 'It's nothing. Just another one of those nutters with a thing about Meggie,' I tell him.

'But they've got your email address?'

'Really, it's nothing,' I repeat.

'It was your sister, wasn't it?' says Mickey, waking up. 'That got murdered.'

'Yes.'

'Pretty, wasn't she? And she was famous. I remember her on that talent show. Wouldn't have thought she was your sister.'

Robbie's hand tightens into a fist, ready to defend my honour. Mickey hasn't noticed. 'I had a mate that got murdered,' he continues. 'Well, it was my brother's best mate's cousin. Punch-up, outside a pub. Someone draws a blade, next thing . . .' and to make the point, he pulls a finger across his throat.

'Mickey?' says Cara. Her voice is soft but her eyes are almost as black as her hair.

He turns to look at her.

'Please sod off and leave me alone. Forever.'

Mickey's face twists, like a glove puppet's. Then he picks up his pint. 'Never fancied you anyway. Stuck-up cow,' then he nods at me and Robbie as he stands up, 'stuck up mates. Oh, and *your* dead sister was way nicer looking.'

Robbie tries to go after him, but I put my hand out to stop him. 'He's not worth it.' I don't add that I reckon that thug could floor Robbie with one punch. Or that Mickey only said what most people think when they realise who I am.

'So, this email thing?' Robbie says.

'Really, it's not an issue, OK? Someone hacked into Meggie's account, and I've had a couple of stupid emails.'

'That's horrible,' he says, taking my hand and stroking it. Six months ago that sensation would have left me unable to speak. 'Lewis could track them down, throw a cyber shit storm at them, if you want.'

Lewis is Robbie's geeky older brother's even geekier best friend. He's one of those geniuses who started their own web design outfit before uni and ended up not bothering to go to college. Apparently he's going to be as rich as Bill Gates, but he's never had a girlfriend.

'No, please.' I let go of his hand to pick up my beer. 'The truth is, I almost like getting the emails. They ... well, they kind of remind me that she existed.'

'Oh, mate,' says Cara, 'of course she existed. She still exists, because we remember her. The whole of Britain does. Even that thicko Mickey knows who she was.'

'Maybe,' I say. 'But no one talks about her any more, do they?'

Cara and Robbie exchange glances, like doctors with a nervous patient.

'We weren't sure you were up to talking about her,' Robbie says. 'We should have asked, though. Memories keep people alive, don't they?'

I hesitate. They are my two best friends in all the world. Maybe I can tell them the thing that scares me most in the world. I take a deep breath.

'If the memories keep her alive, then what happens when I forget her?'

They look shocked.

'You won't,' Robbie says.

I shake my head. 'I won't forget *about* her. But already ... well, I know that one of her two front teeth was chipped but *I can't even remember which one.*'

'The right one,' says Cara, tapping her own slightly nicotine-stained tooth. 'Same as mine.'

'I don't think that's quite what Ali meant,' says Robbie. 'Look. It's not the details. It's how Meggie made you feel that counts.'

He doesn't understand either. The feeling that every time I forget something about my sister, I am betraying her. That I am a poor excuse for a sister. But I should have known there was no point in trying to explain: right now, the world seems an even lonelier place. 'Yeah, maybe. Thanks, guys. Who's on the bar tonight?'

'Dopey bloke with the tats,' says Cara. Then she winks. 'You remember. From the Christmas party. Mr Octopus. He'll do *anything* for me.'

'Good,' I say. 'Because I could really use something stronger than a beer right now.'

8

I tiptoe into the house, hoping to avoid the Spanish Inquisition.

'Alice?' Dad calls out from the living room. I freeze.

'Going straight to bed,' I yell. 'I'm really tired.' I hold my breath.

He grunts 'OK, goodnight then, sweetheart.' I don't suppose he wants to talk any more than I do.

I switch on the laptop, though I bet whoever is behind the whole scam has skulked off into cyberspace like the cowardly hacker he is.

> **Subject:** Re: Re: Meggie Forster wants to see you on the Beach

I stare at the subject line. I can't believe he's replied. Maybe this guy is so stalkery that he'd settle for second best sister?

Or maybe it really *is* her.

Well, obviously I'm not that stupid. I focus on my two choices: open, or delete.

No choice at all, is it?

> **To:** AliceinWonderland@forsterfamily.co.uk
> **From:** admin@soulbeach.org
> **Date:** September 24 2009
> **Subject:** Re: Re: Meggie Forster wants to see you on the Beach
>
> Please, Florrie . . . I've waited so long now

At first, I think I must be drunker than I realised. The text is more like hand-writing than a typeface, and *blurred* handwriting at that, as though the ink has run in the rain . . .

Except it isn't ink, is it? I'm looking at a computer screen, not paper.

But that's not the weirdest thing.

I close my eyes. I imagined it, didn't I?

I open my eyes again, and it's still there.

Florrie

I am Alice Florence Forster. Conceived – oh God, how could they have given me *that* middle name for *that* reason? – in an Italian hotel on my parents' wedding anniversary. Meggie's middle name is London. She was actually conceived in a one-bedroom flat in Shepherd's Bush, but even my mother knew that would be a step too far.

My middle name is a closely guarded secret, known only to six people: my form teacher, my doctor, my dentist, my embarrassing parents.

And my sister.

The only person in the world who can get away with calling me Florrie.

9

Please, Florrie ... I've waited so long now

I read it over and over again. No full stop at the end of the sentence. That is so *not* like my big sister. As well as being a singing prodigy, she got A*s in GCSE and A Level English. No one ever accused my sister of *just* being a pretty face. So her lack of punctuation proves there must be something wrong with her.

Of course there's something wrong with her, you dozy cow. Meggie is dead.

Except I don't think I believe that any more.

I *know* it's her. The same way I knew that scary Cara would be my best friend the minute I saw her in the playground at secondary school, or that Robbie would be the first boy I ever kissed. I *know*.

Everything outside this room is the same – I can hear my father snoring on the sofa downstairs, the only place he can still sleep soundly– but everything in *here* is changed. My heart beats loud and fast. Should I run down, wake him up, tell him that Meggie is with us?

I laugh at myself. Yeah. Show him three emails that prove my sister's immortal. That's really going to help. They'll have me in the loony bin before I can say 'afterlife'.

I could call Cara, but she'd demand to come over even though it's past midnight, and I bet she still wouldn't believe me. Plus, there's no way I am letting her know my middle name is Florence. Not after keeping it secret for eleven years.

Or Robbie? He'd come back here now and hold me the way I need to be held, but he'd probably be texting geeky Lewis behind my back, getting him to block the site, which is the last thing in the whole world I want right now. This might be madness, but it's all I've got.

So that's it, then. I'm on my own.

I scroll down the Soul Beach email, and my cursor hovers over the activation link. My hand trembles and the screen seems to pulse with my heartbeat.

'Hold on, Meggie. I'm coming,' I whisper.

In the distance, I can hear the waves.

10

To maximise true color reproduction, optimize ClearHearAudio, and ensure the best multimedia experience on Soul Beach, we'd love to recalibrate your settings. Is that cool with you too? Click Yes or No.

The idea that heaven might be run by West Coast software nerds makes me smile, despite the fear I'm feeling as I stare at the screen. The fear that this might be for real. Or, worse, the fear that it might not be.

I click Yes, even though I know that'll give whoever or *whatever* this is complete control of my laptop, as well as my emotions. And then I hold my breath.

The beach appears gradually, as though I'm walking through early morning mist that clears with every step I take.

Before I can even see the place, I *feel* it, like an electrical charge through my body. For a moment, it's frighteningly physical, almost paralysing, but then I am warm, fizzy, like my blood has been replaced by champagne.

I blink, and the mist clears, to reveal *that* beach. The one from my desktop. The colours are even more dazzling: every grain of sand is a slightly different shade of gold, so realistic that they seem to shift under my feet as I walk. And the turquoise brilliance of the sea, with white foam cresting on the waves, cools my eyes. The breakers whoosh against the shoreline, and they sound nothing like the artificial waves on Mum's relaxation tapes. These are too real to be relaxing:

forceful and stroppy, as if aware of their own power.

And now I realise. *Those* are the sounds I've been mistaking for anger, for blood rushing through my head. Why didn't I recognise them sooner?

I walk along the beach courtesy of my mouse, though the movement is so fluid that I am hardly aware of it. I scour the horizon for people, but nothing interrupts the holiday-brochure perfection, except clusters of bamboo huts on stilts, and what looks like a deserted beach bar with a palm-leaf roof, a long way in the distance. The bay is enclosed by sharp, green-scrub coloured rocks that rise sharply upwards, protecting the landscape from anything that might spoil it.

I have never been anywhere this breath-taking. I could so easily lie down right here, feel the warm sand mould to the shape of my body, and the healing heat of the sun on my face . . .

Then I remember I'm looking for Meggie.

Anger replaces that rush of pleasure and contentment. That's the first time since May that I've forgotten about her death. I don't think I've even forgotten in my sleep.

So how *could* I forget now?

I rage against myself, furious that I'm so shallow, and then furious with this place for *making* me forget.

'What is this? I don't want to be on a sodding desert island. I just want to see Meggie,' I burst out.

I look around me. Bloody hell. I am in my bedroom, shouting at my computer. I've totally lost it now, haven't I? Or maybe I lost it the minute I believed my sister still existed.

Disappointment comes in waves, harder and faster than the ones on the screen. I'm crushed. I wanted to believe in this, because I can't believe in anything else. But it's nothing but a tropical con trick.

I try to click out of the site, but wherever I move my mouse, I can't find the little x in the right hand corner, and I can't even find the File menu to exit that way. The more agitated I get, the less effect I have on the images in front of me. The water still laps at the shoreline, the sun still bounces off the water, the sand still feels warm between my toes.

Warm?

I look down at my toes. They're resting on my IKEA rug.

The screen has frozen now. All I can see is pale brown. Has the site crashed?

I move my mouse and the blue comes back.

Ah. I'd fallen face-first onto the sand.

As I scramble to my feet, a cloud of dust appears at the edge of my vision. I clamp my lips shut so it doesn't go in my mouth.

Yeah, right. Because virtual sand is really something to worry about, compared to insanity.

I keep walking, keep looking for an exit. The perfection of this place suddenly feels claustrophobic. This isn't heaven. Maybe it's hell. Or maybe it's a virus that's infected my computer: the *Wish You Were Here* virus. Dad's going to go mad if this thing is eating my hard drive. They only bought me the laptop on my birthday.

My birthday. Meggie's *death*-day.

'I don't need this, I really don't need this,' I say, and I realise I'm crying. 'Not on top of everything else.'

The sound of the waves changes.

No.

It can't be.

I move closer to the tinny speaker in my laptop and then I hear it for sure. Somewhere below the waves, there is a voice. It's small. It's frightened. It's hardly recognisable. But it's there.

'Florrie? Is it you, at last? Oh, please. I need it to be you ...'

11

'Meggie?' I whisper her name, unable to believe it's really her.

Nothing comes back. Perhaps I wasn't loud enough. I nudge closer to the mike on my laptop. 'Meggie?'

'Florrie ...' A murmur, nothing more. She sounds different. Flatter, less lively, not at all like my sister. The possibility that she's a hoaxer, that this whole thing is a sick set-up, pinballs round my head again, but I dismiss it; no one would go to this much trouble. It's too crazy.

More crazy than communicating with the dead through a social networking site?

'Are you really there, Meggie?'

'Of course I am. But I didn't think *you* were ever going to show up.'

That's more like her. 'Where are you, Meggie?'

I hear a *very* Meggie-like sigh now. 'Oh, bloody hell. So they were right.'

'They?'

'The others. They said that maybe you wouldn't be able to see us at first.'

'All I can see is an empty beach.' So empty that it feels like the very end of the world.

'Weird. There are loads of us around this morning. The philosophers are having a picnic to your left. The Emos are on the edge of the pier, wondering whether to jump, and feeling extra pissed off that if they do they'll float right back to the surface again like suicidal life buoys.'

Emos? Picnics? So many questions form in my head. I start with the most important. 'Where are *you*?'

'I'm right beside you. I'm touching your right hand.'

I look down at my hand, gripping the mouse. 'I can't feel anything.'

'Well, doh. You are *on a website*, aren't you?' and she sounds so big sister-ish that I smile.

'Where are you now, Meggie?'

'I haven't moved.'

'No, I mean, where are you? Where is . . . this?'

A huge sigh comes out of my speakers now. On the screen, a massive wave breaks on the shore and I think I catch a glimpse of a person in front of it, but then the shape melts away like sea spray.

'You were exactly like this when you were four. *Why does the man in the moon never blink? How can cheese be yellow when milk is white? Why don't humans have wings?* The truth is, I don't have a bloody clue where this is. The philosophers debate it endlessly, but that's not my idea of a good night out.'

'Might you be in heaven?'

I know it's madness but I swear I feel her breath on my neck as she laughs. 'Maybe. It's certainly a version of paradise. We always joke about it being modelled on some icky honeymoon resort. Danny's been all over the Caribbean and reckons it's like that, but then Triti's Indian and she says it's like Goa.'

Danny? Triti? I hadn't imagined my sister having fun in the afterlife. All this time I've been so alone, and now I find out she's got herself a gang of mates again. 'Who are the philosophers?' I rack my brains. 'Marx and Einstein?'

'Oh, no,' she scoffs. 'There's no one *old h*ere. It's our nickname for the really intense bunch who refuse to talk to the rest of us because they haven't accepted that they're here yet. Suicides, we reckon.'

'Suicides? Is everyone there dead?'

'Well, doh.'

It's then I realise I haven't asked her the most important question of all. The one that never leaves me, even in my nightmares.

'Meggie? Who killed you?'

The screen freezes. The early morning mist reappears. The sound of the waves fades, and then the display turns a thousand shades of blood red, like a sunset after a massacre.

YOU HAVE BREACHED THE TERMS AND CONDITIONS OF SOULBEACH.ORG. THIS BREACH WILL BE REVIEWED BY OUR MANAGEMENT TEAM AND THEIR DECISION WILL BE EMAILED TO YOU WITHIN SEVEN DAYS.

'Meggie?' I whisper first, and then scream. 'MEGGIE!'

But I'm back on my homepage, and when I try to click back to the site via my introductory email, my browser simply tells me **The URL you have entered does not exist. Please check your spelling or try later**.

'Are you OK in there, Alice?'

It's my mother, back from Group. For a moment, I imagine telling her that I'm not OK, not at all, and why. The thought makes me laugh, in a hysterical sort of way. 'Fine, Mum. Fine.'

But I'm not fine. I've lost my sister all over again, and I don't know if I can bear it this time round.

12

The questions in my head stop me sleeping until my overloaded brain shuts down at four or five a.m. And then I'm so deeply asleep that Mum has to come in and wake me for school, something she hasn't done since I was in Year Ten.

'Come on, Miss Wonderland. It's like trying to wake the dead.'

I freeze, halfway between lying and sitting up.

My mother freezes too. Then her Grief Buddy training kicks in and she tries hard to smile. 'You know, it's only an expression. It doesn't have any power to hurt us any more than we already have been.'

I can't speak. Now I'm awake, the memories of Soul Beach flood my brain and I wish I was there, with Meggie, and then I remember I've been thrown out of paradise.

Mum sits down on the bed. I know that look. She's building up for a proper *talk*. If I'm lucky it'll be sex or drugs. Anything but . . .

'Olav has set up a new group, for younger people, and I wondered whether you might be interested in trying it out.'

'A group for other kids with dead relatives?' *I can't think of anything worse.*

'Yes!' she says. 'Not like the stuffy group I go to, this is much more informal. There's no theme to the sessions. A chance to chat, that's all.'

'Who would go to something like that?'

She looks hurt.

'Sorry, Mum. I don't mean *you*. But I've got Cara and Robbie to talk to.'

She ignores the suggestion that she's got no friends. 'Well, Olav already has a dozen potential members, all in their teens. I've met some of them at socials, they're a lovely bunch.'

I say nothing. Images of Soul Beach distract me, and I can still hear those waves.

'Alice?'

'Sorry. I'm not really awake yet.'

'No. Of course not.' She shifts on the bed. 'I'll leave you to get dressed. But, remember, however supportive Cara and Robbie try to be, they can't begin to understand. At the group, there'll be people who can.'

'Maybe I don't want to sit on a beanbag drinking herbal tea and snivelling into free tissues. It won't bring her back, will it?' I sound sharper than I meant to.

Mum stands up. 'You're absolutely right, Alice. She's gone, and we all need to find our own way of accepting that. I shouldn't have pushed it. You're entitled to your space. I'm really sorry.'

I wait till I've heard hear her feet going down the staircase. Then I switch on my laptop, and try Soul Beach again.

The URL does not exist.

When I try to access it through my browser history, there is absolutely no trace of any web-surfing after seven o'clock last night. It's as though I never walked on Soul Beach at all.

Could I have dreamed it all, down to the sand between my toes and the sarcasm in my sister's voice? Has grief driven me crazy, like Ophelia in *Hamlet*?

But before I call out to Mum, begging her to sign me up for urgent Olavotherapy, I remember the emails. There they are: the blank one from the day of the funeral, and two from Soul Beach.

Does it make me feel less mad?
Yes.
Does it make me feel any better?
Not even slightly.

Memory is the least faithful of partners.

It's nothing but a convincing story you've told yourself so many times that it solidifies in the mind, and then seems real. Another person's version of the same event could be unrecognisable.

How would Meggie recall our very first encounter?

My version would go like this. A face in the crowd. More than a face. An entire destiny revealed in a single glimpse. Though I never imagined death would be such a part of the way our lives would intertwine forever.

Much later, I did ask her about that first time, but she couldn't even remember seeing me that night, and then tried to laugh off my hurt. She was never a deep thinker. If she had been, perhaps things would have been different. I might have been different. More tender, less quick to anger? At the end, I did see understanding dawn in those pale, perfect eyes, but by then it was too late for her to make up a story that would satisfy me. In any case, the pillow was pressed against her nose and mouth, and it was too risky to let go. That famous voice that could have told me what I wanted to hear, could also have screamed for help. She knew how to project as well as how to whisper.

Ah, there is no point trying to rewrite the past. What's done is done. In the end, what matters is what I believe, and I believe she loved me, no matter what.

13

Seven days of hell. A week has never felt this long, not at Christmas, not birthdays, not ever.

I'm jumpy and foul-tempered and feverish. Mum thought I was sick, but when the Digital Thermometer wouldn't budge from Normal, she lost sympathy. She's still pissed off that I won't join Olav's Teens in Tears sessions, and it doesn't help that Dad thinks I'm siding with him, so now no one's really talking to each other.

Sometimes I feel like the only adult in the house.

Except I haven't been very adult this week. I skulk around, checking my email even more often than usual, but there's been nothing from the Soul Beach Management Team. Assuming they even exist. In between refreshing my account over and over again, my days pass in the usual jumbled way – lessons, canteen, homework, more homework, inane chatter from Cara about men, intense questions from Robbie about university choices. I can't focus on any of it. Soul Beach might not be a computer virus, but it's infected my head. Where *is* Meggie? Is she happy? And will I *ever* hear her voice again?

When I lost her the first time, it hurt like hell, but I swear this is worse.

'What *is* your problem?' Cara finally asks me when we're walking home. It's too hot for the last day of September, and my school shirt sticks to my back.

'What do *you* think?'

She raises her eyebrows. We keep walking. After a bit, she

says, 'I don't get why you've suddenly gone downhill again. I thought you were getting better.'

Yet again I consider telling her about getting onto the site. But she won't understand. 'Oh, I'm *sorry*. I didn't realise that you'd get bored with such a mopey best friend. Better find yourself a more cheerful one, eh, Cara?'

'Come on, Alice, I didn't mean—'

But I don't want to listen. I hear the rush of blood, or the ocean, or whatever it is. I run and I don't stop till I'm home. All I can think about is that at eleven forty-five, it will be *exactly* seven days since I was blocked by the site. So I must get an answer by then. Surely?

I shower. I eat three rounds of toast spread with too much Marmite, but I can't taste it. I sneak some vodka from the freezer but spit out the first sip. I try to do my homework on the laptop, checking email every couple of words . . .

Maybe I'm being *too stupid to live* by believing this could still turn out OK, that the people behind the site will play fair. This isn't Apple or Microsoft or the BBC or—

I click again and for a moment I don't believe what I'm seeing.

There's an email.

To: AliceInWonderland@forsterfamily.co.uk
From: management@soulbeach.org
Date: September 30 2009
Subject: RESULTS OF REVIEW OF REGULATIONS BREACH, SOUL BEACH

Dear Alice,

Following the review of your serious breach of the regulations of Soul Beach, the management has reached the following decision:

1. As a new Visitor on the site, you may not have

had a chance to grasp the rules and regulations, specifically Regulation 4f vvii:

It is forbidden for Visitors to elicit or attempt to elicit information regarding the offline status or history of Guests on Soul Beach, unless the Guest initiates the conversation.

2. Although this breach is serious, the management has decided to allow you back onto the site, on the understanding that any further breach will result in immediate and permanent exclusion from the site.

3. No further correspondence will be entered into.

Your access to the site has been reinstated.

The Management Team

14

The page doesn't load straight away. As I wait, the sound of the waves through the headphones seems more distant than before ...

I'm in a beach hut. No, a beach *bar*. It's empty, but there are lounge club tunes playing, deep red tropical flowers in empty green beer bottles on each of the dozen or so metal tables, and the smell of mandarins and limes heavy in the air. It's intensely seductive, and my breathing slows as the fragrance fills my head.

Fragrance?

'It's Alice, isn't it?'

I spin around, and see a girl behind the bar.

A person! Or, at least, a person-shaped delusion.

When I look a second time, I realise she's older than I thought, late twenties maybe, with dark, dread-locked hair, laughing eyes, and a painfully detailed Celtic tattoo stretching up her skinny left arm, under the spaghetti straps of her green top. She looks like a grungy pixie.

'Who are you?'

'I'm Sam.' She waves at me: the half-dozen silver rings on her tiny fingers cluster like a knuckle-duster on her hand.

'How did you know who *I* was? And how come I can see you? I thought I wasn't meant to be able to see anyone.'

She smiles; her eyes crinkle. 'Everyone can see me, including Visitors. It's only Guests you can't see yet.'

Her accent is Liverpuddlian, like Mr Bryant's. I wonder if I've misheard her. 'Who?'

'Guests. It's what we call the people here. The dead people.'

I flinch. 'I thought we weren't supposed to mention death,' I whisper. 'What if the management hear you?'

She laughs, but I don't feel like she's laughing at me. She takes a packet of cigarettes – Silk Cut – from her apron, and lights one. 'Alice, I am the management.'

I stare at her. 'You?'

'Well, I'm not like *senior* management. But I do work here. I'm kinda part bar manager, part Mother Superior and part shoulder to cry on. Everyone needs a big sister here, sooner or later.'

I immediately think of my own big sister. 'Where's Meggie? Has something happened to her, because of what I said?'

'No, no. She's still here. The reason you're seeing me is so you get the chance to ask a few questions privately. Where we can't be overheard.'

'Questions? Like what?

'Whatever you like, mate. Can't pretend I know everything, but I'll do my best.'

I can't think straight. So *many* questions.

'Oh, Alice. I wish I could pour you a drink.' She looks around the bar, which is better stocked than the flashy Greenwich club Meggie sneaked me into last Valentine's Day.

'It's OK. I've got some water,' I say. It feels like a physical effort to drag my attention away from the screen and back into the 'real world' so I can take a sip. Why is Soul Beach so vivid in comparison?

'Let's sit down,' Sam says, and she pours most of a bottle of red into her glass, before leading me to a table. The bar has a palm-leaf roof, but is open on all sides, and when I sit down all I can see is the sea, and the horizon above it. Tonight the water looks a bright jewel blue, like sapphires, and the sun hasn't set yet, so I don't know which time zone we're in. 'Now. What do you want to know?'

I try to focus. 'OK. Why is Meggie here?'

'She was murdered, right?'

I flinch. It still sounds so wrong. 'Yes. Do *you* know who by?'

'No. No way. We only get the basics, and to be honest with you, it's a bloody good job, because I have a crap memory. And – no offence, because I like your sister, she's a laugh – but there are so many of them, and they've all got a good story, so after a bit, it's tricky to remember who's who, never mind how they got here.'

'Seriously?'

She nods. 'I know I sound a right callous bitch. But, you know, part of helping people settle in is about making sure they forget why they got here, and focus on . . . well, life after death.'

'Is this it, then? Heaven?'

Sam shakes her head. 'Not quite. Look, to be honest, most of what we get told is strictly need to know. But have you heard of limbo?'

'As in, that thing where you dance under a rope?'

She smiles. 'No. The other sort. It's the idea that there's a kind of . . . waiting room between life on earth and eternal life. Or a purification process. Depends on your religion.'

'Purification? Like hellfire? So Meggie did something wrong?'

She shakes her head again; the beaded dreadlocks swing happily from side to side, which feels wrong for the subject. 'No. Not that I know of, anyway. I don't play any part in the whole Judgement Day business. It's a different division.'

'You're telling me that God has *divisions*?'

She pulls a face. 'Sorry, mate. My stupid sense of humour. Look. I know how to mix a Long Island Iced Tea, how to break up a fight, how to unblock the dishwasher, but I don't understand much about the bigger picture.'

'Oh. So what was all that about limbo?'

Sam looks shifty. 'Only stuff I've picked up from all-night 'putting the world to rights' discussions that happen in here. But I do know that all our Guests died with something unresolved. Murders. Suicides. Accidents that weren't all that accidental. I don't know if we're born with our date of death stamped through us like a stick of Blackpool rock, but these kids died too soon, or too violently. I promise you, no one here went peacefully in their sleep.'

I think of the headlines about Meggie: they called her the *Sleeping Beauty Songbird*. Zoe, the girl who found her body, said her hair was laid out on the pillow like a halo, and her skin was flushed, as though she'd had a bit too much sun. 'No one?'

'It might not be heaven, but it's definitely not hell here either,' Sam goes on. 'I mean, look at this place. Free food. Free drink. Non-stop sunshine and beautiful party people. Guitars for those beach-front jam sessions. No stress. *Volleyball.*' She smiles. 'There's every reason for the kids to forget what happened before.'

I really wish I had a glass of her wine in my hand. 'Kids?'

'Oh, yeah. I forgot. You haven't seen anyone yet, have you?'

'Yet. Does that mean I definitely will?'

'Yes, I'd say so. It's kinda of like those stupid Magic Eye pictures. You need to learn the knack. But you will, and then you'll see what I mean by kids. Put it this way, I feel like a right old bag here compared to the Guests.' She looks at her watch. 'I think that might be enough for now, Alice. It's a lot to take in. Plus, you'll be wanting to see your sister, yeah?'

She stands up, picks up her glass and the ashtray. I'm amazed to see it has three stubs in it, just from our conversation.

'No smoking ban in limbo yet then?' I ask.

She smiles. 'I'm the only one who bothers, here. We've got

a fag machine,' she gestures towards the corner, 'but it's empty because none of the Guests are interested.'

'Sam? One last thing.'

She stops halfway to the bar. 'What?'

'If the Guests are meant to forget the past, why am *I* here?'

'Ah . . . .' she walks back towards me, still holding the glass and the ashtray. 'Sometimes people can't accept it. The living-for-now.'

'So I'm here to help Meggie accept her fate?'

'Something like that.' She looks uncomfortable. 'Like I said, I don't have all the answers. And in this particular case, your guess is as good as mine.'

I have a hunch she's not telling me the whole truth, but she turns her back on me before I can ask any more.

'Thanks,' I say, and she looks up from tidying the bar.

'Any time, mate. Megan's by the jetty, I think.'

I realise I'm being dismissed. I take two steps down from the bar to the beach, and when I turn round, Sam is a little shimmery, as though there's a heat haze between the two of us. She's humming along to the music.

'Sam?'

'Hmmm?' She doesn't look up.

'You're not . . . not an *angel*, are you?'

Now she does look up. Her face breaks into the broadest smile, and she begins to laugh. It sounds musical. Almost angelic, I think. But she's shaking her head and laughing so hard she can't seem to stop. When she does regain control, she fights to catch her breath.

'Oh, Alice, you're priceless. Whoever heard of a Scouse angel?'

15

I step onto the sand. The beach still looks empty, though knowing there might be *people* in my way makes me unsteady on my feet.

Even though, in reality, I have my bum parked safely on my pink office chair.

I strain to detect voices, switching the volume up to max, but I hear none. Instead, I feel the same tingle I felt the first time here. It's impossible not to feel awed by this place, even though I know it's not real . . .

As I walk towards the jetty, I hear my 'footsteps' slapping on the sand. I move the mouse faster. The steps increase to jogging speed. I push forward, faster and faster, until I run into the water and splashing begins, in my ears and on the screen, the droplets like tiny seed pearls in the sun.

'Ah, Florrie, you never were much of a swimmer.'

I jump. Really jump, on the screen. Weird. I'm sure I didn't actually move my mouse.

'Where are you?' I ask.

'Look up.'

I peer up towards the jetty, and the sunlight hurts my eyes. 'Can't see you.'

'Yes, well, I know what that feels like. It's been a whole bloody week. What kept you? I won't accept anything less than a red hot date.' Her voice is teasing, but I hear the hurt beneath the bluster.

'That question I asked about . . . what happened.' I stop. I daren't say another word. 'I breached the rules, didn't I?

Even though I didn't even know there were any.'

'Yeah. If it's any consolation, I checked it out. You're not the first it's happened to.' She chuckles. That chuckle made four million people call premium rate phone lines to vote for her. I'd forgotten how sweet it sounds. 'It's their little joke. They make the rules up as they go along.'

I decide not to mention Sam's pep talk. 'Yes, I'm beginning to work that one out.'

'Be careful, Florrie. Take it gently. If you're banned again, it'll be for good, and I don't know if I could cope with being on my own here for ever.'

Her voice breaks on the words *for ever*. The sudden desperation makes me want to cry, but I need to stay in control. 'But you do know that you are, um, no longer alive?'

'Of course,' she hisses. 'But I don't want to talk about it.'

'What do you want to talk about, then? The weather? My A Level coursework?'

'Don't be angry with me, Florrie. None of this is my fault, is it?'

I gulp. 'Of course not. But I feel so frustrated. I can't see you. I don't know where you are. I don't know *how* you are.'

There's a long pause. Beneath the sound of the waves I am sure I can hear low chatter, like a theatre audience waiting for the play to begin.

'OK. You want to know, yeah. About what happened?'

I hold my breath. Does this make it OK, now, for her to tell me? She did initiate the conversation, after all, which must be within the rules of the Beach.

Never mind the rules, am *I* ready for this? For six months, we've had to cope with not knowing about her last few hours on earth. Not knowing if she struggled, if she felt pain. And will I be able to cope with knowing what no one else knows? But this could be my only opportunity, and the question of who took her life from her has haunted me for so long: I *have* to ask.

'Who was it, Meggie?'

'Who killed me?'

I wait for the screen to go black. To be hurled back into cyber-oblivion. But it doesn't happen, so I repeat the question. 'Yes. Who killed you?'

16

'I don't know.'

'*What?*'

'I don't know how I died, sis. Or who killed me, if somebody did. I don't remember.'

Of all the things I thought Meggie might say, this is the one I hadn't considered. 'You *were* murdered,' I say, gently, and then I gulp, because what if even saying *that* is a rule breaker? What if any moment now this beach disappears in a tsunami of oblivion, washing away any trace of my sister?

But I can still hear her breathing beside me.

Breathing. The killer smothered the breath out of her and yet here she is …

'I had sort of figured that one out, from listening to the others here. 'Natural causes' doesn't cut it round the campfire on Soul Beach, put it that way.'

I'm still trying to make sense of any of it. 'So does everyone have amnesia?'

'No. Most people can talk about what they were doing before it happened. Or even how it felt …' she tails off. 'I'm the odd one out. All I remember is going to a party with Tim. A masked ball, big night out, you know. Well, not as big I wanted it to be. We had a row.'

'A big row?' I can't imagine Tim rowing with anybody. He was always so … gentle. I wonder if Meggie said something to provoke him. Maybe that's disloyal, but, as her little sister, I know how infuriating the 'songbird' could be behind the scenes.

'No. I don't think it was. I mean, all relationships, they have their ups and downs. But not big enough to ... Is that what people think? That it was him?'

What am I supposed to tell her? 'Nobody knows.'

She sighs. 'I've tried *not* to think about it. We went to the bar where the ball was, and then I wanted to go to a club and Tim said we should get back early because it was your birthday do the next day. That's how it started. I don't remember how it finished.'

I think of the CCTV images they broadcast on the news, showing the two of them on their way to the masked ball party in the union bar, then Meggie and Tim arguing outside and walking back to halls together, before a final shot of Tim back in the student union bar much later on. 'You left together at about one. That's the last anyone knows.'

'Oh, bloody hell.' She sighs. 'How, Florrie?'

'How what?'

'How did I die?'

'You were ... you were suffocated.'

She gasps.

'What? Sorry. I shouldn't have told you.'

'No, Florrie, it's OK. It explains something.'

'Tell me.'

'Only that I always used to get these nightmares. When I was a kid.' Her voice is hesitant.

'What kind of nightmares?' I ask, though I have a horrible feeling I already know.

'Of, well, of being buried alive. Of fighting for air, and the earth coming down on top of me, and nobody hearing.'

'Oh, Meggie.'

'Don't fuss,' she snaps and I know that warning tone means *don't you dare try to comfort me.*

Instead, I gaze out towards the horizon. The sun is beginning to set, so the light has changed to warmest peach, and the sea is darker, almost green. I don't know what to say.

'Meggie?'

I hear a snuffling in my left ear. 'Meggie, are you crying? Don't cry. Please. I'm here.'

But the crying continues. My sister was *never* a crier. Not even when her brace was fitted, or when she broke her wrist on next door's trampoline the weekend before she was meant to be taking the lead in the school production of *Les Mis*. She still played Cosette, of course, holding her broom with one arm, her plaster cast camouflaged by rags. There was no way the understudy was taking the spotlight off Meggie.

'I wish I could be with you,' I say, but that makes her cry more. And anyway, what use would I be even if I was there? I don't do comforting. I'm the one who always *needs* comforting, whether it's Cara trying to distract me with dirty jokes, or Dad doing the world's crappiest magic tricks, or Meggie singing lullabies . . .

That memory gives me an idea. I've never bothered to sing. Why would I have even tried when my sister was so talented? But, right now, she sounds so hurt that anything must be worth a shot. I take a deep breath.

'*Amazing Grace, how sweet the sound . . .*'

My croaky voice reverberates in the headphones. It's not a sweet sound *at all*. I try to whisper tunefully instead.

'*That saved a wretch like me.*'

She's stopped crying, at least. I keep going, the words coming back to me phrase by phrase as I remember it was *her* song, the one that made the headlines after she performed it so beautifully in the second episode of *Sing for your Supper*. She reduced grannies to tears with her sincerity, even though behind the scenes she joked around, wondering smuttily what exactly was so amazing about Grace . . .

'*I once was lost but now am found,*
Was blind, but now, I see.'

I hum now, because I don't know the second verse.

And she takes over.

'*Through many dangers, toils and snares ... we have already come.*

T'was Grace that brought us safe thus far ... and Grace will lead us home.'

Her voice falters over the word home, but she's sounding like Megan *Songbird* Forster again. I don't need to *see* her any more, because hearing her is enough to make me remember everything that's important about my sister.

'*When we've been here ten thousand years ... bright shining as the sun.*

'*We've no less days to sing God's praise ... than when we've first begun.*'

When she finishes, I clap next to the laptop microphone. 'Oh, Meggie, it hasn't affected your voice,' I say.

'What hasn't? Being dead?'

I don't say anything.

'I haven't sung once, you know.'

'What?'

'Since I arrived ... here. Not once. It's not that kind of place. Climbing up on the jetty and doing my diva thang is not the way to keep a low profile, eh?' She's back to being funny, sarcastic, *normal*. I feel better momentarily, then immediately I feel worse. She shouldn't be trying to cheer *me* up. It's her that's dead.

'You don't have to pretend, Meggie. You don't have to protect me any more.'

Another pause. I can *definitely* hear people now. Have they always been there, in the background, and it's taken me this long to decipher the sounds?

'All right, then. I feel like crap, Florrie. Lonely, and desperate. I get up every day and the sun is shining in the same perfect way, not a cloud in the sky. Like in that bloody song:

53

When we've been here ten thousand years. Maybe there's no escape, and I wasted the bit of life I had, and there's not a single thing I can do about it.'

'Oh.' I want to tell her how many millions of people miss her, and how that must be proof that she didn't waste a second of her life. 'I'm so sorry, Meggie. Are you in pain?'

'No. Nothing physical hurts at all. Here ... How can I put this? Everyone is whole. Undamaged. Some of them died horribly, but there's not so much as a ripped shirt. Though there's the odd pair of deliberately ripped jeans.'

'Good.' It's only now that I imagine how the place could have been if they weren't whole, a beach crowded with the dead, bits missing or hanging off, bleeding into the sand. I try to block it out, to think instead of questions that might help me understand and help me *see*. 'How many is *everyone*?'

'I don't know. Sometimes it seems like a few dozen. But sometimes hundreds. The beach, well, it kind of goes on for ever. Take a look yourself.'

I move the mouse through three hundred and sixty degrees. The view is turquoise and gold, like Tutankhamen's breath-taking death mask. Apart from the pier and the beach bar, and the clusters of bamboo-and-palm beach huts, there's nothing but beach and sea and sky. Oh, and the hundreds of other people I can't see.

'Can you see *me*, Meggie?'

A pause. 'I can see a shadow. A you-shaped shape. And I knew straight away it was you because ... I don't know. If I say you've got an aura it sounds wanky, doesn't it? And just cos I'm dead doesn't mean I've gone all new-age. They say you might get clearer, or you might not. But in my head, you're there, right down to the cowlick to the left of your fringe, and the big spot you always get between your eyebrows.'

I hear the sadness in her voice. 'Shows what you know,'

I say. 'The antibiotics the doctor gave me finally kicked in. I haven't had a spot since April.'

'You're growing up, Alice.'

She only ever calls me Alice when she's being serious. 'Yeah.'

The silence between us is heavy.

Finally she speaks. 'I ought to let you go now, baby sis. It's quite draining, isn't it, being back together and knowing that it could end at any moment?'

I'm about to argue that I want to stay, but I suddenly realise I do feel dog-tired, and when I look at my watch, it's almost midnight. I've been on the Beach for nearly three hours. How did that happen? It felt like minutes. The best, yet worst, minutes of my life.

'I'll go. But I'll be back tomorrow, if that's all right?'

'All right?' She laughs. 'I can honestly say that you turning up on the Beach is the most wonderful thing that has happened to me since I died. Sweet dreams, Florrie.'

And she's not pretending. I can hear the truth in her voice.

'Sweet dreams, Meggie.'

17

'Three questions are enough to find the truth. With just three questions you can bring down a government, reveal an affair, unmask a killer.'

Mr Bryant's words slice through my daydream.

Unmask a killer? Talking to my sister again has put finding her murderer back on the agenda. All I think about is that, and her, and the Beach.

'So now, in groups of four, I want you to plan an interview for one of your favourite celebrities. One that will reveal more than ever before. But only in three questions.'

Mr Bryant claps his hands together, like he's applauding himself. I used to like his classes, the way he at least tries to be entertaining, unlike most of our teachers.

But now I resent the fact that I have to listen to his cheesy lines, when all I want to do is be on Soul Beach, with my sister.

At lunchtime, Cara and I take our Diet Cokes out onto the school field so she can try to top up her fading tan in the thin autumn sunshine. The Goth look has been abandoned – 'the guys who like it are all depressive morons' – and she's spent two entire Saturdays having her black hair turned to honey blonde. She's also on a caffeine-only diet, in preparation for a date with a personal trainer, and I'm eating nothing in sympathy.

Despite the sun, I can't stop shivering. On Soul Beach, the virtual rays are so strong they make my face tingle.

'Amazing weather, isn't it? Like being on holiday,' she says.

I nod half-heartedly.

'What's up, chick?'

I shrug. 'The usual.'

'You know . . . maybe your mum's right, yeah? About giving the counselling a go. Because this is not getting any better on its own, is it?'

I stare at her. *How dare she?* But before I can say it, she holds up her hand.

'Sorry, sorry. Forget it. None of my business. I couldn't possibly understand, etcetera, etcetera. Pretend I never mentioned it.'

It's not like Cara to back down. 'Am I that bad?'

She tries to smile. 'I don't have any other mates with murdered sisters to compare you to, and I'd be a crap friend if I got the hump because you're snappy. But I do miss the old you. The one that never stopped taking the piss.'

I try to take in what she's said. 'I miss the old me, too.'

She puts down her Coke and puts her arms around me. Usually that would be enough to make me cry, but worse than that, I feel nothing. Well, I feel her patting my back like you'd pat a baby to soothe it, but I'm separate somehow, like someone in a gallery looking at a painting of a girl comforting her grieving friend.

Eventually she pulls back. There are tears in *her* eyes.'

'Better?' she asks.

'Yes,' I lie.

'It'll get easier. We're young, Alice. Things can't stay like this for ever. One day something wonderful will happen that'll make you forget about everything else, and then you'll know you're getting better.' She smiles at me.

I don't have the heart to tell her I'm not looking for something wonderful in this world any more. Because I already sense that I've found all that I need on the shore at Soul Beach . . .

18

After school, I sneak in through the back door, hoping to find something in the fridge to fuel my next walk along the sand.

My parents are lying in wait in the kitchen. *Uh oh.*

Dad hasn't changed out of his suit, and is sitting at the breakfast bar with a pile of paperwork. Mum has that 'fresh from the gym' glow, even though I know she's been at group most of the afternoon. Mental workouts are so much more stimulating.

'Hi,' I say, trying to sound rushed. 'You wouldn't believe how much homework I've got for tonight, so I'll get on with—'

'We need to talk about Meggie,' Dad says. I freeze.

How did they find out? I log out of my account every time I leave my room, even if it's only to use the loo, and I've adjusted my chair so it's impossible to see what's on the screen if you peer through the crack in the doorway, as my mother often does before she goes to bed.

'Oh?' I say.

Mum pulls out one of the stools and I climb onto it. I haven't sat here since I was nine and she used to make me proper breakfasts, with toast fingers and boiled eggs. I went through a skinny phase and she wanted to feed me up. It worked a bit too well, to be honest.

'They've got him, finally,' Mum says.

'He hasn't been charged, Bea. They're just—'

I interrupt him. 'They've arrested Tim?'

I feel the blood drain from my head. It's a good job I am sitting down, or I'd be on the floor like a puppet with its strings cut.

My parents are nodding, my mother more enthusiastically than my father, even though Mum is all about human rights: marching against the war, against extraordinary rendition, against the Burmese government. Yet she's the one who decided Tim was guilty straight away.

I can't believe it. There is nothing in the world I want more than for Meggie's killer to be brought to justice. But this isn't justice.

'Fran from Family Liaison called,' Mum says.

'She said not to read too much into it,' Dad adds hastily

'Come on, Glen. Why else would she call if they don't think they've nailed him?'

It's not the first time Tim's been questioned, but *everyone* was questioned after she was found dead: the caretaker, the barmen, the mates she used to hang out with, the people she passed in the CCTV footage that last night. They even interviewed Zoe and Sahara, though the papers had already decided it was a man.

But this is different. This is the first time he's actually been *arrested.*

'She was only calling to warn us in case the media turn up. No more, no less.' Dad doesn't think he's guilty, either, and no one accuses *him* of fancying Tim.

Mum sighs. 'I went online and my support group all say there must be new forensic evidence. Anyway, never mind our bickering, how do *you* feel about it, Alice?'

I want to scream, *He didn't do it.* But even if I could trust myself to speak, Mum wouldn't listen. So I say nothing.

She looks mildly irritated. 'Well, you know where I am when you want to talk.'

'Thanks.' All I *want* is to be out of this room, to be back online, with Meggie, because these days that's about as close to normal as I get.

Dad starts to pack up his papers. 'I'd better go. Partners' meeting.'

Mum turns on him, her face twisted with rage. 'I can't believe you're even considering working while the police have Megan's killer in custody.'

'Bea, you know as well as I do that if they had the evidence, they'd have charged him on day one.'

'Unbelievable! You really don't care . . .'

And I feel that drifting again, the sense of floating above the room, watching my parents argue bitterly, as they never, ever did when Meggie was alive. But their shouts are fading, and instead I hear the sea whispering, and I swear I can almost feel a breeze on my face.

I push myself up from the stool, my legs still weak, and slip past my parents. They barely notice me go.

19

As I switch on my laptop, my craving for the peace and beauty of the shore is stronger than ever.

It's only been ten days since I first walked at the water's edge, but already I don't know how I could survive reality without my refuge on Soul Beach, and the miracle of hearing my sister's voice again.

As the page loads, I realise I don't know how I'm going to tell Meggie about Tim. Should I even try? Does she deserve to know – or will it hurt her even more?

And yet, there's nothing to tell yet. This is Tim we're talking about. The first of her boyfriends to treat me like a human being, instead of Meggie's dumb kid sister. He talked to me about the big things: my plans, my ambitions, my ideas.

That's not how a killer behaves, is it?

I'm trying to work out how to play it with her as the beach appears at last, and I gasp . . .

I can see *people*.

Hundreds of beautiful people.

It's like a beach party on a music video: sun worshippers clustered round the bamboo beach huts and splashing about in the turquoise water. So much for my refuge . . .

I don't move forward. I'm too busy staring. Everyone here is young, exactly like Sam said: teens and early twenties. And not just young: gorgeous, too. There's a rainbow of hair and skin colours, and they're all wearing slightly preppy clothes. The boys are in cut-off jeans or baggy surfing shorts – no skin-tight Speedos in sight – with either bare chests, laundry-white tees or linen checked shirts.

The girls are more colourful, wearing bikinis in bright primary colours, or patterned spaghetti-strap sundresses. They're swimming, or surfing, or lolling around on beach towels. I see one guy with a Spanish guitar, singing an indie hit from last summer. He has a sexy voice, with a slight accent. Russian? Czech? A Japanese girl sits next to him, tapping an improvised beat on a tiny set of drums, and the others hum a soft accompaniment.

I think I preferred the beach empty. There's something *disturbing* about perfection. And the creepiest thing is that they all look so familiar. I suppose it's because of the model looks – and yet I'm sure there's something more than that. I recognise them at a deeper level: a flutter of the eyelids, a pout, a flick of the hair.

There's a kid over there who reminds me of the drum and bass star who was found dead in his hotel room after some serious partying. And that German girl who was all over the headlines last year when she was kidnapped because a gang was after her dad's scientific formula or invention or something.

Did she ever turn up? I have a feeling her ear was couriered, on ice, to his lab.

She looks around and looks right through me. No, that girl was ordinary, even in the picture her family gave to the papers. This girl here is a supermodel. And she has both her ears ...

As I move, I notice that they *all* look straight through me. But then perhaps I am not worth paying attention to, with my normal face and my normal body. *Their* bodies are perfect: no sunburn, no cellulite, no sign of how they might have died.

No Meggie, either. I look for her Alice in Wonderland halo of hair. (I deserved that hair to go with my name, but instead

I got impossible kinks that even Mum's GHDs can't iron out.) My sister must fit right in here, with her curves and her heart-shaped face that never needed make-up, not even under the harshest studio lights.

But if the surfers and the sunbathers here are all dead, then where do *average*-looking teens go after death? The ones with thick ankles or frizzy hair? Before Meggie died, I'd never thought about life after death, but if there is a judgement day, shouldn't it focus on good deeds, instead of sex appeal?

'Florrie?'

I spin round.

Oh my God . . .

Meggie, a hundred times more beautiful than before.

Her hair has lightened in the sun, so it's even fairer than it is in the picture of her as a baby Mum keeps on the man-telpiece. Normally, Meggie just has to look at the sun to burn, her one flaw, but right now, only her face is pink, cheeks the colour of garden roses. Her body is a flawlessly airbrushed bronze.

We reach out to touch each other at exactly the same moment . . . but my hand strikes the screen, and hers drops like a stone through empty air.

'Oh, Meggie. I didn't think I'd ever see you again.'

She's struggling to answer. She reaches out her arms a second time, but of course, there's nothing there. Even if we weren't online, I've seen enough movies about ghosts to know you can't *feel* them, beyond a half-imagined breath in your ear or the sensation of their eyes watching you.

'Bloody hell,' she says, moving backwards like she's been slapped. 'I don't know why I did that. You look so real, that's all.'

'Do I?'

'Yes. Oh yes. I was frightened you might stay a blur, but you're not. You really are here. On the Beach. With me.'

It's then I realise that the light on the built in web cam is glowing for the first time since I got to Soul Beach. So part of me is here, in my bedroom, hunched over the screen, and then a virtual me is on the sand. I struggle to make sense of it. 'What am I wearing?'

'Oh, the usual,' she says. 'The usual for here, that is. Today you're in a bright red t-shirt that makes your eyes look greener, and a short denim skirt that shows your *very* lovely tanned knees.'

'They're not tanned at all. The weather's been crap this summer.' Though I only know that from newspaper headlines; I've hardly left the house.

'Well, your tan looks pretty fab to me, Florrie. Then again, everyone looks fab here.'

'I noticed. Where do the mingers go? Is there a separate heaven for them?'

She looks serious. 'I've heard it's on a rubbish tip, and, when you get there, you have to scavenge your own clothes from among the tin cans and the rotten food.'

'Really?'

'Oh, God, Florrie, you're still bloody gullible, aren't you? No, there's no audition to get onto Soul Beach. The good thing about being dead is that suddenly you're perfect. Look .... ' and she lifts up her ankle, '... my trampoline scar.'

She runs her finger along untouched, hair-free flesh.

I look closely. 'It's not there.'

She laughs. 'No. And I haven't had a single spot. No periods, no PMT, no headaches, no hangovers. There's booze here, of course, but it doesn't affect you in any bad way, and after a while most people don't bother to get drunk, because everything here is so damned *wonderful* already.'

I suddenly notice that there's an odd shrill tone to her words.

'Unlimited booze but no one gets wasted?'

Meggie nods towards the group of Scandinavian-looking blond kids sitting on a rug having a picnic further along the shore.

'Look closer. What do you see?'

I stare at them for ages, trying to work out why they make me feel so uncomfortable. The picnic is incredibly lavish, the rug laden with bright green salads, fresh juicy peaches and nectarines, barbecued burgers and chicken, baguettes, chocolate cake, strawberries and cream.

For the first time in days, no, *months*, I feel properly hungry; it all looks so mouth-watering. Then there's the booze: jugs of ruby red sangria with oranges floating amongst the ice-cubes, cans of beer in a bucket, bottles of white wine with condensation frosting the glass.

Then I realise what's wrong.

'They're not drinking. Or eating. Are they on drugs?'

'No,' Meggie replies. 'But after a while ... it's hard to explain. It doesn't really satisfy you like it did before. I guess that's something to do with not being alive.'

Another thought occurs to me. An awkward one. 'What about *sex*?'

She laughs loudly now, no more tension. 'Oh, there is *that*. Risk-free and available whenever you fancy it, especially with the newbies when they first get here. They're rampant when they realise there's no need for condoms, no STDs, no pregnancy worries.'

I try not to think about whether my sister ran wild to begin with. 'But you can actually feel touch? Between ghosts I mean.'

'Shhh!' She looks alarmed. 'Don't use that word. We're not ghosts. I don't know what we are. Lost souls, maybe? But we're not *ghosts*.'

'Sorry.'

Meggie smiles. 'Don't be. It's too weird, at first, isn't it? Anyway, yes, sex does feel good here. Not quite the same. A bit ... distant, somehow. You know when you kiss a new person for the first time, it's always different, even though it's only a variation on the same slobbery theme?'

I've only kissed two boys, but I don't tell her that. 'Hmm?'

'The sex here is so easily available and so ... samey that I miss something real, something as ordinary and messy as snogging. Plus, it's extra weird because everyone here is gorgeous. Different colours, different looks ... yet we're spookily similar, like mannequins. Highly shaggable mannequins, but all the same ...'

'Meggie! You never used to be this coarse.'

She shrugs. 'That'll be the company I keep. Speaking of which, would you like to meet some of my new best friends?'

20

Her new best friends are sitting on the bamboo steps of the beach hut, in the shade of a giant palm. They hug Meggie as though they haven't seen her for years, but ignore me completely – which strikes me as incredibly rude, though it does gives me the chance to study them.

There are three friends: two boys and a girl. The girl is Indian and very petite and pretty. I'd guess she's around my age, but she looks older, thanks to enormous boobs that are barely contained by her orange-and-white striped bikini. She wears a huge amber-and-crystal necklace that draws the eye down to her cleavage, and dangly earrings that move softly in the breeze like wind chimes. Despite her brown skin, there's an odd bluey sheen to her, as though she's slightly translucent. For a moment, I imagine I can see her skull, but then I realise it's just the sun shining on her sharp cheekbones.

Sitting next to her is a tall, skinny guy with Italian colouring. His lilac cotton shirt is unbuttoned to show toned abs, and his gestures are larger than life. There's something superficial about him, somehow.

But when the other guy looks straight through me, I shiver. I can't take my eyes off him. He reminds me of someone famous. Leonardo di Caprio, maybe. He's chunkier than his friend, and shorter, with blond highlights running through slightly curly hair. Not my type at all, but those eyes seem so knowing, as though he understands everything but wishes he doesn't. They're old eyes, though the rest of him is young.

What is it about him that's so intriguing? Then I realise.

This guy with the knowing eyes is the only person I've seen on Soul Beach who doesn't look airbrushed: compared to the rest of the clones, he's almost normal. Still cheesily handsome, yes, but his hair is messy, and his baggy white t-shirt is crumpled and not quite as wash-day bright as everyone else's. And as Meggie leans forward to greet him, he seems more awkward with the air kissing than the other two.

Meggie releases herself from the Italian stallion then looks puzzled for a second. 'Oh. Shit. Sorry, sis, I forgot. They can't see you until I introduce you. Not sure why. I think they're worried that Guests might get jealous if they never have a Visitor of their own. You're the ultimate accessory, believe me.'

She grins at them. 'Guys, allow me to introduce my sister, Alice.' Meggie sounds proud of me in a way I don't ever remember her being when we were both alive.

They turn in the direction of her hand but they still don't seem to see me. 'Oh,' she says, flustered. 'There's obviously something I'm not getting right here.'

'You have to use our names,' explains the guy in the white t-shirt. 'It helps control who can see her and who can't. Like privacy settings on Facebook or whatever.' American. *Posh* American. Definitely not my type.

'Right. In order of residency, then. This is Triti, usually known as Pretty Triti. She's been here longer than any of us.' The Indian girl blinks, then smiles and steps forward.

'You're Meggie's double!' she says, air kissing me. Not that I feel anything at all. 'I love your skirt.' I was expecting a soft Indian voice, but instead her accent is upper-class English, with just a hint of Cockney.

'I love your bikini,' I say. I want to add that it's a miracle of engineering, but she might take that the wrong way.

'And this is Javier, from Spain.'

Javier is the flamboyant one. He waves lazily but doesn't

move. 'I would give you a hug, but, you know how it is.'

'I thought you were Italian,' I say.

He scowls moodily, like a bad actor. 'I hate Italians. All show. No substance.'

Which seems rich, coming from a dead person . . .

'And last but not least, Danny.'

'Hi, Alice.' He stands up, like the well-brought-up boy I'm sure he is. Taller than I expected. Eighteen, maybe? Either in his last year at school, or his first year at some elite American university.

And then it strikes me that he's not at university any more, because he's dead. With Meggie, it doesn't seem so strange, because I've had months to get used to her death. But being introduced to people who aren't actually alive is one of the weirdest things that has ever happened to me . . .

His all-knowing eyes meet mine. They're a soupy green, but the colour isn't what holds my attention. It's the intensity, the longing. I don't think it's because *I'm* beautiful: I do know what lust looks like, but this is something else.

I suppose it could be a lust to be alive again.

I force myself to look away. 'Hello, there.' I say to them all.

Javier doesn't try to hide his boredom, but Danny smiles. 'I've heard a lot about you from your sister. Good to see you here. Hope you're not too freaked out by . . . well, by the obvious freakiness of the whole set-up.'

'Sit down,' says Triti, making space for me on the steps. 'Megan's so pleased that you've shown up, finally. She was starting to think you'd never reply to her messages.'

'Completely understandable, though,' says Danny. 'Don't feel bad, Alice. I tried to contact my little brother the same way but I never heard from him.'

'There was never any point in me trying to contact my brother,' says Triti. 'He never liked me when I was alive.'

I look at Javier. He shrugs. 'Only child.'

I nod. It figures. 'So, is it only sisters and brothers that are allowed to come?'

'Well, there's no handbook when you arrive, but I asked around,' says Danny.

'One way of passing the long lazy days,' says Javier.

'I think it can be anyone you have a strong bond with, who also happens to be young,' Danny explains, 'otherwise they wouldn't be allowed onto the Beach.'

'We do not want to see wrinkles or anything that *sags*,' says Javier.

'Ignore him,' Danny says. 'We all do. Seriously, though, the bond seems to be stronger with blood relatives. People have tried to contact friends, but none have shown up so we don't know whether it ever works.'

Something else occurs to me. 'I haven't seen any laptops here.'

My sister smiles. 'It's a bit more basic than that.' She nods back towards the beach, where a couple of girls are standing by the water. One is holding a bottle, the other is trying to scribble something onto a piece of paper that flutters in the breeze. She folds up the paper, kisses it once, and then takes the bottle from her friend. The note goes inside, then the cork, and after another kiss, she tosses the bottle into the water. It bobs about for a while, before a wave sweeps it away. The girl stares at the sea long after the bottle disappears.

'Messages in bottles?' I ask.

And then I remember how Meggie's hand-writing looked so odd in that final email. *Almost as though the ink had run.*

'The Management's idea of a joke,' says Javier.

Danny ignores him. 'Mostly we never hear anything. Maybe they get lost in the oceanic post. More likely our loved ones can't believe the messages are real. But occasionally a bottle washes back up with a reply.'

'Like yours did,' Meggie explains.

'We think it has to do with the depth of the connection between the Guest and the person they're trying to contact. The deeper it goes, the more chance there is of them washing up here.'

'Yeah, such a deep connection that most Visitors leave Soul Beach after a week, maybe two,' Javier says flatly.

'Javier, don't,' says my sister.

He shrugs. 'Better she knows, huh?'

'Why do they leave?' I ask.

They all look awkward now. Triti frowns. 'Maybe they're banned by the site for breaking the rules. Or for making a Guest unhappy. That happens sometimes.'

'Yeah, or maybe the bond isn't as deep as they thought. Maybe they don't have anything in common any more. It must be hard to take, seeing us living in paradise, while they have to deal with all the boring responsibilities of the real world,' Javier suggests. 'And, anyway, we are not very entertaining to watch. All we do is screw, swim and sit around talking crap.'

'Speak for yourself, Javier,' Meggie says. 'You're a grumpy sod.'

Javier stands up. 'Maybe I need more sleep .' And he laughs drily, then walks off towards the sea.

'Why was that funny?'

'We don't need sleep at all,' Danny says. 'Sure, the sun rises and sets, and then most of us do lie on the beach or in a hut when it's dark, but that's more out of habit, we don't need to. We never get tired. People have tried running for hours, until their body drops, but the brain, no. It never switches off completely. So we can't blame tiredness for our moods.'

'What's his excuse then?' I ask.

Triti frowns. 'You'll learn.'

Meggie shakes her head. 'Lighten up, Triti. Right now, I'm feeling pretty bloody ecstatic because my sister's arrived and

I've missed her like hell. This place does feel pretty much like paradise with her here, so please be nice.'

'Sorry, I'm *always* nice usually,' says Triti with an apologetic smile. 'Nice is my middle name. Bye, Alice. See you around, I hope.' She shuffles away, her earrings tinkling as she walks. From the back she looks thinner, more like a long, lean shadow than a person, but then that's not surprising after what my sister said about no one bothering to eat.

Danny stands up. 'Guess you guys might like to be alone. Nice to meet you, Alice. I'll have a word with Javier. Make sure he remembers his manners next time. We're normally great to be around, I promise.'

He looks at me with those green eyes and that longing again. I try not to return the look, but it's too late. I feel like I'm falling through thin air, with nothing and no one to catch me.

21

'Well? Do you like them?' asks Meggie, when he's disappeared into the crowd.

'They're ... interesting,' I say, guardedly. Actually, Javier strikes me as completely self-centred, Triti is such a blank canvas that she barely seems to exist except for those boobs and her huge jewellery, while Danny is the only one I'd be interested in talking to. But I don't tell Meggie that because I know my sister will take even the tiniest hint that I think Danny's nice as a sign that I fancy him *to death* – no pun intended – and tease me for ever. Like she did with Tim.

Tim. I shiver. I'd forgotten all about what's happening in the real world. How did that happen?

'They're cool when you know them,' Meggie says. 'Maybe you didn't see them at their best. It can be tough. We're like a family ... a huge, really dysfunctional family. But we're all we've got.' She whispers. 'How *are* Mum and Dad?'

I bet they're still bickering downstairs, but I decide it would be wrong to tell her that, or to tell her why, much as I'd love to share the burden. I figure she has enough burdens of her own. 'They're ... fine. Well, not fine exactly. Not after everything that's happened, but they're coping in their own ways.'

She gives me an odd look. I never could get away with lying to my sister, but she doesn't challenge me. Instead she folds her hands together, almost like she's praying.

'You won't leave, will you, Florrie? You won't lose interest in me. Not like other people's Visitors have?'

I smile, because already I cannot imagine ever wanting to leave the Beach, or her. 'No. Besides, you're the most entertaining person I know. We'll always have things to talk about. There's ... love. And music.' I pause as I realise that I'll only ever be able to talk about music that dates from before her death. 'And theatre and books and ... well, loads of other stuff.'

She laughs, for just too long for it to be genuine. 'Eternity lasts a bloody long time, Florrie. We're going to need a lot of small talk.'

I can't think how to reply.

She smiles. 'You look tired again. Maybe you should go; I don't want you failing your exams on my account. But come back tomorrow. Tell me about school and telly and, I don't know, the clothes you've bought and the university you want to go to, and ... I almost forgot. Tell me about the garden.'

'The garden? As in, our *back* garden? When you've got this to look at?' I wave at the beautiful beach.

'You haven't noticed, have you? Listen.'

I listen. I hear the waves and the chatter, like before. 'What am I supposed to be hearing, Meggie?'

'Nothing. That's the point. Apart from the fake waves and the fake trees, there's nothing here but us. Not another breathing thing. No fish, no insects and no birds. It's like whoever designed it ran out of time.'

'That's it. *That's* why it feels so weird.' Suddenly this beautiful place seems a little darker.

She nods and I realise she looks close to tears. 'Oh, Florrie,' she says very quietly. 'I never realised I'd miss the screech of bloody seagulls quite this much.'

There's nothing I can say. I look at her face, trying to memorise every detail in case this is the last time. The more I learn about the place, the more I worry that I can't count on anything on Soul Beach.

'I'm so sorry, Meggie. I wish there was something I could do to make it better.'

'You make it better just by being here, Florrie. Believe me.'

I nod. 'Thanks for saying that. It means a lot to me.'

'Sleep tight, mind the bugs don't bite,' she says, and I click on the Log Out button before she sees me crying.

But then, before she disappears, I notice *her* eyes. Her irises are super-blue, but the whites aren't white any more. They're a violent blood-red. Then that redness spreads like a blush across her face, as though she's drowning in blood. It's so horrifying that I have to close my eyes.

When I open them, the beach is fading away and I realise I am sweating and shaking. I fight to remember my beautiful sister, but, when I shut my eyes again, all I can picture is a Meggie with crimson skin, gasping for breath.

22

The press are outside our door tonight. Dad waits until he thinks there's a full house – local reporters, that guy from the *Sun* who lives round the corner, two cameramen who've been here so often I bet they've saved our address as 'home' on their sat nav – then he walks out and stands in front of the double garage, the same spot where he's given his mini press conferences before.

'I appreciate you have your jobs to do, but as usual we won't be making any form of statement apart from to say that, obviously, we appreciate the kind messages we continue to receive, and we all long for any development that will help solve the mystery of our beloved daughter's death. Any further queries will be handled by the police press office. I'd appreciate it if you'd consider leaving all of us in peace, especially our daughter, Alice. Thank you.'

He ignores the shouted questions about how we feel and whether we think Tim's guilty, as he comes back into the house. I'm in the kitchen making a sandwich. Mum's at Group. I bet she'll be top of the bill tonight.

'How are you, Alice?' Dad says, pouring himself a very large glass of wine. 'Would you like one?'

He doesn't usually offer. I'd been planning a late night trip to Soul Beach, but he looks like he needs some company. 'OK.'

My father pours a lot less wine into my glass, and we sit down in the dining room, because the living room has a huge window and we have an unspoken understanding that it would be bad for the reporters to see us drinking together. *Underage Booze Shame of Tragic Songbird's Sister* is a headline we could probably do without.

'It's been a while since we talked properly,' Dad says.

'Hmm.'

'This business with Tim. I just don't see him as a violent boy. I know your mother says we never know what people are capable of, but it seems to me that the police are clutching at straws.'

'Right.' What does he expect me to say?

'You don't think he killed Megan do you?'

I shake my head. 'No. It makes no sense that he'd kill the person he loved. And I never did fancy him, whatever Mum says.'

Of course, he was attractive – Meggie would never go out with someone ugly. He had pale grey eyes and brown hair that always looked messy and glowed like embers in the sun. Oh, and a permanent five o'clock shadow – not because he was a poseur but because he had too much on his mind to remember to shave every day. But there was never anything flirtatious about my friendship with Tim. We liked each other, no more, no less.

Dad smiles. 'Your mum says silly things. She's … vulnerable.'

'And I'm not?'

He smiles. '*Touché.* I'm sorry, Alice. You're falling through the cracks at the moment, and that's not fair. We'll make it up to you. Things will settle down …'

'No they won't.'

Dad rests his hands on his knees, which means he's about to impart some gem. He must do this with his clients when they're buying a house. *Weighing up all the information, I feel it would be prudent to look into the shared boundary issue …*

'Alice, I don't have much faith in the average PC Plod, but

the detectives on Megan's case seem bright and they really want to solve this. One day soon, it will be over and we can focus on the good memories of your sister.'

'You're crazy if you think that'll be the end of it.'

His right hand twitches on his knee but he doesn't say anything. He nods, so I carry on.

'In Year Ten we did a Media Studies project on press intrusion. There was a family with a murdered daughter, not even famous like Meggie was, and the press never left them alone. The trial and the retrial and then the anniversaries. One year on. Five years. Ten years. Journos chasing them for comments whenever some other kid got killed. It'll be the same for us, and there's nothing we can do about it.'

He takes a sip of wine. His face is colourless, as weary as my grandfather's. Dad hasn't had a proper night's sleep since Meggie died. He feels he should have been there, to look after her. Sometimes I hear the creak on the stair at two a.m., when he realises he's not going to get another wink and goes down to watch Sky Sports with the sound off. He doesn't even *like* sport.

'Doesn't that make you angry, Dad?'

He sighs. 'What makes me angry is that I used to have two beautiful daughters, and now I have one. What makes me angry is that someone thought they had the right to snuff Megan out. The press,' he waves in the direction of the gathering outside, 'they're an irritant but maybe they keep up the pressure to find out who did this. I can forgive them an awful lot for that.'

I take a sip of the wine, not because I want to, but because it seems the right thing to do. I wish I could tell him that Meggie is all right. Well, not all right, but not alone either.

But I know this is *my* secret. These are my two worlds, as important as each other, but I am the one who must choose

78

what Dad and Mum and Meggie can know, and what is best kept from them.

Yes, Soul Beach feels like the most incredible blessing, but it occurs to me for the first time that it could also be a burden ...

23

In London it's dark and rainy. Fat drops fall steadily on the reporters below my bedroom window.

But on Soul Beach it's scorching.

I can't *feel* the heat, but I can see it, a desert haze that makes the shore look unreal. The place seems different to me tonight, and it takes a moment or two to remember what Meggie said about there being no animals here. But that doesn't mean I don't still tingle with excitement when I take my first steps.

As I walk, I notice that the people on the beach are lying in small clusters, not moving. And then it strikes me: they look as though they're all dead.

'Alice?'

I look round and see the American guy with the sad green eyes.

'I'm Danny, remember? Your sister introduced us yesterday,' he says, holding out his hand, then withdrawing it again. 'Sorry, I keep forgetting that we're on different planes.'

'Is that what you think? That the Beach is a kind of parallel universe?'

He shrugs. 'What do I know? I'm a simple American homeboy. I don't think about the bigger things, they make my head hurt.'

I stare at him. Our eyes meet, but this time he looks away first.

'That was a joke,' he says, kicking at the sand.

'Oh. Sorry. I didn't know Americans did irony.' *Why did I say that?*

His eyes narrow, then he laughs. 'Believe it. I spend hours trying to make sense of why I landed up here. Doesn't get me anywhere, but hey, it passes the time ...' He nods at a group of beach boys, asleep next to their boards. 'And it sure beats the alternatives. Surfing's for dummies.'

'Right.' I thought he was the only one of Meggie's friends I wanted to meet again, but now he's here, he makes me feel unsettled. There's something too restless about him, or maybe too raw.

Is it possible to feel unsettled *in a good way?*

'I think Megan is ... um. Having a lie down. With a good friend. I can go and find her if you like?'

'Yes, I'm sure she'd like to know that—' and then I realise what he means by a *lie down*. 'Oh. No. No, that's fine. I can log off and try later.'

His smile is still broad, but now his eyes are more guarded. 'You don't have to leave right now. It's cool to chat to Visitors.' He leans in a little closer. 'After a while here, Guests get kinda one track. Half of them want to talk about books I've never read or movies I've never seen or singers I've never heard of, and the other half want to screw. I mean, I don't say that to boast. Seriously. I say it to prove how desperate folks get around here.'

Danny's deadpan delivery makes me laugh out loud. He smiles again and my sadness is gone, just for a moment.

'So, you'll wait with me?'

I nod. Maybe he's not so difficult to be around after all.

'Fancy a tour?'

'Sure,' I say, glad of the breeze. I know it's virtual, and yet ...

I follow him, past the groups of tanned bodies, as beautifully draped across the sand as bronzes in a museum.

'Those are the musicians,' he says, pointing to two clusters of people. 'Choir on the left, the ones with neater hair. Rock on the right. Every day they try to muss up their bangs and they wake up all shiny and tangle-free. Both are good, though. Sometimes they sing at the same time, like a weird competition. That's not so good.

'Over there is the beach bar, but I guess you know all about that.'

I stare at him. 'How did you know?'

'It's where all the Visitors go first. Kinda like an induction. I do my research.' And he taps the side of his nose.

'What else do you know?'

He sighs. 'More than I want to, Alice, that's for sure. Some questions I wish I'd never tried to answer.'

I open my mouth to ask what those might be, but he puts his finger to his lips and shakes his head.

'Let's go by the jetty,' he says.

'If there's a jetty, does that mean there are boats?'

His eyes cloud and for a moment he seems ... empty, as though there's nothing there, no sight, no knowledge, just a blank. Then I blink and he's smiling. 'Do you see a schedule?' And he laughs.

There's no one else by the jetty.

'Too hot for most people today,' he says, and I know it's because I have a vivid imagination, but when we stop, sweat is trickling down the back of my neck.

He sits at the very end, looking out to sea, and I join him. The sound of the waves becomes louder, and when he dips his feet in the water, I hear splashing. His feet are pale and bloodless in the sea.

I wonder how Danny died.

'It won't always be this hard for your sister,' he says. 'I arrived nine months before she did and it's tough at first, adjusting to your new ... *status*.'

'What's the biggest shock?' I ask. 'I'd like to understand.'

'Ah, you're sweet.'

'Don't patronise me.'

'I wouldn't dare. But if I'm honest – and maybe this is jealousy because no one's shown up for *me* – I don't know if it's a good thing, letting family visit. No offence.'

'None taken. Why?'

'Because there's *nothing* you can do to help her. Plus you'll never understand, unless it happens to you, which is the last thing Megan would want.'

'I can *try* to understand.'

'Sure,' his voice softens. 'But trust me, you won't. Here is *forever*, right. No exit. I don't know if you ever come to terms with it. I haven't.' And he kicks the water so forcefully that it splashes in my face. It's cool and refreshing.

I brush the seawater away. Even though, of course, it doesn't exist.

'Is there really no way out? No one ever leaves?'

He shrugs. 'Not while I've been here. There are rumours.' He laughs, but it's a bitter laugh. 'Look around you, Alice, this is like a giant open-air university dorm. Of course there are *rumours*. It's like a hobby for some people. Making stuff up. But I don't know if I believe them.'

'What do the rumours say?'

'That you'll only get away if . . .' he leans in close, 'if *whatever landed you here in the first place is resolved*, back in the real world.'

'Right.' I don't understand, but I drag myself back to that 'real' world and scribble down what he said on a heart-shaped Post-It. Maybe it'll make sense later. 'And that's all?'

He looks at me evenly. 'You guys aren't Catholics, are you?'

'Church of England. And only then to get into the right school.'

'Well, they accept all gods on Soul Beach. Or no god at all. But at church sometimes people talked to me about limbo.'

'Limbo?' *That* word again.

'He's not started on his religion shtick, has he, Florrie?'

I look around and there's Meggie, looking slightly flushed. The weather or her 'lie down'? None of my business, I suppose. 'He's just keeping me company.'

Danny gets up. 'It's only a theory.' He winks at my sister, then leaves. His legs are strong and powerful, and there's something in his walk that's different from the surfer swagger of the other men on the beach. He's more ... upright, somehow, like a soldier or an athlete.

Meggie takes his place next to me, hugging her knees to her chest. 'Whatever he tells you, ignore it, sis.'

'OK,' I say, not wanting to ask about her appearance – her messy hair, crumpled clothes. I don't like thinking about what happens when I'm not here.

'So good to see you, Florrie. You're the only thing that feels real to me these days.'

I look at her face, to see if she's messing about, but she's absolutely sincere. 'I know. It's like having you back ...'

We don't feel the need to say anything else. The water slaps against the sun-bleached wood of the jetty, and all the doubts and the questions I had after talking to Danny disappear. We are sisters, hanging out. *Like we used to.* Meggie and Alice.

And then I realise that it's not quite like we used to, because before it was always me doing what she wanted: waiting on Meggie, waiting for Meggie, waiting for Meggie to notice me.

It wasn't that my sister was horrible, not at all. She was just the first, and so like every other younger sister, I would always be *her* first audience.

But here on the Beach it feels different. She needs me as much as I need her. More, maybe. For the first time in my life, I feel like we're equals, like we understand each other ...

I hear a knock at my door. *Shit.*

I push the laptop screen down as far I can without it

shutting down, and mute the sound and the mic in case Meggie says something.

'Alice?' It's my father.

'I'm doing my homework.'

'Yes. I know. Sorry to disturb you. It's just that Fran's here and she'd like to talk to all of us together.'

'I'll be right down,' I call back.

I wait until his footsteps are gone, and then I switch the microphone and sound back on. 'Meggie?'

She looks at me, her big blue eyes as trusting as a baby's.

'Need to go. Sorry. I promise I'll be back soon.' I try to sound like it's no big deal.

She flinches a little. 'OK.' Her voice is small.

I blow her a kiss, log out and then as I close down the laptop, the dread grows, and I feel like I've fallen into an icy lake.

Fran? This can only mean one thing . . .

24

Fran the Family Liaison officer is sitting on the edge of the sofa. She looks uncomfortable, but then that's nothing new. I think someone told her once that she's not allowed to smile when she's with 'her' bereaved families.

But my mother's eyes are bright, the precise same shade of blue as Meggie's.

'It may not be the news you were hoping for, Mrs Forster.'

Mum blinks.

'Tim Ashley has been released without charge.'

I try to keep my face neutral. Dad catches my eye: I can tell he's trying to look neutral too. But Mum looks broken.

'It's not the end. Honestly. Try to think of it as just another step closer to finding out who killed your daughter,' says Fran, wearing that expression of professional concern that makes me want to slap her.

'We all know who killed her,' my mother hisses. 'But you lot are too bloody incompetent to make it stick.'

'Bea . . .' my father says softly.

'I'm going out,' she says, brushing his arm away.

'Wait,' says Fran. 'The reporters are still outside.'

Mum's face is furious. *Scary* even. 'I'm not going to be trapped in my own house by those scum. It's not like I'm the guilty one, is it?'

We follow her into the hallway, Dad trying to change her mind. But when she opens the front door, the driveway and the street are completely empty.

'How did they know?' Mum asks.

Fran shrugs. 'We try to keep things under wraps, but I guess the news got out.' I realise she's carrying her bag and coat. Planning a fast exit, I think. I wish I could leave too.

My mother hesitates on the doorstep. Her anger's gone, now, and her shoulders slump. Fran opens the door, slips through. 'I'll be in touch, hopefully with more positive news.'

Dad takes my mother's arm and this time she doesn't swat him away.

'Brandy,' he says, and she lets herself be led back inside.

We all have a brandy, and my mother doesn't even given my father a dirty look for pouring me one. She can't sit down. Instead she paces like a zoo animal, mumbling under her breath.

'If you've got something to say, then say it, Bea,.' Dad tells her.

She tuts. 'I can't talk to you about this, can I? You'd rather go on a *Tim Ashley is Innocent* march than admit he might have killed her.'

I want to leave but I can't. I don't trust my legs to hold me up. The brandy has left an evil, woody taste in my mouth and I want to be sick.

'Maybe I was wrong,' Dad says.

Maybe I was wrong, too. Perhaps I was fooled by Tim's shyness. Wasn't Hitler meant to be a mild-mannered vegetarian, when he wasn't committing genocide? Perhaps Tim only pretended to be interested in me as some kind of sick smokescreen.

My mother sits down next to me. Then she opens her arms and, let's face it, it would be heartless of me to turn away. When she hugs me I smell Meggie's perfume, Coco Mademoiselle, which Mum wears when she's missing my sister so much that she can't bear it, and wants to remind herself that she was real, once. And then she whispers,

'They'll get him in the end, Alice, I know they will.'

I let her hold me, but all the time I'm thinking, well, *how*, if they've held him and questioned him and threatened him and he still hasn't admitted it?

And that's when it occurs to me.

Tim might just tell *me* the truth . . .

They should have bottled how Meggie smelled.

Honey and lemon to soothe her throat after a performance. Chamomile shampoo for that silky blonde hair. And last night's party always clinging to her clothes, last night's perfume sticky on her skin.

Sometimes I try to recreate the smell, to help me remember. But for all my alchemy, there's a missing element, always. The element that made her, her.

Meggie would have been turned into a brand, had she lived. There would have been a reality show, an autobiography, a range of novels, perhaps. And definitely a signature perfume. Not under her own name, of course. Meggie is too harsh a name. It would have been called Songbird or something even more crass. And it wouldn't have smelled of her at all. Instead, it would have been sickly. Sweetness and light with no edge.

A lie, because the Meggie I knew, especially at the end, was more than sweetness and light.

At least I saved her such indignities.

25

I count to three. Then I pull away from my mother's arms.

'I'm really tired, Mum.'

'Of course you are,' she says, and then she finally notices the brandy Dad poured for me earlier, and gives him a dirty look. 'Sleep tight, sweetheart. Tomorrow it will all seem better.'

She doesn't believe that any more than I do.

My father hugs me briefly, silently.

On my way upstairs, I know the only way I'm going to feel better is by seeing Meggie again, even though it's only twenty minutes since I left her.

Outside my room, a wave of nausea hits, and I only just make it to the bathroom in time.

Afterwards I throw water into my face, and try to drink it from the tap, to wipe out the revolting taste. Is it insane to believe that Tim might talk to *me*? That our friendship might make him trust me?

I scrub at my face with a flannel. It's ridiculous. This isn't a re-run of *Buffy* or *Scooby Do*. Perhaps I am losing it, to imagine he'd confess just because I ask him nicely.

But then again, perhaps what makes me different is that I'm pretty much the only person out there who *wants* to believe he's innocent. I can't imagine him smothering my sister, ignoring her struggles, and then calmly leaving her digs to get pissed in the student bar, making sure he's caught on the CCTV to give himself an alibi.

That's not the Tim I know. We all thought he was one of

her phases, when she brought him home only a few weekends after starting at uni. Every previous boyfriend had been flashy, in love with himself, but Tim was so *straight*, right down to his name. After years of Rafes and Joshuas and even a Merlin, Meggie fell for a Tim who hated parties but loved cooking, who felt more at home on a protest march than in the booze-filled green room behind the scenes on *Sing for your Supper*. Incredible.

But gradually it started to make more sense. The other men treated her as a trophy; Tim treated Meggie as a human being. He opened doors for her, let her choose the best seat in a restaurant, carried her suitcase. Some people would find so much attention suffocating, but she lapped it up. He adored her and she adored him back. They were supposed to be the University Sweethearts who fell in love in term one, married on graduation, stayed together for ever. They didn't fall out when she started to get famous, not even when one of the gossip columns printed a picture of the two of them with the headline *Surely The Songbird Could Do Better Than This?*

I knew the truth behind the cruel headlines, or at least I thought I did: that he was a million times better than the arrogant poseurs and hangers-on who were trying to edge into her life. That he was kind and gentle and judged people on *who* they were rather than what they could do for him. Other-wise why would he bother with me?

Unless, of course, I was just a gullible little girl who he could fool with a few casual questions about my GCSEs and my favourite movies? If he could manipulate me so easily, what might he do if I show up on his doorstep?

I can't go to see him. It's an insane idea.

And yet, I need to know who killed my sister, and why. It has to be worth the risk.

I tiptoe back to my room, my head still fuzzy from the

brandy in my system. I have to log on now before I lose it completely. I move the laptop onto the bed.

I need to be on the Beach.

I wait for the buzz, for the strange, half-pleasurable, half-fearful sensations that Soul Beach awakens in me. I cannot imagine anywhere in the crappy real world feeling *this* good again. I picture Meggie, squinting into the sun, and then, behind her, I imagine Danny, his green eyes seeing into my soul . . .

But I'm not on the sand. I'm in the beach bar. It's dark, except for ripples of moonlight that shine in through the open sides of the building.

'Sam?' I call out.

She pops up from behind the bar, looking even more elfin and otherworldly in this light. She's holding a roll-up and she looks slightly guilty.

'Taking a break?'

Sam nods. 'R and R. It's been hellish for the last few hours, if you'll pardon the joke. Maybe the management are playing around with the thermostat, but it's feverish here.'

I smile, though I couldn't be less interested in the temperature. 'Have you seen Meggie?

'She left the bar, maybe twenty minutes ago, when they decided to go for a late night picnic. What's the rush?'

'I . . . it's Tim, her ex-boyfriend. Well, he was still her boyfriend when she died. The police have been questioning him and now he's been released. '

'That's why you've landed in here first, then, I guess. So I can remind you that you mustn't say anything to her about it.'

'Another of the pointless rules?'

'This one isn't pointless. How will it help her to know what's happened when she doesn't even remember how she died? Will it make her any happier?'

I consider this. 'But the police think he killed her. Everyone does.'

Sam takes a drag on her cigarette. It changes her face shape, makes her look cruel. 'Doesn't sound to me like you do.'

I stare at her. 'Why do you say that?'

'Hunch. Always been my speciality, hunches. But anyway, go on.'

'You said before that people are here because they've died unresolved deaths. So once the death is resolved, doesn't that mean people leave?'

'Who told you that people leave?'

'Danny. I don't know his second name. American.'

'Oh. Danny Cross. Hmm. I should have known it would be one of the big *thinkers*. They cause so many problems. '

Danny Cross. I write his name down. Maybe if I can find out why *he's* on the Beach, it'll help me understand why Meggie is, too. 'Did he get it wrong then?'

She walks to the side of the bar and I join her. The beach looks real again, now, all the strangeness I felt after Meggie told me there were no animals, no birds, has gone. The waves seem to call out to me. *Jump in, the water's lovely.* I've never skinny dipped, but I can understand why you would here.

'Look, mate, I told you before, everything is need to know. All I do is make it as good as possible so that the kids never *want* to leave.'

'But some do.'

She sighs. 'Some want to leave, yes. And a few, a very few, find a way out. But mostly, this is for eternity, and the ones who do best are the ones who learn to stay in the moment. All the kids who've tried to keep track of how long they've been here lose count after a couple of years, and then hate themselves for it. It doesn't help.'

'And the ones who do find the escape hatch? Are they the ones who kept trying?'

'No. It's not that simple. There are Guests who are desperate to leave but never do, and some who loved it here, but then simply didn't show up one morning.'

'So it *is* about something that happens in the real world.'

She blows a pungent smoke ring. 'Real is a relative term, Alice.'

'In my world, then?'

Sam looks away. 'I've probably said too much already.'

'So ... if I do something that helps to resolve what happened to Meggie? Like, I don't know, work out who killed her. Would she disappear?'

'Don't do anything you wouldn't do anyway. It could be dangerous. Things have effects you could never predict.'

'But ...'

She seems to be thinking something over. 'All I'll say is that I think you might be right about resolution being the key. But resolution doesn't always mean what you think it means. As Confucius might have said.'

'Confucius?'

She waves the comment away. 'Some old Chinese guy. You know your trouble, Alice? You read too much into things. Half of what I say is as pointless as you'd expect from a girl who's been up all night.'

'And the other half?'

She tuts. 'Give it a rest, will you? Tell you what, it's a good job you're only a Visitor. You'd go crazy here.'

'I'm going to find her,' I say, quietly.

Sam stands next to me, and the stink of cannabis is almost overwhelming. 'Go on, Alice. And when you do, tell her jokes and happy stories, enjoy the time you've got with her. If there's one thing I've learned in this bloody place, it's that you never know what you have till you lose it.'

26

If Meggie has an inkling that anything has changed back 'home' then she's not letting it show.

I find her lying on the jetty, staring up at the crescent moon, while three guys gaze at her like she's a mermaid who's been washed ashore. I look for Danny or Javier but they're not among her admirers. These men are toned and honed and, in the blue lunar light, their skin reminds me of marble. Plus, their poses are too deliberate, as though they've chosen the best positions to show off their muscles. Funny, I hardly know Danny at all but I cannot imagine him doing that: though I am not nearly so sure about Javier.

I have to remind myself that in real life they probably weren't nearly as cute, so they're making the most of the novelty of being gorgeous. I guess I might do the same if I looked so good.

Then again, while I'm here, maybe I do.

'Meggie?'

She looks up and for a moment, she frowns, the way she used to when I walked into her room without knocking and found her posing in her underwear in front of the mirror, holding a banana to her face instead of a microphone. But then she smiles so kindly that I realise I must have been wrong.

'Oh, Alice, you're back already, that's terrific!'

The beefcakes don't look round, and I'm about to say something about their rudeness, when I remember that of course, they can't see me.

Megan stands up. 'I shan't bother to introduce you to these three,' she says, stepping in towards me for an air kiss. She whispers, 'They're not very bright or interesting and to be honest, I've already forgotten their names myself. I had wanderlust. Wanted a break from the intensity of the usual gang.'

She walks ahead of me, back towards the bar. 'Good to see you again so soon, baby sister. Taking a break from your homework?'

'Something like that. You know what it's like at home,' I say, even though she doesn't, not any more. If she walked up the driveway to our house now, she wouldn't see any difference: same peeling paint on the garage door, same garden statue of a kissing couple next to the pathway (not my parents' choice, but it had been concreted in by the previous owner and there's no shifting it).

Inside, though, everything feels topsy-turvy, like a parallel world where evil has reversed all the settings so that *happy* and *family* have changed to *sad* and *strangers*.

'Tell me what's been happening on telly,' she says.

As I try to remember the latest storyline from her favourite soaps, it's a struggle to pretend any of it matters. But I need to do it, for her sake. Funny to think that only a month ago I would have been ecstatic about being able to talk to her about *anything*, however banal.

'Hi, girls.'

I know it's him before I turn around: *Danny Cross*. In the semi-darkness he looks older, more serious. He catches me staring and I blush. The one consolation is that I don't think he can see me blushing, because I'm not *really* there.

'Hot still, isn't it?' he says.

Oh. I look at the web cam light, glowing mischievously. Evidently Danny *can* see my face. I hope it's been given the magic Soul Beach airbrush, so that I look as stunning as the Guests. 'Is it?'

My sister sighs. 'Ugh, it's always hot here, even after sunset. I never thought I'd dream of rain.'

I turn, peer out of my real window in my real bedroom: a storm has begun, and I didn't even notice. The dense, dark sky keeps splitting open, the thunder coming a second or two later. The eye of the storm must be close.

'We could go to the bar. At least they have ceiling fans,' suggests Danny.

As we enter, Sam drags herself up from a chair to mix their cocktails, but she doesn't acknowledge me beyond a half-nod. I realise that our conversation was strictly private. It's not as though I'd dare repeat it anyway. Not with so much at stake.

I watch my sister extra closely as she sits down with her mojito, and I try to commit every millimetre of her to memory. Because if I do go ahead with my plan to corner Tim, and if that *does* resolve anything, I could lose her all over again.

But where will she go *then*? Will she no longer exist, or is there *another* place beyond the Beach?

'. . . has she always been such a daydreamer?'

Javier and Triti have joined us at the table, and Javier is waving a hand in front of my face.

'Sorry. Miles away.'

'You mean light years, don't you?' says Javier. The others laugh.

Lightning flashes outside my bedroom window, almost dazzling me I'm so close to the eye of the storm now, and thunder follows immediately. No one on the Beach flinches, of course.

I feel got at. 'It's not easy for me, either, you know.'

'What? Being alive? Oh, poor *you*.' Javier has fixed me with his eyes, like a jaguar sizing up its prey. I look up to my sister but she's smiling at him.

'Javier, leave her alone.' It's Danny who stands up for me.

A sly smile crosses Javier's unshaven face. 'Sweet.'

'What?' says Danny.

'Love across the divide. It's like a movie. But they're doomed.' Javier mimes playing a violin, and Triti and Meggie pull faces, but they're *oh, you're too funny* faces.

Rain is lashing against my window now, loud as bullets.

'Ignore him. He's a dick,' says Danny.

'And you are proof that Americans have no sense of humour,' Javier replies, stretching out his long legs, and yawning.

Meggie smiles at me. 'Don't listen to either of them, Florrie. Apparently they've been at it ever since they got here.'

'I wouldn't say that,' Javier replies.

'Did you arrive at the same time, then?' I ask.

Danny nods. 'Yeah. A year ago. Kinda like twins.'

'Twins?'

The idea seems grotesque, that you're twinned with someone who died around the same time. Though I suppose it's every bit as significant as the day you're born.

Javier stands up and walks round to where Danny's sitting. He puts his arms around Danny's neck and gives him a kiss. 'He ain't heavy, he's my soul brother, huh?'

Then he blows me a kiss too. 'Don't break his heart,' he says to me as he leaves the bar. Triti follows him like a faithful lapdog, without saying a word.

More flashes – one, two, three in succession – fire up the sky. Usually storms scare me a bit, but I don't feel that way now, because reality feels so much less real than the Beach.

'Sorry about him,' says Danny. 'I, uh, ought to be getting along too. But come back soon, huh, Alice.' His smile is warm, like lazy summer afternoons, and he holds my gaze for a moment too long. I look down.

Then he slopes off.

My sister is looking at me in a funny way. It's the expression she always gets when she's about to say something clever. 'You like him,' she says languidly. 'And you two would make a lovely couple. If it weren't for the obvious problem—'

I interrupt her. 'Don't say it. Not tonight.'

'Eh?' she looks surprised. 'Oh, *that*,' she says, dismissing the whole life/death divide with the flick of a hand. 'No, I didn't mean that. I meant the altogether more fundamental problem that Danny Cross is even gayer than Javier.'

27

'Gay?'

She yawns. 'That's my theory, anyway. It'd explain why he and Javier are so prickly around each other. And why Danny never bothers to chat up the girls here.'

I feel disappointed somehow and that in turn makes me feel silly: why should it matter to me either way? Anyway, it could simply be that Danny doesn't bother to flirt with other Guests because Beach life seems so pointless to him. He almost said as much to me. I could say that to Meggie, but she'll only take the piss and decide it proves her stupid theory that I like him.

Well, I *do* like him, but not in *that* way. Her other friends make me feel awkward and stupid, the way I used to when she was fifteen and I was twelve and I could hear her catty mates laughing at me.

I wonder if Javier and Triti do the same when I leave Soul Beach?

Suddenly I feel exhausted. It's been quite a night, with all the Tim drama, but I can hardly explain that to Meggie. 'Listen, I know this is a rubbish excuse, but I have to get an assignment done for first period tomorrow, so I have to log off.'

'Not like you to leave stuff to the last minute, Florrie.'

'No, well, maybe I'm not such a swot these days.'

I see it in her face – the moment when she understands why school work seems like the last thing I can be bothered with, how her death has made my life seem like a charade. But she doesn't say anything.

I'm about to blow my usual kiss, when I think about what Sam said in the bar. 'I love you, Meggie. You'll remember that, won't you, even when I'm not actually here with you?'

'Daft cow, of course.'

'I know it's soppy, but I'm going to say it every time I see you. We can't know what will happen in the future, can we?'

'OK, serious girl.' She nods. 'Look, it's enough that you're here. It's *proof*, isn't it? I'm the only one of my friends who has a Visitor. That means something, Florrie. So you don't have to keep telling me. I *know*.'

And I know better than to argue any more, so we air kiss.

'Come back soon, Florrie. Missing you already.'

I log off and instantly regret it. I want to go back and say even more. I don't care if she takes the piss. But when I try, the site is down. *Soul Beach is undergoing maintenance. Please try later.* Maybe there are virtual cleaners picking virtual litter up from the virtual sand. Or maybe the whole thing is my imagination anyway, so when I'm not 'there', the site no longer exists.

I go to the window. The storm has moved on, but I can still see lightning in the distance, towards central London, and the sky is the colour of brick. My own world looks so much less convincing than the Beach does.

I wonder if it would be easier if I was always there? With Meggie. *With Danny.*

I shake my head, to shake away the fuzzy brandy feeling and the stupid thoughts. The heart-shaped Post-It on my desk catches my eye.

It has his name written on it: Danny Cross. Though for all I know, he's no more real than the Beach and the tooth fairy. I want to Google him, but that's what stupid kids do when they fall for the floppy-haired singer in a stupid reality TV band.

It's what people did all over the world, in their millions, over Meggie.

Then I think of Tim. I guess he'll be back in his flat by now. Is the storm raging over *his* bit of the London sky? Can he sleep? Is he thinking about Meggie, about Mum and Dad, about me? Fran telling us the news feels like weeks ago, even though it's only a couple of hours. I click onto the *Daily Mail* website, and the *Sun*, and then the BBC news front page, but there's nothing there about him being released.

And then my fingers are already typing *Danny Cross* into the Google search box before I realise what I'm doing. Other words appear next to it, as the search engine tries to guess what I will type next. *Danny Cross son of Vincent Cross, Danny Cross Cross Enterprises, Danny Cross plane, Danny Cross accident.*

And then, *Danny Cross death.*

My throat feels tight, as though someone has knotted a scarf around my neck and is pulling hard. He's real. And he's dead.

When I manage to breathe again, I'm light headed. I search for *Danny Cross death* and a list of pages pops up, along with the suggestion that I could try narrowing it down to *Images* or *News*.

I click on the first link, which takes me to a page on an American TV website, headlined *Magnate's son feared dead in desert crash*. Before I can read on, I notice the photograph.

Now I realise why Danny looked familiar. *I've seen this photo before.*

This Danny wears a tuxedo and white shirt, and a black bow tie lies loose on either side of his collar. His clothes couldn't be more different to the ones Danny wears on the Beach, but the smile is the same. Confident, but not arrogant. Intelligent, but challenging, too. The eyes are different, though. They're still green, but there's none of the longing that drew me in the first time he looked at me on the Beach.

I remember this picture of him from the papers, though I don't remember many details of the story. Back then, death seemed irrelevant to me. Now I skim-read: private jet, en route to a family party, aerial searches, father's business growing despite recession, one of America's most eligible bachelors, ready to take up a place at Yale.

I'm numb. I don't know what I was expecting. Or perhaps I do. Maybe I never expected to find a Danny Cross at all, never mind one whose digitally reproduced eyes twinkle back at me right now. It makes it . . .

Real.

It makes Soul Beach real. I only realise now that I hadn't completely believed in the place, or that I was really talking to my sister. After all, every detail could easily have sprung from my grieving mind.

But *this* couldn't. I look at the date on the news story: just over a year ago. The timing fits.

What was I doing then? Lying by a pool at a resort in Greece, on the last family holiday before Meggie went to college. Mum had to use the guilt card to persuade her to come and I even had to skip the first week of term to fit in with my sister's hectic social calendar, but once we got there, she was her usual shiny self. I had nothing to talk about except what GCSEs I'd be taking the next year, but she still let me tag along with her newly formed gang . . .

I click some of the other links. After the plane went missing, it took the search teams a day and a night to find the crash scene. When they did, Danny was in the pilot's seat, a long way from the wreckage, and his dad's pilot had ejected, too, still in the passenger seat, bolt upright. That's when I remember a detail I must have taken in at the time: the fact that the son of a multi-millionaire was arrogant enough to believe he could fly a plane without training. He paid the price for his vanity.

The photograph below it shocks me. Metal confetti lies across an arid desert landscape, and it's impossible to tell this used to be an aircraft: it also seems completely crazy that the two victims wouldn't have been smashed to smithereens, too, but that's what it says.

The articles mention the pilot as an afterthought. He left a widow and two young daughters. Hardly anyone went to *his* funeral, yet it takes me only a couple of clicks to find a video of Danny's from the local news channel in Boston.

I feel a sharp stab as I watch his funeral, because it reminds me so much of Meggie's. Danny's father is stocky and serious, more like a bodyguard than a billionaire in his mourner's suit. His mother, a blonde trophy wife, looks sedated as she walks in slow-mo into a whitewashed chapel. Danny's brother is fourteen or fifteen, moon-faced and clumsy, the kid brother who was surely only ever meant to be in the shadows, and has suddenly become heir to an empire.

And what an empire! The voiceover explains that Cross Enterprises includes chemical works and drugstores and a small selection of dot com companies, 'purchased on the advice of Danny, who was widely seen as a hot prospect within the business world'.

Inside the chapel, huge banners hang from the beams, showing Danny's face. A choir of girls dressed in the royal blue and crimson uniform of his exclusive private school sing an 'inspirational' song I don't recognise. Half of the congregation are on the brink of tears. A Botoxed pastor gives a sound-bite about lost promise and God's unfathomable ways.

Then the video cuts to a long shot of the Cross tomb, the grieving family like stick figures at this distance. The voice-over mentions a childhood sweetheart, and I see a pretty girl with chestnut hair step forward to throw something – flowers, earth? – into the grave.

See, Meggie? He's straight.

There are more headlines linked from this page: a report blaming the pilot for the accident, because he allowed a kid to take over the controls. A rumour that Vincent Cross was planning to sue the pilot's family for recklessness. Then a final story denying the rumour, and stressing that Mr Cross had gone to considerable lengths to ensure the widow and daughters would be provided for. Between the lines, the message is clear: Vincent Cross is one of the good guys.

I watch the funeral footage again, with the sound off, trying to make sense of it all. Like my sister, Danny died a violent death, one that made him more famous than he had been alive. And, like my sister, his face sells newspapers: the two of them had it all but readers can take some warped comfort from the fact that neither Meggie's brief fame or Danny's huge fortune could stop them losing everything.

OK, they're not Kurt Cobain or Princess Diana or Che Guevara. They weren't alive long enough to become real legends, and they'll be forgotten or replaced by the next tragic teen sooner or later. But their deaths did say *something* to people about life, however briefly.

Is that why they're on the Beach?

28

I wake up with a pen in my hand, and loose pages of unreadable scribble scattered across the duvet and the floor.

Last night I spent hours trying to make sense of the rules of the Beach, but I must have been in a kind of trance. The few words I can decipher trigger vague memories of my frenzied searching for details about Danny and his death. Oh, and my theory that Soul Beach is a collection of kids who found their fifteen minutes of fame when it was too late for them to enjoy it.

My head throbs. I open the laptop and go online again. If Javier is Danny's death 'twin' then it should be easy to find out about how he lost his life, too. On the news search page, I choose the date I now know that Danny died: September thirteenth. Then I type *Javier + Spain + death*.

I wait. Nothing appears in the auto-complete box, and so I press *return*.

Your search terms have not returned any results for this date. Would you like to widen the search to include other dates?

Could Javier or Danny have arrived a few days apart, and then got confused? I press *yes*, and a page loads with thousands of results, most of them in Spanish. I click on auto-translate and, *finally*, there's a headline from a Barcelona newspaper, in broken English:

Boy, 17, dies in fall of tragedy during fiesta, drugs suspected

I scroll down the short article. *Javier Natera Fernandez*. The dead teenager is ringed in a family photograph: mother, father, a boy, a small girl and a baby on a beach, all grinning at the camera. It must be an old photo because the boy is no more than ten – the defiance in his eyes is absolutely familiar. It's *our* Javier.

But didn't he say he was an *only* child?

There's another picture, of a roof terrace just visible from street level. Six, seven floors up. I imagine Javier falling ... falling ... Was he pushed? Did he call out, wave his arms to try to get some resistance against the air?

'Alice? Are you up yet?'

The house is coming to life beyond my bedroom door. The fan whirring in the bathroom, the boiler firing up for Mum's shower, Radio Four in the kitchen. Funny. Those sounds haven't changed since Meggie died.

Yet now I think about it, I realise the sound of the waves is always there in the background. A reminder of what I'm missing ...

I'm running late, but I crave the Beach so deeply that I don't care. I log in quickly. My mouth is dry and instead of the familiar rush of energy, all I feel is dread. I can't explain it: maybe it's guilt at snooping into the lives of bereaved families, which surely makes me no better than the gawpers at my sister's funeral. Or maybe it's fear that I've somehow broken the rules of the Beach again, by meddling in someone else's affairs.

Either way, I am convinced something is wrong ...

Soul Beach is quiet. Hard to know what time it is 'there' but I'm guessing somewhere around four a.m. There's a hint of dawn on the horizon, but the bodies on the beach are slumped, and even the waves seem to whisper *shhh*.

No one stirs as I pass. Most of them can't see me, after all. As I increase the pace with the mouse, my footsteps speed up, slapping against the sand until I begin to pant – it really does feel as though my lungs are emptying as I get faster. I remember what Meggie said to me, about the beach stretching on for ever, about no one ever finding the edge.

Finally I see Danny, half-sitting, half-lying against the side of a beach hut, his shoulders slumped and his eyes closed. The images of him in his tux, and then of his plane smashed against the desert like a broken insect, come back to me and the contrast is so shocking that I have to look away. I stalk around the other side of the hut, and find Triti and Javier asleep in one another's arms. He's so long and lean, and she's tiny, but they both look like little children, their mouths slightly open as they breathe. What happened to devastate his family so completely?

And then I look inside the hut, through the gap between the door and the bamboo frame.

She's on her own, a sheet half wrapped around her. How strange. I've seen Meggie in the nude a thousand times, I've bathed with her, compared freckles (thousands on me, no more than a dozen on her). But this feels wrong. Like spying.

I put the laptop into sleep mode and shuffle into yesterday's clothes. I try to reason with myself: at least she's still here. At least I can still talk to her. A few moments ago, I thought I might have been banished from this paradise, so I should be glad.

But none of that improves my mood. I wish . . .

I try to stop myself thinking it, but it's too late. Sometimes I almost wish I was dead, too, because at least then I wouldn't feel so left out.

29

The news about Tim being let out is all around school.

I feel the stares as I go through the gate, and when I'm outside sixth-form block, I'm attracting so much attention that I have to check I remembered to put on my jeans.

'Alice!' Cara cuts through the crowded corridor and gives me a hug. I wriggle free, though with her at my side I do feel less exposed. 'I heard about Tim. Need a coffee?'

'I'm late already.'

'Screw that. The teachers'll let you off anything today. Make the most of it, chick.'

Before I can argue, I'm being swept towards the common room, which is empty because anyone up this early has a class to go to. Cara makes me a coffee, and when I sip it, it tastes of booze. 'Ugh!'

'Medicinal,' she explains. Cara's mother has one of those drinks cabinets that just keeps on giving. 'Plus, we've got History, haven't we? I need something to get through that even on a normal day.'

I take another sip. 'I appreciate the thought, but that's disgusting.'

She sniffs, then tastes, and pulls a face. 'Shit, you're right. I guess that means we're not teen alcoholics, then.' She walks over to the sink with the mugs and pours them down the drain.

Cara sits back down again and reaches into her bag, pulling out a packet of chocolate biscuits. 'Plan B.' She makes a big pile out of them on the table in front of me. 'The leaning tower of digestives. We can't go to History until we've finished them! Agreed?'

I nod.

'Do you still think Tim's innocent?' she asks.

I turn the question back onto her. 'Do you?'

She shrugs. 'He never seemed the murdering type to me, though I admit I'm not the best judge of men. I thought he was a bit dull. Maybe he had an awful temper that none of us saw. His hair was sort of ginger, wasn't it, and they say they're the worst. Maybe he did it but didn't mean to.'

No. Not Tim. '*Maybe.*'

'You don't sound like you believe it. Do you suspect someone else?'

'Just because I'm her sister doesn't mean I know who killed her, Cara. I don't have a sixth sense.'

She sighs. 'Sorry.'

'It's all anyone can think about when they see me. *Oh, look, there's Alice. Oh, wasn't it terrible what happened? Poor Meggie, so talented.* It was bad enough when she was alive – *Let's hear you sing, Meggie. Alice, you can mime* – but now it's unbearable.' And then I realise how that sounded. 'Sorry. I'm such a bitch.'

Cara nods, and eats half a biscuit before she speaks. 'I only asked because in the pub you said you were fed up with no one ever talking about Meggie.'

'Oh.' I see her point. 'Sorry.'

'No. *I'm* sorry. Today's an exception, Alice. Sure, there'll be times like this when it's all anyone can think about. But if Tim did do it, they'll get him in the end. He'll go to prison and then you can live the life you were always going to have. Which reminds me. Have you started on your UCAS form yet?'

I take a biscuit myself. I didn't eat this morning and I feel slightly faint. But it tastes like cardboard. 'No. Maybe I should go to Greenwich, like Meggie.'

'So you can be even more paranoid about people always thinking of your sister?' Cara shakes her head, then stands up. 'Sometimes you're your own worst enemy. I'll put up with it, I'm your best mate. But not everyone feels that way ...'

'Are people saying things?' And then I wonder if she means Robbie. 'Has Robbie been talking to you?'

'No. He's too loyal. But it doesn't mean he's *not* getting pissed off, Alice. And don't think for a second that the Megan thing will stop other girls getting their claws into him. I've already heard whispers that people think he's fair game because of the way you treat him.'

She waits for my reaction. I feel nothing. 'Thanks for the warning, Cara.' I stand up too. 'If we don't go to History now, we might as well not bother.'

She grabs my hand. 'Don't leave me, Alice. *Please.* I feel like you're slipping away.'

I stare at her. 'Don't be daft, Cara. I've got enough on my plate without you saying weird stuff.' I walk out of the common room, feeling wired from the sugar rush. I know she's right. That I'm going to lose Robbie to some competitive bimbo from Year Eleven. But I don't think I care enough to try to stop it happening.

Somehow I get through school, ignoring the whispers, and then I walk home alone.

Today the sky's so grey it merges with the pavements, and the humidity plasters my hair to the back of my neck. I crave colour: on Soul Beach, it will be blue and gold and sunshine and salty sea breezes that blow away any stickiness. If it isn't actually heaven, then it must be pretty damn close. I suddenly feel slightly impatient with Meggie. What *exactly* is wrong with eternal paradise?

OK, too much of a good thing might get samey, but given a choice between hellfire and tropical loveliness, most of us wouldn't hesitate. Trust Meggie to find something to complain about.

There. I've said it. Meggie could be a bit of a moaner.

Death smoothes away people's faults. Meggie was beautiful and talented and generous and funny. No one could resist her. That much we're allowed to talk about. But she could also be moody. And selfish. And patronising. Even, occasionally, unkind. She was a human being, but now that she's dead, she's a saint.

Mum didn't sit me down and say *do not speak ill of the dead*. It happened naturally. It's only now that I've got her back that I can admit how maddening she could be on the rare occasions when she wasn't the centre of attention.

Is that why she's so miserable on Soul Beach? On earth, her voice and her beauty made her special. Even before *Sing for Your Supper*, she stood out. But now she's just another pretty face in an ocean of them. I've heard the kids jamming by the shore, and no one on Soul Beach sings off-key.

Now she knows what it's like to be me.

No, that's not fair. I have a future, she doesn't. I can't even begin to understand how she feels. But then isn't it torture for her when I'm on Soul Beach? My presence is a reminder of what she's lost. Perhaps she even wonders why it had to be *her* and not me. God knows, I wondered it myself in the early days.

Maybe *that's* why Visitors stop going back to Soul Beach. It's not because the living get bored hanging out with the dead. It's because they realise that the dead don't want a constant reminder of what they've lost.

30

'You know I'd never put pressure on you, Ali. It's just that ...'

We're sitting on Robbie's bed. He texted me after hearing about Tim from some kids in his school, and insisted I come over. But now we've somehow stumbled into The Big Conversation, the one we've been avoiding for months.

It's just that ... he can tell my heart's not in it, and that must be pretty tough on his ego.

It's just that ... whenever we kiss I feel my body shutting down or, worse, I feel horrified. Of course I haven't told him that, but he's not stupid.

It's just that ... he knows the difference between the way I used to respond, and the way I tense up now when he touches me. He'll stop and we'll sit up and mostly we'll pretend it never happened. When we first got together, we could talk about anything. Now *everything* embarrasses us.

'Do you want us to break up?' I ask.

'No,' he says, but I don't think he realises he's nodding even as he denies it. 'I know it's not the most important thing in a relationship, and I love you so much, but I fancy you so much and ...' he stops speaking. 'Sorry.'

I put my hand on his. 'Don't apologise. We're not fifty, are we? We're meant to be having the time of our lives.'

'We were so brilliant together.'

Were.

I breathe in sharply when I realise he's talking in the past tense. It's one thing to imagine I'll be so mature if he wants us to split up. It's a whole other thing now it's actually happening.

'I love you, Robbie.'

But if I loved him, I'd *want* him. Maybe I'm in love with the memories of how he made me feel before it all went wrong. Now, nothing makes me feel anything any more. Nothing except Soul Beach.

'I love you too, Alice.'

He's on the edge of tears and those kissable lips are drawn tight, as he tries not to break. I can't let him cry. I know what I have to do for him. I shut my eyes.

'But love doesn't mean it's not over between us, Robbie. We'd have split up months ago if you hadn't felt sorry for me. Well, I'm a big girl now. I'll cope. We'd have split up when we went to university, anyway. Everybody does.'

He stares at me, unable to believe what he's heard. That makes two of us. I am surprised at how easy it is to play the bitch.

'Is that really what you think?' he says eventually.

I shrug. 'I've watched my parents start hating each other since Meggie died, but they're married. They have to work on it. We don't. Sometimes it's best to have a clean break.'

He doesn't know what to say. Maybe he's relieved. After a few seconds, I swing my legs off the bed and push my shoes back on.

I did this, so why do I still want him to say something to rescue *us*? But he's not even looking at me. I lean forward to kiss him, because it seems like the right thing to do, and out of habit he kisses me back properly and I pull away.

'No.'

I walk out of the door and down the stairs and I don't even look round when I hear Robbie's mother come out of the kitchen to ask whether I want a coffee and a slice of homemade carrot cake.

I'm on my own again, the dusk turning the streets even greyer than before. I close my eyes, longing to hear the waves that remind me that there's more to life than this pretty crappy reality.

But it's not the waves I can hear. It's Meggie.

Florrie.

And I answer her in my head. *I'm on my way ...*

31

October stinks of bonfires and rotting leaves.

Of cemeteries.

But the Beach has the same, impossible fragrance it always does, a seductive cocktail of ozone and fruit punch and sea-washed bamboo.

'What time of year is it, Florrie?'

My sister and I are sitting together a little way from the bar, under a palm so huge that the shady area underneath feels like our own private hideaway. I come here twice, three times a day now: morning and afternoon, plus the briefest of trips before I go to bed.

It's as much part of my routine as brushing my teeth, though a lot more enjoyable – I can't imagine *not* doing it. As for Meggie, she seems happier than she did when I first arrived, more like herself. I think it might be because of me . . .

'Er. You really don't know?'

She opens her eyes. 'Look around you. The weather's always the same, so I lose track. Anyway, Sam in the bar says it's better that way. The Guests who mark each day with a line in the sand will never accept what's happened.'

'It's autumn. October.'

'My favourite. *Christmas is coming and the goose is getting fat!*' That's the other thing that's changed: Meggie sings, now. In fact, it's almost impossible to stop her.

I don't tell her that Christmas this year will be unbearable without her there.

'Hey guys!' She calls out to Javier and the gang, who are walking past. 'Guess what. Summer's over!'

They head towards us, and I try to fake a smile. I prefer it when it's just Meggie and me: not only because Javier is annoying and Danny unsettles me and Triti makes me feel fat. But also because now I know how the two boys died, I can't get two images out of my head: that debris-strewn desert where Danny's plane crashed, and Javier as that sweet, solemn boy whose life ended with a fall from that rooftop.

'Don't you guys just love winter?,' she says, as they sit down on our blanket. *Uh oh.* Looks like they're sticking around. 'Darker nights in cosy pubs. Halloween. Bonfire night.'

'And Diwali,' says Triti. 'The festival of light.'

'Thanksgiving,' says Danny. 'Best dinner of the year. Ah, I remember how it felt to be hungry, the smell of Mom's turkey roast drifting up from the kitchen. So good.'

Javier shrugs. 'I am more of a beach bum. Winter is crappy. Having to stay indoors, ugh, in the bosom of the family. Not my scene.'

I remember his lie about being an only child. What else is he lying about?

'Don't be such a misery guts,' my sister says. 'Summer's fine, but too much of any good thing is rubbish, as we all know.' She laughs, and the others join in. 'Tell us what it's like, sis. Are the shops decorated for Christmas yet?'

Her face glows like a little child's, waiting to hear for the millionth time how the reindeers will hover over the roof of her house, while Father Christmas sends presents down the chimney.

'The adverts have started,' I say. Actually, I've been trying to ignore the Z-list celebs who waltz across the TV screen like they've swallowed a sleigh-full of Prozac. If I'm in the room with my parents – an increasingly rare occurrence these days as they're rarely in at the same time – we all stare at the floor, like we used to when someone started having sex on screen. Right now, images of family celebrations are more painful to watch than X-rated action.

It suddenly occurs to me that if Meggie had still been alive, she might have featured in those ads herself ... The terrible boy band who came second to her are advertising breakfast cereal *and* a new karaoke game.

'Tell me, tell me,' she demands, and even Javier looks up.

So I lie. I tell them what I think they want to hear: about shops full of pumpkin lanterns and witches' hats, about long-range weather forecasts for a white Christmas, about plans for London's biggest ever fireworks display on New Year's Eve. In reality, I barely notice anything about the outside world, or think about the future if I can avoid it.

'Fireworks,' says Triti, wistfully. 'Can you imagine how beautiful they'd look, here? Reflected in the sea at night? It would be so cool!'

'Oh yeah. Love it. And what are the chances that when the cocktails are flowing and the fireworks go off, the clothes will come off too. An entire beach full of exhibitionist skinny dippers,' Javier says. 'How *fantastic*.'

For the first time since I got here, I actually feel the same way as Javier. From what I've seen, most Guests need no excuse to show off their newly flawless bodies.

As they begin to reminisce about winters past, I check my watch and when I see the time – past midnight – I am glad of an excuse to leave. 'Sorry, guys and gals. It's past my bedtime.'

Javier doesn't look up, but Danny does. 'I wanted to hear more about your plans,' he says. 'About your *real* plans.'

The way he looks at me makes me wonder if he can tell I'm lying to get away, even though my own sister can't.

'Well, I'll be back tomorrow, same as I always am.'

And Meggie stands up and gives me the warmest of smiles – even broader than the one she wore whenever she got through the heats in *Sing for Your Supper*. 'My little sister,' she says. 'I don't know what I'd do without you, Florrie.'

32

Getting up for school these days is harder, and not just because it's dark in the mornings.

Since Robbie and I broke up, I can't be bothered with make-up. Sometimes I don't even brush my hair. On the Beach, I always look gorgeous anyway.

Another reason to love it there.

Cara hasn't disowned me yet, though she's told me about a thousand times that *my* grungy look is bad for *her* image, especially now she's adopted cheerleader chic. Sometimes I try to talk to her about big stuff – whether she believes in life after death, or parallel worlds, and she just sighs and says, 'The hoaxer who sent those bloody Soul Beach emails has a lot to answer for.' And then she very obviously starts talking about clothes or music or make-up – 'You know, the stuff you used to love, Alice. *Normal* stuff.'

As if normal is something I'd still actually want.

After class, I keep my head down. I prefer to walk home alone. I don't want to gossip or talk about boys, and I especially don't want to hear about Robbie seeing someone else. I hate reminders of the life I used to have.

'Wait, Alice.'

Cara is there, with a tall, skinny guy I half-recognise. A new boyfriend? These days she churns and burns her way through them so fast that I can't keep up with their names, though I try, for her sake. It's not *her* fault that her best friend has turned into the very worst kind of beach bum.

She's walking alongside me, keeping up, even though I am

going as fast as I can. 'Look who I bumped into,' she says. 'Remember Lewis?'

I nod at the guy, without slowing down. 'Hi.' I wave. 'Sorry, I'm in a hurry.'

I do remember him now. He's the geeky one, Robbie's brother's mate. Rich as an Arab Prince, so the rumours go, though you'd never know it to look at him. Old trainers, no label jeans, dirt-brown stand-on-end hair. Thick, curious eyebrows that are twisted in a permanent question. He seems to be going out of his way to look ordinary. Maybe that's to stop the gold-digging girls coming after him and his bank account.

Cara's getting out of breath – the nightly sessions with the cute fitness trainer didn't last long – but she's not letting me get away. 'Don't go, Allie. It's been ages since we chatted.'

I stop suddenly. 'Is this an ambush?'

Lewis looks down at his dirty trainers. Cara says nothing.

'That'll be a yes, then, will it?'

Cara shrugs. 'You can call it that if you like. I'd call it your friends being worried about you and wanting to help.'

I can't look her in the face. Is this what I've become? The kind of person who accuses her best friend of ambushing her, when all Cara wants is to let me know I'm not alone.

Little does she know how far from alone I am.

I'm about to apologise, when I realise *why* Lewis is here. 'Robbie sent you?' I ask him, and despite what's happened, it makes me feel a bit dizzy to know my ex still cares.

Lewis looks up briefly. His eyes are incredibly dark. Like a camera lens, they seem to reflect myself back to me, and I don't know if I like the person I've become.

'*I* asked Robbie to talk to Lewis,' Cara explains. 'It's that phony site, isn't it? You were doing OK until you started getting the weird emails and now I can't even talk to you any more.'

The mention of Soul Beach makes me catch my breath. It's *mine*. My secret. The only thing that's keeping me going. 'Rubbish. You don't know what you're talking about, Cara.'

I turn my back on them.

'Alice, your mates are worried about you.' It's Lewis.

I sigh. I wish people would just give me up as a bad job, it'd make things so much easier. 'I don't know what they've told you, Lewis, but I just happen to be a normal girl with a dead sister and I can't help it if my friends don't think I'm getting better fast enough for their liking. Do I really look so shallow that some crappy emails would make any difference to how I feel?'

He holds out his arms as if to say, none of my business, I'm only doing someone a favour. Funny, I remembered him as ganglier and *nerdier*, but he seems self-assured.

'It's nice of you to play Good Samaritan, but I promise you I don't need help from you, or from the Pope or from Barack Obama or the Tooth Fairy. I need time, OK, and if my mates are getting impatient, well, that's their problem, not mine, right?'

Cara shakes her head. I can't be sure but I think she might be about to cry.

'Right, Cara?'

This time when I turn round and walk away, I mean it. Even though I can feel tears in my own eyes, and even though I know that this time I really have gone too far, I try to convince myself it's for the best. Yes, she's my friend and she's trying to do her best for me. But perhaps being cruel to be kind is better for her. She can find new friends.

I can't find a new sister. Meggie, and the Beach, must come first.

When I log onto the Beach, I can't make sense of what I'm seeing at first. My screen lights up with flashes of cherry pink, ice white, sherbet lemon. And the noises are thunderous.

On the sand, a hundred or more Guests are standing and pointing upwards, and the chatter's so loud it almost drowns out the waves.

Fireworks!

Tropical flowers bloom in the night sky, then fade away again in an instant. Beautiful, but gone too soon. It wouldn't take one of the smarty-pants philosophers on the Beach to see the parallels.

But the kids – and they look like young children right now, the candy colours reflected in wide eyes – are too thrilled to think morbid thoughts. The sky is deepest navy, as though it's been darkened especially. Why wouldn't it have been?

On Soul Beach, everything is possible.

I glance round, looking for Meggie, but the first person I see in the distance is Triti. As I watch, a sapphire firework explodes. It seems to flash through her like an x-ray: it's almost like I can see every one of her bones.

'Florrie! Over here.'

I weave through the crowd towards my sister, dodging between the spectators. Even though they can't see or feel me, it seems rude somehow to walk *through* the Guests, as though they don't exist.

Danny smiles when I reach my little group of friends, but then looks away again without his usual soul-searching stare. 'I thought you were gonna miss the party.'

'What's the celebration?'

Triti speaks without moving her head; her gaze is fixed on the heavens. 'They knew it was what we needed, somehow. To cheer us up.'

Meggie raises her eyebrows at me, but says nothing.

'And is it working?' I ask Triti.

'Oh, yes! I feel so different. Alive.' Then she giggles at her own joke. 'Well, kind of.'

I laugh, too, but my brain is buzzing. This must mean that They – whoever 'They' are – listen in to every conversation on the Beach. I should have known that anyway, after they banned me from the site the instant I asked the wrong thing, but the idea that every stupid exchange that I have with Meggie is being recorded, monitored, pored over . . . well, it freaks me out.

Though I suppose the alternative is worse: if the site is a hoax, then some creepy hacker knows everything I've said to my sister online.

I chase the thought away. This *can't* be a hoax. It feels more real than real life.

'Hey, day-dreamer? You coming with us?' My sister reaches out, as though we could actually take each other's hand. 'We're feeling claustrophobic.'

Javier rests his fingertips on Triti's elbow, guiding her like she's blind, because she's refusing to look anywhere but up. We head towards *our* palm tree. Meggie, Javier and Danny sit down, but Triti stays standing, hypnotised. Meggie leans across and whispers in my ear, 'You want to know her story, don't you, Florrie?'

I jump slightly. 'I'm not allowed to ask, though.'

'Anorexia,' my sister says, still whispering, though Triti looks so distant that she wouldn't hear if we had a loud-hailer.

Anorexia makes perfect sense. She's so slight, almost translucent. And now, in the light of the fireworks, I catch a glimpse of downy hairs covering her limbs. I've seen that before, on a girl I knew at school who refused to eat.

Before that girl, I always thought anorexics did it to be the centre of attention, but she treated not eating as some kind of terrible competition with herself, one she'd lose even if she won. I only realised when she was taken out of school that she didn't want to be noticed at all. She wanted to be invisible.

'That's tragic,' I say. There's so much joy in Triti's face

right now that it's impossible to believe she could have willed herself to die. 'But if she chose not to eat ... if she *chose* to *die*, then how is her death unresolved? What's she doing here?'

Meggie shrugs. 'I don't make the rules, sis.' And she lowers her voice still further. 'And if I did, would I still be hanging out round here, however pretty the bloody fireworks?'

I freeze. 'I thought ...' I don't stop, because it seems such a stupid thing to say, that I thought she might have got used to being dead. That she might even enjoy hanging out with me these days. 'You're still that unhappy, then?'

I think she realises what she's said, now, because she plasters the fakest of fake smiles onto her face and shakes her head. 'Scrub that. Nothing makes me unhappy so long as you're around, Florrie.'

I don't believe her. 'Is there anything I can do to make things easier?'

'There is ...' Meggie hesitates. 'No, it's not fair to burden you.'

'Burden away,' I say. 'Seriously. Anything.'

'How would you feel about going to Greenwich?'

I stare back. How would I feel? *Terrified yet oddly excited.* It's not as though I hadn't considered it myself already. I'm as desperate to get the answers as she is. Even if that involves putting myself at risk. 'To see Tim?'

She nods. 'I know it's a huge thing to ask, but there's so much unfinished business, Florrie. Not just with him, but with Sahara as well. We hadn't really been talking before ...' she hesitates, '... before I died, not for a while. I want her to know I cared about her. Valued her as a friend. And Tim. He should know that I loved him.'

'Even though he might have ...' now I'm the one hesitating, because the threat of being banned from the Beach again hangs over me as the worst thing I can imagine in the world.

'*Especially* because he might have. I think, well. If you saw him, he might tell you things. Things that might lead to ...' she whispers, 'a resolution.'

A resolution. I remember what Danny said, his theory that the Visitors here can only escape if something changes in the real world.

'But then I might lose you again,' I say, before I can censor myself. 'Lose the Beach. Lose what matters.'

Meggie smiles at me sadly. 'You'll never lose me, Alice. Not now we've spent so much time together. But I understand if it's too much to ask. I shouldn't have said anything. Don't worry about it.'

'No, I'll do it, I promise.' Because the truth, I realise, is that I've always known a showdown between me and Tim would be inevitable. I need to know what really happened, and my own selfishness at wanting to keep my sister where she is – where I can see her and talk to her – has to come second to resolving this.'

She mouths *Thank you*, then claps her hands and the others look round. 'I reckon the show's nearly over, boys and girls, so how about the Old Dog and Duck for a pint of bitter before closing time?'

They laugh at her fake cockney accent and scramble back to their feet, and they're off again, towards the beach bar. I hold back. Am I a coward, not to have visited Tim already? No, it's not that, because physical harm doesn't scare me at all. In a way, I'd almost be relieved if Tim turned on me, because then at least I'd know for sure just *what* he really is. And have an answer to that question that's dominated everything for seven months: *who killed my sister?*

As I watch my sister get further away from me, and then disappear into the bar, I feel a pang of loss, and that's when I know I must go, whatever my fears about facing life without her.

Love – real love – is about sacrificing your own needs for someone else's.

It'll be a test. I can only hope I'm strong enough to pass it.

I turn back towards the sea, and realise I'm not alone. Triti's still here, too. She's staring at the sky, which has turned a strange rusty colour, from the gunpowder.

The others are laughing and joking in the bar. The fireworks seem to have had an effect on everyone. I don't feel like joining in, so I say goodnight. But now I'm lying in bed, and it's like they're still with me.

I think of Triti and Danny and Javier. But mostly of Meggie and Tim.

And wonder whether I can bear to let her go . . .

33

I'm not the kind of girl who bunks off school.

And, despite her backchat and bluster, neither is Cara, so I can't ask her to come along for the ride. For an amateur like me, the risk of discovery is high: the teachers are already on my back about my falling grades, creepy Olav is dying to get his hands on my neuroses, and Mum is building up to another Big Talk about my Future. As if I care . . .

Still, a few detentions are the least of my worries, compared to confronting the chief suspect for my sister's murder.

Better not to think about that right now.

I slip out of school after registration and take the back roads where none of Mum's friends live. Instead of using our nearest station, I walk to the next one along to catch the train. I sit in the front carriage, facing the wrong way, behind a dog-eared copy of *Metro*. When I realise no one else is getting in, I let the paper slip and watch the world. It's been raining, which makes the browns and greys of the bricks and pavements even more depressing. Winter's almost here, and I feel like it'll be the longest of my life.

Already I crave the Beach, even though I was there only two hours ago. I decided to make up a story to explain to Meggie why I might not be around later, rather than get her hopes up about my trip to Greenwich. Right now, I can't see how it can end in anything *but* disaster.

Yet I have to try. I promised her, even though by then she wasn't listening. And she's not the only one who needs answers.

When I get on the little toy-train carriage on the DLR towards Cutty Sark, I begin to shiver. I'd decided not to try to contact Tim before coming, in case he went to ground. But how exactly will he react when I show up on his doorstep? Even Cara, who loves living dangerously, might have had something to say about me taking a suspected murderer by surprise.

Shit.

The train cuts between the skyscrapers of Canary Wharf, which look less real to me than the huts on the Beach. I put on more make-up, so I look older.

I think of what that awful bloke of Cara's said in the pub, about not believing I was Meggie's sister. And it makes me laugh, because for so many years, I woke up every morning hoping my eyes had lightened overnight from pigeon grey to baby blue, or my hair had self-ironed itself to match hers.

Now, for the first time, I'm glad to be ordinary.

'White wine spritzer, please.'

The barman weighs it up. Despite my kohl and my mascara, and all the crap I've been through this year, I still look like a schoolgirl who knows nothing about anything, unless you count AS Level Media Studies.

But I can't be the only underage drinker here: this is the pub where Meggie used to take me to meet her friends when I visited her, and it was always full of teenagers from the local sixth form too. I came here because I'm not ready to face Tim yet. I need to remember how things were between him and Meggie, and steel myself for what I have to do. And I never drink during the day, so the wine might be enough to give me the courage to do this crazy thing.

The barman shrugs to himself, then turns his back on me to make my drink. The bubbles in a spritzer will disguise the taste of the wine, and anything will taste better than this fear.

'Ice?'

I nod. He puts the glass down, and I can see the little cracks in the ice cubes and the vapour rising inside the glass.

I nod.

'Say when,' he says, as he tops up the wine with water from the siphon. Was *he* working the night that my sister died?

'When.'

'So you're a fresher, then, are you?'

I stare at him. 'Um . . . yes. Sorry, I said When!'

Could he have recognised me?

He looks at the glass, which is overflowing. 'Whoops.' He pushes over the drink. 'Three fifty, please. Nah, make it three. I'll throw in the fizzy water for free.'

I gawp. 'Oh. Thanks.'

'So what are you studying?'

I gulp. 'Um. Media.'

He grins. 'Cool. I'm gonna see you on TV, then, am I?'

Oh my God, he's chatting me up. And I thought he was checking me out because I was underage, or because he knew who I was. I haven't really noticed him properly till now. Twenty-two, twenty-three maybe. Fair haired. An open face. Kind-looking. A practical joker, I bet. Plays football on a Sunday. Likes classic comedy and stadium rock.

Before it happened, I might have fancied him. I'd certainly have been flattered – barmen have that confidence, and that power, that Cara at least finds pretty irresistible. But it's not happening for me any more.

'Not on TV, no. I'm more a behind-the-scenes kind of person.'

I take my drink and walk away, quickly.

'Hey, blondie?' he calls after me, and I prepare my brush off. Meggie always had a good line, a way of making it clear they had no chance, but leaving them with a smile on their faces.

I can't think of anything.

I turn.

'You forgot your change.'

I take my drink outside. The benches are damp from the rain showers, but the sun is brighter here by the bend in the Thames than it was back home. I see the flashy towers of the bank buildings on the other side of the river, and then the Dome to the right. This was Meggie's favourite pub, and Greenwich was her favourite place. It *is* beautiful here, but the majestic limestone Old Naval College buildings and the bright green lawns seem tainted now. How could they *not*?

I'm not alone out here. Most of the other drinkers are male smokers: not just students, but tourists and office workers. Last time I was here, I thought the guys who were smoking looked sexy. Now I think they're stupid for wasting what life they have. Don't they know what happened to my sister?

The students, the tourists, the barman. It could be any one of them who killed Meggie, couldn't it? Maybe I'm turning into a man hater. After all, if I can't trust a man as gentle as Tim . . .

I shiver.

A couple of guys check me out, and I look away. They're not ugly – Meggie always joked she chose Greenwich because it had the cutest selection of guys on her open day – but I'm not interested in *this* life. I want the airbrushed loveliness of Soul Beach.

I shake my head, like a dog trying to clear water from its ears. This is madness. Soul Beach isn't real.

For the first time, it hits me: the Beach is changing me, just as Meggie's death did. Spending time there might be making things worse.

No! No way. Giving up on the Beach isn't an option, and not just for Meggie's sake. It's all that's keeping me going right now.

I finish my drink. I'm more awake, from the bubbles or the wine or both. It's time to go. If I don't go and find Tim this minute, I'll lose my nerve. I put the glass down, take out my map, work out the fastest way to the halls.

That's if he still lives there . . .

How stupid am I? I haven't thought this through properly. Is it likely he'll still be in halls, two floors from where Meggie died, after what happened? And if he's not, then what do I do? Knock on doors until I find him? And when I do, all I have to protect myself is a schoolbag full of Media Studies textbooks.

I shiver again. I shouldn't be here. This is crazy.

And that's when I feel a hand grip my shoulder.

'Alice Forster? What the hell are you doing here?'

34

I jump about a metre in the air, before I register that the low growl belongs to a woman.

I turn round. 'Sahara!'

'Hello, Alice,' she says, her voice heavy with sadness. 'Oh, Alice.'

Sahara opens up her muscular arms and holds me too tightly against her chest. She's one of those sporty, Amazonian women. We used to joke that she could be Meggie's bodyguard.

Yet right now there's something so needy about her that I feel like I'm the one comforting her.

Finally she pulls away and there are tears in her eyes, catching in her impossibly long lashes. 'Oh, God, when I saw you just then, Alice, it was like her ghost.' She blinks, and two teardrops bridge the eyelash dam, to tumble down her slightly pitted cheeks.

'But I don't look anything like her, Sahara.'

'You do. Honestly.' She looks at me again. 'OK, maybe you don't. It might have been the way you were sitting. Or *where*. You know this is *her* place, don't you?'

I feel irritated by the ominous way she says it. 'This is *everyone's* favourite pub, isn't it?'

'No. I mean this is her *place*. Her *bench*. She always sat exactly where you are, leaning forwards like you were doing.'

'Really? I guess I must have sat here with her that time I visited and then I just sat here again out of habit.' But my skin feels as though a million ants are marching across it, because I remember that the night I visited it was pouring with rain, and we took refuge indoors, watching the smokers through the window.

'You drinking?' she says, eyeing my glass. 'You're only sixteen.'

I tut. 'I bet you never drank underage, Sahara?'

She thinks about it. 'No, actually, I didn't. I was a goody-two shoes.'

So was I, I think, and suddenly I see myself as she must see me, sixteen, sitting on a bench, drinking alone. 'People change.'

Sahara gives me an odd look. Then she says, 'Do you want to join us?' She nods back towards the pub, and I see a group of students at the far end, sprawled on sofas. Why didn't I notice them before? 'Everyone here knew Meggie, if that helps.'

I hesitate.

'Though Tim's not there, of course,' she adds.

No, I think, but one of them might know something about how I can find him.

Or – and this makes me shiver – one of them might be the killer.

35

'OK.' My voice trembles as I agree.

Sahara takes my arm, and leads me inside again. 'Look who I found outside,' she says, and there's a possessive edge to her voice that makes me feel like a show-pony.

'Hi,' I say, waving awkwardly.

'Come on, sit down here,' she says, patting a two-seater sofa and sitting down next to me. *Too* close. 'You remember everyone? Lisa was in the same tutorial group as Meggie.'

A girl with curly hair waves at me. Is it just a myth that people with curly hair can be unpredictable? She doesn't look the murdering kind.

'Simone and your sister were going to start a band together, remember, before the TV show came up?' Sahara reminds me.

Simone raises a glass to me. 'So sorry.' She's tiny, could barely squash a fly, never mind suffocate my strong, healthy sister.

'Then Adrian, my boyfriend.'

He actually gets up, offers me his hand, and when I shake it, he puts his left hand over the top, just like the vicar did at Meggie's funeral. It feels warm, almost comfortable. 'You know, I still can't believe it,' he says.

I shake my head. 'Me neither.

I've never really noticed him before, but his face is one of those that draws you in slowly. He has high cheekbones, skin so pale he could be Scandinavian, and light brown hair that's swept back from his face like a fighter pilot's. He's too good looking for Sahara, I think, and then dismiss the thought. I don't fancy him, but he seems like a gentleman, somehow.

Not him.

Around the table we go, and I weigh each person up. Su-Lin, a Chinese girl with a lazy eye was out of the country when the murder happened. Jules, who knew my sister from the uni open day and tracked her down as soon as they both arrived as freshers, is too sweet, almost in awe. Meggie had that effect on people, drawing them to her like moths to her flame.

I feel the absence of Tim, and someone else.

'Where's Zoe?'

The others look away. Sahara reaches out to touch my hand. 'She ... left college. It was too much. The memories. She's gone travelling or something.'

Zoe found my sister's body. Unlucky enough to be the first one back to the shared flatlet after the party, she'd passed Meggie's door, noticed it ajar and then pushed it open. Later, she told the press my sister looked like an angel, with her hair like a halo around her flushed face. The police ruled her out, but then they were all looking for a man ...

Could there more to her quitting college than trauma?

I notice, then, that no one is speaking, or looking at me. Alice the party pooper strikes again. I don't blame them. I wouldn't know how to make small talk with me, either.

Adrian rescues the situation. He makes a show of looking at his watch. 'Shit. Late for my lecture.' He stands up, and the others scramble to their feet, too, swigging the dregs of their drinks, and mumbling more condolences, before leaving the pub, even though I know the chances of *all* of them having lectures at the same time are tiny.

Only Sahara remains. As we watch them walk towards the exit, their body language changes. They jostle and joke as they disappear into the light.

'Why did you come here, Alice?' Sahara asks. 'Tell me, please. I might be able to help.'

Can I trust her? Meggie and Sahara met on their first day at college, because they'd been allocated to the same flat in halls. They were always in and out of each other's tiny rooms. I don't know if the friendship would have lasted – I hadn't even realised they'd fallen out before Meggie died. My sister certainly thought Sahara could be needy and emotional, but maybe emotional isn't a bad thing in a person you want to confide in.

'I wanted to see you. To let you know my sister really cared about you.'

Sahara smiles. 'I knew that anyway. But thanks.'

'I know she regretted the argument you had.'

Her face changes. 'What?'

'You fell out. Before she died. But she didn't mean it.'

'We were fine.' She pushes out her bottom lip like a child sulking. 'We'd just both been busy with other stuff.'

What am I meant to say now? That I *know* they rowed, because my sister specifically wanted me to come and see her. 'Well, anyway, I know she'd have wanted you to remember her at her best.'

Sahara is staring at me. She looks almost hostile. 'You came all this way to tell me *that*? You could have told me at the funeral.'

'I know ...' Then I realise: if anyone knows where Tim is, it will be her. 'I came to see Tim, as well.'

'Oh.' She looks startled. 'Does he know?'

I shake my head. 'I thought he might not want to see me.'

'Only I think he's meeting Adrian later.'

I stare at her. 'I didn't know you two still had anything to do with him.'

She shrugs. 'I don't. Adrian does. Too bloody much. He even lives with him now, off-campus, which means I never visit his place. It's the only thing we argue about. We almost split up over it.'

That was the other thing Meggie always said: that Sahara had a way of making her problems seem like your problems. That she didn't know when to stop blabbing.

But right now, I'm not sure that blabbing's a bad thing. 'That must be hard.'

'Mmm. Yeah, I think Tim did it, Adrian doesn't. Or he thinks we shouldn't jump to conclusions, anyway. Which is easy for him to say because he wasn't Meggie's best friend, was he? He doesn't get nightmares about discovering her body all lifeless and ... swollen.'

Sahara bursts into such loud tears that everyone looks round at us. I hope no one recognises her from all the TV news interviews she did afterwards.

'There, there,' I say, reaching out even though I don't want to. It wasn't even Sahara who found Meggie, though she arrived just minutes after Zoe did. And as for being her best friend ... I feel irritated by that comment. It's as though she's trying to pull rank over me.

I shouldn't have told her. All I want now is to get away, try to find Tim myself. If I hurry, perhaps I could follow Adrian. 'I need to get back.'

Sahara stops crying almost as suddenly as she started and I prepare my leaving speech. 'Already?' she asks. 'But what about Tim?'

'Maybe it's not the best idea for me to see him,' I lie.

'No,' she says darkly. 'He might get cross.'

It feels as though someone's running an ice cube down my spine. 'Did he often get cross?'

She shrugs. 'Not often, but ...' And then she shakes her head. 'Forget it.'

'It's not that easy to forget, Sahara.'

I wait for a few more seconds, then I stand up.

She puts her hand out. 'Don't go. I can let you see it, if it'd help?' Her voice is muffled but urgent.

'See what?'

She blinks hard, then leans forward. Her eyes blaze.

'Meggie's room.'

36

I'm fighting to stop my teeth chattering, because I don't want Sahara to see.

It's not as though I haven't been there before. I even slept in that room when I came to stay with Meggie, sandwiched into the single bed between the wall and my giggling sister, listening to drunken punch-ups on the street underneath her window.

But now it's different.

'You can get in there?'

Her brown eyes are wide and proud. 'No one's supposed to. But Meggie gave me a spare key because she was always forgetting hers.'

Sahara is desperate to show me. But do I want to see it?

I find myself nodding, and she takes my hand and marches off along the Thames, then back through the college grounds, past the arched temples to learning, towards the modern halls. It's still lunchtime – now I definitely know Adrian was lying about being late for a lecture – and students laugh and flirt across the campus, which makes the gravity of what we're about to do seem even more obvious.

I'm out of breath by the time we're back in the lift and going up to Meggie's floor. It smells of hot engine in here, and on the walls there are posters for the Last Beach Party of the Season featuring tropical palms and hula-hula girls, and I wish I could magic myself out of here and back to my bedroom, and Soul Beach.

The lift takes an age to get going, and as my breathing

slows I look at Sahara. She's staring at the steel doors. Her jaw is locked in determination.

As the lift gears crunch, something slots into place in my head, too.

Could Sahara have killed my sister?

My brain seems to be working at treble speed. An argument before the murder. Sahara's weird excitement at showing me this place. The fact she showed up just minutes after the body was found . . .

'I want to get out,' I say, in a whisper.

'That's fine, we're here,' she says.

'Right.'

As we step out, I search in vain for a video camera. Even though I know there aren't any, because the CCTV trail of my sister's last minutes stopped three streets away. The uni rejected the whole idea of extending surveillance on the grounds of privacy, but surely the police have added cameras on the main road now. *Cameras that might show my last minutes.*

'Are you all right? We can take our time.' Sahara is smiling broadly, revealing her goofy teeth. Was she jealous of my sister's effortless prettiness? Of her success?

I try to calm myself. It's rubbish, of course it is. The killer was obviously a man. One who wanted Meggie all to himself. Tim or . . .

Sahara has taken my arm, and pushes me up a few carpeted steps. The wooden door to the flatlet is the same, but the glass panel in it is papered over from the inside, with a sign saying NO ACCESS. 'They had to cover it up because all the freshers came here to gawp. Especially late at night. Some have even convinced themselves they've heard your sister singing.'

'So no one's living in any of the rooms now?'

I try to calculate how loud I'd have to scream to be heard from here.

'Nope. No one's on the entire floor. They've left it closed

for this year as a mark of respect. Or to ward off the ghouls.'

Ghouls like Sahara?

She hits the down button on the lift, 'So no one will realise there's someone on the third floor,' then glances around, and when she's sure no one's lurking, uses the key to let us both into the flat, closing the heavy door behind us.

It's stifling in the corridor, hospital hot, and completely airless. I'm not sure I could get enough oxygen into my lungs now to scream, even if I wanted to.

I don't want to. It'd be mad. Sahara's no more a killer than Tim is, surely. They're just students. Bystanders.

'Something's different here,' I say, surprised at how high my voice sounds. Then I look down at the grey concrete under my feet. 'What happened to the carpet?'

'Forensics took it,' Sahara says. 'Don't be shocked, but they took quite a lot away.'

She puts the key in the door of Room A, and pushes it ajar. 'After you?'

Oh, God, why did I let her bring me here? I don't want her behind me. She could . . .

I feel a firm push in the small of my back, and I fall against the door, which swings fully open. 'Ouch.'

'Sorry, Alice. Don't know my own strength sometimes.'

Meggie's room is completely stripped out.

No longer a room, but a cell – the floor the same rough grey as the corridor, the walls a dirty cream, with cleaner patches where the furniture and pin board used to be. Like ghosts. Everything soft has been removed – the curtains, the bed, the carpet. The tiny bathroom pod that all the students moan about, because you can't have a shower without soaking the loo roll, is still there, but when I open the door, the toilet, basin and plastic walls have been hacked out.

But it's not the bareness of the space that upsets me. It's the *feel*.

'You can feel it too, can't you, Alice?'

I swing around. Sahara's eyes are boring into me, though at least she's not carrying an axe or a pillow and there's no room for either in her bag.

I shake my head. 'Feel what?'

'It's like an aura, isn't it?'

'No,' I lie. I'm not admitting anything to her. Even if she had nothing to do with my sister's murder, she seems to be getting a kick from her death.

But the horrible thing is that Sahara's right. There is an aura, even though it's exactly the kind of airy-fairy term that Meggie would have laughed at. There's evil in this room, or, at the very least, an intense darkness despite the sunlight now streaming through the locked window.

Even if I didn't know my sister had died in this place, I would have sensed the complete absence of good here. But is it the room, or is it Sahara? I try to tap into it, to reach out for a clue about what happened. Who did it ...

I hear waves. The waves of Soul Beach. They're almost a reassuring sound now, because they're always there, if I choose to tune out the everyday noises of 'real' life. But above the crash and hiss of the seawater I swear I hear laughter. Meggie's? No, the sound is too cruel. It must be someone else's.

'Alice?'

I am falling, falling through the darkness, and though I fight to open my eyes it's as though someone has covered my face and is pressing down on my nose and mouth so I can't breathe. Everything is dark and I taste and smell blackness, the dank clay stink of earth in my face and hair and ...

'Sorry, but I have to do this.'

I feel a sharp pain across my cheek, shocking enough to make my eyes pop open. No more darkness, no more mocking laughter, just Sahara with her hand in mid-air and her face apologetic.

143

'You slapped me!'

'I didn't *want* to!' she hisses. 'But you'd gone all weird. You were swaying and then you started scratching at your face and . . .'

I look at my fingers; they're bent like an animal's claws. I half expect to see soil under my nails.

'What happened to you, Alice? Did you sense what happened to Meggie?' She sounds curious, rather than anxious. Suddenly the whole idea of her being the killer seems mad.

I shake my head. 'No, of course I didn't. It's just the white wine.'

The expression of disappointment on her face irritates me so much I want to slap her right back. Now I feel safe, but so, so angry with her, and with myself for coming, for getting myself into such a state.

'I want to get out of here, Sahara. But not before you've got rid of that bloody key. It's not right for you to have it. Apart from anything else, you're contaminating evidence they might not have found yet.'

She clutches it to her chest. 'No.'

'If you don't give it to me, I'll tell the college.'

Sahara scowls at me. 'You wouldn't.'

'I would. It's not doing you any good. How often do you sneak in here?'

She shrugs. 'Once a week or so. I talk to Meggie.'

I hold out my hand. Suddenly I feel so much older than her. 'She's dead, Sahara. She can't hear you.' I cross my fingers.

'You're mean. And you're making a mistake,' she says, but even so, her hand creeps towards mine and she drops the key into my open palm. 'You need to lock up behind us. Or they'll know someone has been here.'

As we turn to go, I take one last look at the room and I feel the darkness once more. 'No one is coming back here, Sahara. No one.'

Afterwards, I pretend I need a coffee, and of course, Sahara offers to come, but I bark back, 'Alone,' and finally she gets the message. I wait until I've seen her disappear back through the gate of the uni.

I should still try to find Tim, but where do I begin? I could hang around waiting for Adrian, then follow him back to their shared flat. Or skulk around the grungy cafés Tim always liked. But the chances of either plan working are slim, and I need to be back home before it gets too late or Mum will want to know where I've been. She's keeping a closer eye on me these days and I'm cutting it fine already.

'*I promise I will come back, Meggie. I will find him,*' I whisper, ashamed of my own weakness. But now the decision's made, I know it was the right one; I need to be razor sharp and prepared for my encounter with Tim, and right now my head's too full of ghosts and fears to get the answers I need. Instead I walk towards the Thames, the key in my hand so cold that it feels like it's destroying the hot skin of my palm. The clouds have cleared completely now and the water is still as a mirror, reflecting the heat of the sun.

I lean against the railing, and hold the key at arm's length. All I need to do is let go.

Something's changed. I spin around, convinced there's someone behind me, but the nearest people are tourists, eating ice cream, despite the wind. There's nowhere to hide here, no refuge, yet that sensation of being watched is unmistakeable.

'*Go away,*' I whisper. '*Whoever you are.*'

The feeling goes as suddenly as it came. I look down once more. Even though the river water doesn't seem to be moving, I hear waves again, but this time they're softer, more soothing.

I'm about to release my grip when I hear a whisper.

'*Not yet, little sis. Hold on. The time will come.*'

My hand closes back over the key, almost without me thinking about it, and the iciness of the metal makes me shiver.

37

I get on the train, exhausted and defeated. All the way home, I try not to sleep, but my head keeps dropping and the brief moments before I jolt back awake are full of grotesque images: Meggie's face red and swollen, Danny's whole but lifeless body sitting in an ejected seat in the desert, Triti's skull clearly visible under skin that's the same pale blue as airmail paper.

I shouldn't have gone.

And yet, knowing that the key is in my bag makes me think that perhaps I have achieved something. I just don't know what.

I run from the station as there's no point going back to school now. All I want is to be back on the Beach, where my dead friends are restored to beauty and eternal life. I want to hear their laughter, see their smiles.

But as I turn the corner into our street, I see a man sitting on our garden wall. It must be a journalist. Actually, that suits me fine. There's nothing more likely to cheer me up than the chance to mouth off at some creepy reporter.

It's only once the guy sees me, and stands up, that I realise it's Lewis.

'Are you stalking me?'

He stands up. Or should I say unfolds himself? He's taller than I remembered. 'I may be a geek, but I'm not a sex pest.'

Despite – or maybe because of – everything that's happened today, that makes me smile, but I try to stay stern. 'So what are you doing here?'

'I promised Robbie I'd have another go.'

'What, have you got super-human powers or something?'

He smiles. 'It has been said. But, admittedly, not by women. He's worried about you.'

'Yeah. So worried that he dumped me.'

Now he looks at me, but sideways. 'From what he told me, it was more like you didn't leave him much choice.'

Was it?

'How long have you been hanging around? The neighbours are really pissed off with us for attracting so many undesirables. First the police. Then the press. Now you. You're at high risk of being given an ASBO.'

'I've been here an hour or so. Thought I'd catch you on your way home from school. But seems you're running a bit late . . .' he gives me a meaningful look. He *knows* I've bunked off. What else might he know? 'I could do with a glass of water, or something.'

I sigh, and unlock the front door. 'Mum?' I call out, but there's no reply. I glance at him and leave the door open long enough for him to come in.

He follows me into the kitchen, and I take a glass off the draining board and fill it with lukewarm tap water. He takes it off me, but doesn't drink.

'So what part of *I don't need any help* didn't you understand last week?'

Lewis frowns. 'I understood. I just didn't believe you.'

'Oh.'

He pulls out one of the stools and sits down at the breakfast bar. He seems even bigger in here, more confident. 'I knew your sister. A bit.'

'So what? Half of Britain thinks they knew my sister.'

'Fair point. But, you know, we were in the same year, our circles intersected each other. Like in a Venn diagram.'

'You weren't kidding about being a geek, were you? So were you friends?'

'Not exactly. Admired her from afar, like most of the guys round here. She grabbed what she could from her life. She'd have hated to see you like this, withdrawing from life, turning your back on your mates.'

Shows what you know, I think. Meggie and I know that what *really* matters is sisterhood. 'I'm not.'

'Robbie thinks you are. So does Cara. That's two against one. Geeks like me know that the numbers never lie.'

God, he's persistent. 'Supposing I *was* finding it hard, what exactly do you think you can do about it? Are you going to bring her back from the dead?'

'Cara tells me someone's already done that.'

I stare at him. I wish I'd never said anything to Cara; I don't want to run the risk of anyone getting anywhere near the truth. The best that might happen is that he'll think I'm a crazy person who hears voices or something. The worst is that he could take me seriously.

'I got one stupid prank email. It's nothing.'

'Just one?' He knows I'm lying.

'OK, a couple. And when they arrived, I was in a state because of the funeral, so for a day or two, I *did* think they were real. But obviously it's complete rubbish. I am moving on, but at my own pace, and everyone's going to have to be a bit more patient with me.'

Lewis looks at me, his dark hair hiding part of his face. I can't work out if he's genuinely shy behind all the bluff, or whether he's actually a poseur.

'What?' I say, when he stays silent.

'I'm not sure I believe you, Alice. But I guess it is your business, if you want to handle it on your own. If you think you can ...'

Can I? The alternative is to trust someone else, like I tried to with the neurotic Sahara this afternoon, and look what happened then. I shudder. 'I can,' I tell him. 'Thanks for caring, though.'

He looks like he's about to say something else to me, but then he stands up. 'Fair enough. Thanks for the water.' It's untouched on the worktop. 'You don't need to see me out.'

I wait till I hear the front door close. Alone again. I expect to feel relieved, but I'm still jumpy. Mum'll be home soon, so I do need to go upstairs, out of the way, because I don't want to have to lie to her about 'how school was today'. Maybe a shower will help me feel a tiny bit better.

It's only when I step into the hall that I see the card on the console table. I assume it must be a taxi ad, but when I pick it up, the card is too thick. I see the name *Lewis Tomlinson* and a mobile number embossed in chrome against a deep blue felted background. *Expensive.*

I turn it over. He's written *Call me anytime. I know I could help. L*

Yeah, right. I put the card in my pocket. I'm never going to call him, but I need to throw the card away *outside* the house, because the last thing I need is for Mum to find it in the bin – she already carries out random searches through the rubbish to try to keep tabs on Dad's terrible diet – and start interrogating me on why a random IT geek is offering to help me out.

Before that night, I'd never lost control.

And it hasn't happened since. Not even a hint that it could happen again. Until today.

Meggie made me lose control that first time, so perhaps it is no surprise that her sister might remind me of how it felt. The family resemblance is not obvious, but genes are about more than the same button nose or the same curve of the chin.

Seeing her was exhilarating. If anything, she is more appealing than her sister was, because little Alice has no awareness of her power. Her sharpness. Her potential . . .

I won't let it take me over, though, not like the last time. The pleasure is so fleeting, and the consequences and the subterfuge so exhausting. So I must control myself. Learn from my mistakes.

Better that way for everyone. But especially for Alice Forster.

38

On the Beach, the smoky smell is so strong that I check behind my laptop, to see if it's over-heating.

No. Just another hallucination . . .

There's a haze above the sea, which at first I think is from the heat, but then I realise it has a strong yellow tinge to it.

The first familiar face I see as I walk towards 'Meggie's' palm tree, is Triti's. She's sitting stock still on the sand, ignoring everything that's going on around her. At first I think maybe she's doing some yoga thing, but then I notice the tears streaming down her face.

'Triti! What's happened?'

She keeps staring ahead. 'Nothing.'

'It doesn't look like nothing. Shall I go and get one of the others?'

She gives me a nervous glance. 'No! No, I've bored them to death with all of my problems already.'

I sit down beside her on the sand. 'You haven't bored *me* yet.'

Her hands are locked together in her lap. 'It's nothing.'

'Are we stuck in an echo chamber or something?' I ask with a smile.

She looks at me, and her big brown eyes look flat. 'Here. This. The same nothingness, every single day, for eternity. I can't cope with it any more.'

I stare at the sand, trying to think of an upside to nothingness. The smoky smell gets stronger and I realise what it is. Gunpowder. 'But it's *not* always the same, Triti. What about the firework display. I've never seen you so happy.'

'Yeah, exactly.' She spits out the words. 'Fireworks now and then. Hey! Maybe we can even get turkey at Christmas if we shout loud enough.' She stares up at the sky, as if that's where the power is.

I want to ask her about the past, but daren't risk getting banned from the site. I have to put my sister first, even though seeing Triti like this almost makes me want to weep myself.

Eventually I say, 'Meggie told me. About what happened to you.'

'Yeah, we've all got our tragedies. Mine's no worse or no better than anyone else's. Except I did it to myself, didn't I? I've got no right to moan.'

'Something *made* you do that, though, Triti. No one would do that unless they were desperate.'

Have I gone too far? I wait for the beach to fade away.

Triti laughs bitterly. 'Desperate? Or just desperately selfish? I'm not a victim, except of my own vanity. Or stupidity.'

'It's not that simple, is it? Perhaps it would help to talk to some of the other people who did the same.'

'Other anorexics? I haven't found any.'

'But surely if you're here there *must* be others? Or suicides?'

She shrugs. 'Yeah, there are. But not as many as I thought there'd be. Just topping yourself doesn't win you a place in forever, but I don't know what that X factor is that gets you a ticket to *paradise*.' The bitterness in her voice is painful to hear.

'I wondered if it might be fame? Or at least notoriety.'

'I'm not famous. Why would anyone have heard of me? Over-achieving Indian girl dies of anorexia. At our school, anorexia was almost as common as acne. That's not going to make the headlines, is it?'

I want to tell her that it *should* make the headlines, that it's an awful story. But I realise that's too simplistic, too glib. Triti is making a choking noise, a swallowed cry.

If only I could help her.

Danny's words come back to me: *you'll only get away if whatever landed you here in the first place is resolved, back in the real world.'*

Could I try to resolve things for Triti? And, by testing the theory, find out if I can do the same for my sister?

'Triti. If there *was* a way out of here, would you take it?'

The choking stops. 'Like a shot,' she whispers.

'Please don't raise your hopes, or anything, but there might be something I could try. If you're absolutely sure. Because I don't think there'd be any going back.'

'Oh, Alice—'

I realise too late that she's reaching out for me, and we watch, horrified, as her hand drops through space onto the sand with a painful slap.

'I forgot,' she says, and her voice sounds so tiny and desperate that I feel an emptiness opening up inside me. 'But believe me when I tell you that I have never been surer of anything in my life.' She manages a warped smile. 'Or in my death.'

Maybe I am crazy to offer – to think a sixteen-year-old can change *anything* – but I know I can't leave her to suffer like this. 'There are no certainties, Triti. I could be wrong. It might make no difference. But I will try, I promise you that.'

'Thank you.' She nods, then closes her eyes and I feel as though she's a long way off, even though we're still right next to each other. Perhaps I should ask for more information, but then the threat of being banned from the Beach is always hanging over me. And if I am banished forever, then I can't help Triti, Meggie or myself. I must take it slowly.

I push myself up off the sand, to look for the others. They'll be expecting me. But even as I walk towards the jetty, I wish I could take just one night off.

After just a few minutes with Triti, everything feels different. Bleaker. It's going to take all my acting skills to laugh and joke and pretend that the Beach is paradise right now . . .

39

My cousin Laurel is very, very drunk, but nobody minds. That's what you do at your twenty-first. It wouldn't be much of a party here in the real world if you could remember any of it.

Her little sister Stacie sidles alongside me. 'She looks like a bloody Barbie doll,' she says, nodding towards Laurel.

Considering that Stacie has fake tan, fake nails and new fake boobs which were an eighteenth present from her step-dad, this seems a bit rich.

'So long as she's having fun.' On the stage, Laurel rocks backwards and forwards on her silver heels, and I wouldn't bet on her staying upright for much longer.

Stacie and Laurel are Dad's sister's daughters, from the WAG side of the family tree, but even though they couldn't be more different from Meggie and me, we've always got along.

'So where's the sexy Robbie then?' Stacie asks.

I shrug. 'I wouldn't know. We finished.'

Her eyes widen. 'No way! You shouldn't have let him get away.'

It's obvious she thinks that Robbie was well out of my league, that I'll never get a lucky break like that again. 'Right now other stuff in my life feels more important.'

'Yeah, I know, but . . . Alice, the right bloke is going to take your mind off everything. When you're with them, you can't think of nothing else, not even what happened to Meggie. Sooner you find a bloke, the better.'

Considering that Stacie loves fake *everything*, her faith in true love is always surprising. 'Is that what it's like with David?' I ask her.

Her eyes go funny, like she's stoned. 'I felt like half a person until I met David. Now I'm like, a whole one. I can't wait till he's back from Kabul. I think he's going to propose.'

David's a soldier – Stacie always said she thought she'd marry a man in uniform.

'See, it wasn't like that with Robbie,' I tell her. 'He was lovely, and kind, and very cute, but . . .'

'You never felt like any joke he made was the funniest thing you ever heard?'

'I guess so. At first.'

'OK. Did the rest of the world stop when you were with him?'

'No.'

'You never dreamed of what your kids would look like? Knew that you'd give up pretty much everything else in your life if you could be with him?'

Part of me thinks it's funny how she's swallowed the lyrics of a thousand love songs. 'No.'

'Did you feel violently jealous when you saw another girl even talking to him?'

'A bit annoyed, maybe.'

'But not like you could scratch her eyes out, or lamp her one?'

I smile. 'No.' But part of me *is* jealous that life for Stacie is so black and white.

She touches me on the shoulder. 'Fair enough. Doesn't matter how cute he is if he's not the One.'

'You really believe we all have a soul mate? One single person for each of us? No compromises?'

'Of course.'

'But people change, don't they? I know I'm a different

person to the Alice I was before Meggie died . . .'

'The right boy will love you even if you change.'

'It seems a bit random. To think you can only ever meet one person. What if your paths never cross?'

'You sound like my mum. Don't get all cynical, Alice. Boys hate that. You'll know what I mean when you find him, I promise. Then you'll go, bloody hell, Stacie was right all along.'

And she smiles at me, all-knowing and wise, as though she's ten years older than me, not thirteen months.

'Thanks.' I don't tell her what I'm thinking: that I don't even want to find the One any more, because everything seems so meaningless when you know that nothing except the Beach lasts for ever. And that forever isn't something I'd wish on my worst enemy.

Sometimes I do want to tell people, to warn them of what lies ahead, to make the most of now.

'Though, Alice, hope you don't mind me saying this, but I reckon you'd stand a better chance of finding him sooner if you did your hair and thought about a spray tan. I mean, we all know what you've been through, and we're all worried about you, but you're really pale. '

'It's the end of October, Stacie. Of course I'm pale.'

'So what? Ever heard of faking it? God, I bet you don't wax in winter, either, do you?' She casts a horrified look down at my jeans, as though there might be a jungle of hair lurking underneath. 'The thing is, you never know when you're going to meet the One. Or where. So you need to look great at all times, just in case. Best bit of advice I could give you, Alice.'

And with that, Stacie does an elegant turn that wouldn't look out of place on *Strictly Come Dancing*, and heads towards the stage just in time to stop her big sister tumbling onto the dance floor below.

40

After the tackiness of the party, the Beach is a breath of fresh air. Somehow the Guests look more natural, plus, no one's going to slag me off for not being orange or depilated enough.

'Hey, Alice. Good to see you.' Danny is under our tree, playing solitaire.

He smiles so widely that for a moment it even cancels out the awful yearning in his eyes. But only for a moment.

'Keeping busy?' I sit down, facing away from the shoreline.

'Non-stop here.' His smile drops and for a second all I can see is desperation. Do they all feel like this, behind the grins and the jokes?

I turn back towards the sea where, in the distance, the beautiful girls and boys are splashing each other in the surf. It's a stunning day. I mean, it's always stunning here, but today in particular the sky seems an unbearably perfect blue, and the coastal breeze offers just the right amount of relief from the warmth of the sun.

The coastal breeze? How can I possibly be feeling it when I am sitting in my stuffy, centrally heated bedroom miles from the sea?

'Can I ask you something, Danny?'

'Sure.'

'It's about Triti.' He nods at me to continue. 'At the weekend, I talked to her before I met up with you guys. She seemed so ... hopeless.'

He begins to pick up the cards fanned out on the blue chequered beach towel. 'We've all tried talking to her. Javier first. Then Meggie. Then me. I'm always the last resort.' He laughs. 'Not too hot at cheering people up.'

'What happened?'

He's shuffling the cards. 'Javier tried a few jokes. Meggie tried pointing out the good stuff about paradise. I played it straight. Said we all had bad days, just like we did when we were alive. That even though we have peachy bodies and clothes that never need pressing, we're still the same underneath.'

'Do you believe that?'

He looks up at me. 'Sure. Whatever the hell we are, we're not angels. You've only gotta listen to Javier for a few minutes to know that.'

I smile. 'True. Nothing angelic about him.'

'I'm no nicer. Scratch my surface and you'll find a snob. I was brought up in a family where we felt we were better than everyone else. Now I'm here, it's hard for me not to judge the jocks and the male models and the bikini girls.'

The way he says it makes me feel self-conscious. 'And me?'

He looks at me steadily. 'No, Alice. You're different.'

Something about his directness makes me blush. I look away. 'Am I? I mean, apart from looking frumpier in a bikini, how am I different?' When I look up again, I realise he's still gazing at me.

'You need to ask?'

'I just did, didn't I?'

'It has nothing to do with bikinis.' He shuffles the cards some more. 'Apart from anything else, you happen to be alive.'

'Oh. That.' I laugh. 'Sorry.'

'Not just that ...' Danny seems to be thinking something over. He shakes his head. 'Ah, let's go back to Triti, huh? It's so much simpler. She's in a bad place right now. Think about it. When life got too much for her, whatever the reason, she made a choice to keep shrinking and shrinking until she was nothing.'

How can he describe the decision to starve yourself to death like it's no bigger deal than choosing your A Level subjects?

'What kind of a choice was that? What about her family?'

Danny frowns. 'Maybe it was her family that made that choice inevitable. Who knows? My point is, here the choices are meaningless. What colour tee to wear today. Whether to hang out under this tree or that one. Hell, even eating isn't a real choice if you never feel hungry. She's stuck. We all know she has to accept that, but it doesn't make it any easier.'

'And if she doesn't accept it? If she can't?'

'I didn't design this place, Alice. If I had, I sure as hell would have introduced a Game Over option, for when we can't take any more. OK, so then the Beach would only have the jocks and the bikini girls left, because anyone with an IQ bigger than their chest size would take the opt out. Leave paradise for the dumb ...'

'You're being judgmental again, Danny.'

'Just a sign of how relaxed I can be around you, baby.'

Funny how good knowing that makes me feel. But I push the thought away. 'Baby?' I make my voice mocking.

'It's what I call all the girls.'

'Are you *flirting* with me, Daniel?'

The cards he's shuffling explode from his hands, scattering across the sand. His head stays down as he picks them up again.

'Wouldn't dare. Anyhow. Back to Triti. They made a dumb mistake, with the fireworks. Gave her the idea that she had some control. It's bad for everyone. It's ... disruptive. That's why the weather's so good today, I think.'

'As opposed to every other day when the sun shines,' I say, pretending I hadn't noticed.

He leans forward. 'No. It's different,' he whispers. 'One

thing I noticed. They use the weather here. If everyone's edgy, they make it so hot that it dampens us down. Right now they're going heavy on bliss.'

'They?'

He shakes his head. 'They? God? Your own twisted imagination? Who knows? But hey, Alice, if this is all your twisted imagination, do you think you could imagine up a video game or two for me? I sure miss Grand Theft Auto.'

I laugh. His sense of humour makes *me* feel better, too. When I'm with Meggie, I feel responsible for her, especially now I've decided to see if I can change things for her. But with Danny it's like I'm the one being looked after.

'I don't think there's much I can do about that. But . . . well, you know your theory. About resolution in the real world affecting stuff here?'

Danny stops laughing. 'Uh-huh?'

'I think it could be time for me to test it out. I might be able to help Triti.' I stop there, scared to say more in case I'm jinxed or banned.

'You know what, Alice? If you're serious, then that makes you even more special. Because I think you might be pretty much the *only* person who can rescue Triti from forever.'

41

I'm fighting to keep my eyes open, but I'm too excited to sleep. I need to know what I can find out about Triti. And after what Danny said, I feel important. Special. For the first time in ages – maybe even in my whole life – I might just make a difference.

I drag the laptop onto the duvet. The bedside lamp's off, so Dad won't see any light under the door when he gets up for his two a.m. pace. Instead, I surf by the glow of the screen.

Google tells me that Triti is either a Hindu name meaning a moment in time or a wish, or that it's a disease. But when I add *anorexic* to it, or *London schoolgirl* or death, nothing comes up. I can't give up now, especially after what Danny said. I am *the only person who can ...*

Perhaps I'm on the wrong track. Triti said herself that she was a nobody, but there's nothing to stop Guests making up stories, even creating whole new identities for themselves when they arrive on the Beach. Dead people can lie and cheat just the same. What was it Danny said: *whatever we are, we're not angels.*

It makes my head spin. The person whose death I know most about is Danny, so I replay the news report about his funeral, to see if there could be some clue I've missed that might explain Soul Beach. But no: just the same sobbing class mates, and the same hushed reporter whispering respectfully, and the same giant-sized photographs of a handsome, happy Daniel Cross giving his million dollar smile straight to camera.

But then I spot that the sidebar of related stories has a new addition.

CROSS HEIR INVESTIGATION NEARS END: NEW VIDEO!

I click through. It buffers for a second or so, and then I gasp.

Danny is at a barbecue. *With a girl.*

'*This exclusive video of Cross Enterprises heir Daniel Cross reveals for the first time the loss that devastated not only his family, but also the many young people who loved the boy predicted to be one of America's rising business stars.*'

The reporter sounds really pleased with herself, even though the video's been filmed on someone's camera phone and is jerky and low res. Danny has his arm around the girl, who is chestnut-haired and petite. The same girl I saw at the funeral? That time, she was too far off to tell.

But she doesn't take her eyes off him once as he poses for the camera, holding up a bottle of beer and laughing.

'*Kiss her, Dan, kiss her for the camera.*' The guy with the phone is calling out instructions. Danny seems to hesitate before he leans down and plants the softest, briefest kiss on the girl's lips.

'*These pictures, taken just weeks before the airplane crash that killed both eighteen-year-old Daniel and his father's pilot, show a confident, happy young man. But was that very confidence his undoing?*'

The phone camera pans across from Danny to other un-dead, un-rich kids, and then the report switches to footage of the crash scene, where the wreckage is scattered across the yellow earth. The shape of the plane itself made a dent in the sand on impact, keeping its form, just about, like an upended jigsaw.

There's an interview with an investigator, who says that the destruction was so total that there's little chance of ever knowing quite what happened, but that witnesses spoke of Danny taking the controls even before he took off.

And then the reporter almost explodes with excitement. *'And XCT Live News has obtained another exclusive picture which appears to corroborate those reports.'*

A photograph. Danny sits in the cockpit of his father's plane, which is bigger than I expected: the aerial shots of the wreckage gave no sense of scale. The picture is taken by someone standing outside the plane, and in the seat next to Danny, there's a beefy man with a too-broad smile, his arm placed proprietarily on the back of the pilot's seat.

Something about this whole video unsettles me. It's the same sensation I felt when this all started, when I stared and stared at Meggie's first email but couldn't see that the time it was sent was also her date of death . . .

'This photograph, taken on the afternoon of the ill-fated final flight, suggests Daniel had already decided to take control of his father's airplane before it left the ground. With terrible con- sequences for the real pilot, himself, his family and, who knows, maybe America too?'

The mobile phone footage repeats over her last words, which are spoken in an overly dramatic whisper that even Sahara couldn't manage.

Is it that photo that's making me uncomfortable? Or some- thing else?

The report ends, and I click on it again, but this time I mute the sound, not just because I want to kill the semi-hysterical reporter, but also so I can focus on the images, on any clues that I've missed.

But as I watch, I realise what's got under my skin: it's *her*. It's the teeny-tiny chestnut-haired home girl, with her delicate little hand locked around his waist and her goo-goo eyes fixed on the prize.

There's *nothing* between them. Any idiot could see that.

The stupid reporter is exaggerating for the sake of the story.

And when he kisses mini-girl, my anger disappears, replaced by a feeling like I'm falling through space. Is this how Danny felt as he plunged to earth? Or . . .

As the final shot replays, finishing on a freeze frame of the moment when his lips meet hers, I remember what Stacie said to me at Laurel's party, and I realise. How can a girl with as many GCSEs as me be so stupid about real life? It's not about the picture. It's not even about some psychic hunch or mystical clue.

It's jealousy, plain and simple.

42

I slam the laptop shut.

Stacie's soppy questions ring in my ears, louder than the waves from the Beach have ever been.

Did the rest of the world stop when you were with him?

Does it? The real world means nothing to me when I'm on Soul Beach, and up till now, I've assumed it's all about being with Meggie.

But is it possible that Danny is the other reason why I can't stay away? And if it is, then what does that say about me?

You never dreamed of what your kids would look like?

No. That really would be very, *very* weird.

Knew that you'd give up pretty much everything else in your life if you could be with him?

If I wanted to be with Danny, I'd be giving up on life altogether. I'm not that foolish.

And yet, haven't there been times lately when I've felt that Soul Beach is the only place I want to be? Even though it's terrified me to admit what that would actually mean . . .

Did you feel violently jealous when you saw another girl even talking to him? Like you could scratch her eyes out, or lamp her one?

Well, that's a yes, for sure. So: two yeses, one maybe and one no. Stacie would say that's not nearly enough to be certain.

But me? I lie in the dark and I think of Danny and I know that the way I feel when I'm with him is a million times stronger than the way I felt with Robbie.

No, scrub that. It's another emotion altogether.

Shit. I think I'm falling for a dead guy.

43

In the morning, I realise how ridiculous it is: of course I don't *love* Danny. I'm just lonely and fed up and maybe that's what's triggered the kind of embarrassing crush I thought I'd grown out of in Year Eight.

But still, I don't feel like taking my usual pre-breakfast stroll on the beach, so I head to school early. No one notices. Dad's already left for the office – probably because he can sleep there undisturbed – and Mum is up to something. She keeps humming, which is always a bad sign.

Just outside the school gate, my mobile rings. *Withheld number.* I'm about to let it go to voicemail when I get this awful terror that it could be Meggie, on some kind of Soul Beach emergency phone, worried about why I haven't turned up on the Beach yet.

'Alice? Is that you?'

A man's voice. Not a wrong number, but a man who knows my name. Those four words feel like a precise kick below my ribcage. I almost double up.

'Who is this?' I whisper, once I can breathe again.

A nervous laugh. I'm about to hang up when he says, 'It's Adrian. Sahara's boyfriend. Remember, from the pub?'

My fear turns to irritation. 'Yes. I do. But couldn't you have texted? I've got enough to worry about without calls from people I don't know.'

'I'm really sorry to call out of the blue,' he says, and he sounds it, which makes my heart beat slow a little. 'And yes, I knew it might stress you out, but I've made someone a promise and it's something that might help you too.'

'How?' I'm sceptical, though actually, he sounds genuine.

'Sahara told me that when you were in Greenwich, you'd come to look for Tim?'

Meddling cow. 'She had no right to tell you.'

Those moments in Meggie's room come back to me: the darkness and the panic. I never want to go there again, never want to talk to Sahara. *But if you don't, you'll never know* ...

'Listen, you're right, maybe she shouldn't have told me.' His voice is still calm. 'And, you know, maybe I had no right to mention it to Tim either, but I thought it through for ages and I did mention it. And, well, he says he does want to talk to you.'

I stumble back against the school wall. Suddenly it's the only thing that feels solid. What did my sister say? *He might tell you things.*

'Tim? When? I can come now.' Before he changes his mind.

'Hold on, Alice. It's not quite that simple. He's pretty sure he's being followed by the police.'

'*What?*'

Ellie from my Media Studies class walks past. She gives me a smile and I realise how normal I must look, for once. Like a hundred other girls, sneaking in a call from a boy before racing into class.

'I don't know if it's true, or if he's being paranoid, but ever since he was released from questioning, he says he's been seeing the same guys tailing him. Plus a car is always parked in the road opposite our flat. I'm pretty jumpy too, to be honest.'

It's hard to imagine detectives following Tim around, as he goes from library to corner shop and to the greasy spoon he always preferred to Starbucks. They must be so bored. Unless, of course, I'm wrong about him, and he's spending his days torturing pigeons and preparing himself for his next kill.

'God.'

'That must sound shocking, after what you've been through.' His voice is kind.

'I guess it does, yes.' I remember what Sahara said about her and Adrian arguing over Tim. 'Do *you* think he did it, Adrian?'

There's a pause. Around me, the stragglers are racing into school, watched by the head of Year Seven, who is always eager to get a few more names on her late list so she can sentence them to a week of litter clearing.

Adrian sighs. 'I guess I'm ninety-nine per cent sure he's innocent, or I wouldn't be living with him.' He tries to laugh. 'I was the only one willing to, mind you, but on the plus side, he's a good cook, and always cleans the loo. Do murderers clean the loo?'

I pretend to laugh, but really I'm wondering how Tim copes with being notorious. He always loathed the limelight. 'What about the one per cent? The bit of you that's not sure?'

'Thing is, Alice, since your sister died, I've found it impossible to be a hundred per cent sure of anything or anyone. Even good friends.'

'I know how that feels.'

'I bet you do. So, did I do the right thing? The last thing I want to do is upset you even more.'

'Yes, yes, you did. Thank you. I definitely do want to see him, so what should I do next?'

'Tim needs to find a time when he can feel safe. I'll text you because he thinks his phone's being tapped.'

'Are they even allowed to do that?'

'I guess anything's OK if it they think it'll help catch Meggie's murderer.'

I nod to myself. 'I guess. Will he call soon?'

'I'll talk to him. I think he's nervous about what you'll say.'

'Thank you so much for doing this for me, Adrian. Tell him ... tell him all I want is the truth.'

'Don't we all, Alice. Take care.'

He rings off, and I stare at my phone until I hear a loud tut and see the head of Year Seven walking towards me. 'Just because you're in the sixth form, Alice, doesn't mean you're immune from litter duty. I'll count to three. One ...'

I scoot in through the gates, even though I couldn't give a toss about litter duty or registers. When I reach the corridor outside Mr Bryant's classroom, everyone's waiting because he's late himself.

Ellie sidles up to me. 'So what are you doing about Saturday?'

I gawp at her. No one but Cara bothers to invite me anywhere these days, and even she's on the point of giving up. There must be some stupid house party on Facebook that they've included me in, as the charity case. Or the freak show.

'Quiet night in. As usual,' I say, praying for Mr Bryant to show, and breathing a sigh of relief when he does, dropping his papers and fiddling to find his key.

My classmates look at me like I'm an alien. Just because I don't want to go and get drunk with them and fend off slobbery advances from tongue-tied sixth formers from the boys' school, or my classmates' sweaty older brothers.

I really don't think *I'm* the freak around here.

44

There are two dark estate cars on the drive when I get home. Mum must be playing host to her grief cronies.

I take my shoes off in the storm porch, hoping to slip past, but before my key's even in the lock, my mother is there, wearing a manic smile that suggests she's either been at the sherry *or* she's about to try to talk me into something I don't want to do.

'Darling! How was school? I'm so glad you're back in time, as there are some people here who'd love to talk to you.'

When she gestures towards the living room, I notice a ghostly glow through the gap in the door. Bloody hell, what's she got herself mixed up in now? Has she ditched Olav for a bunch of occultists? Are they holding a séance?

'Go on, Alice, no one's going to bite your head off.'

I step into the room, and am immediately dazzled by three enormous lights on stands, all directed at Dad's armchair, which has a table next to it, with three of Mum's favourite pictures of Meggie carefully arranged on top. There's a cup of tea, too, even though my mother never drinks it.

Then I take in the other people: a man behind a large video camera, another with headphones, plus two women, one with a clipboard and the other wearing the expression of super-sympathy that I've seen too many times in the last few months.

'Hello, Alice. How *are* you?' asks Ms Super-Sympathetic so sincerely.

I look at her suspiciously. 'What are you doing here?'

Mum's behind me. 'It's a tribute, Alice. The new season of

Sing for your Supper begins this Saturday and the programme wanted to record something about Meggie.'

This Saturday. That was what Ellie must have been talking about. Not a party at all!

'Yes,' says super-sincere whatsherface. 'We didn't think it would be right to ignore the huge contribution she made to the success of the last series. And her millions of fans will be expecting something.'

And her millions of fans won't exactly do your audience figures any harm either, will they? I think. But I turn around instead of saying it out loud. 'I don't want to, thanks for the offer.'

I try to leave the room, but Mum's in my way.

'I think it's what your sister would have wanted, Alice.'

'How do you know?' I want to tell her that I'll go upstairs right now and ask my sister, but funnily enough, I don't. I want to ask her why there are three pictures of Meggie on the table but not one of them has *me* in it too, but I don't. And then something else occurs to me. 'And what about Dad? Is he doing it?'

Mum looks away.

'You haven't bloody told him, have you?' I realise. 'This family, God.'

She lets me pass, and I run upstairs. I know there's only one place I can go where I'll feel normal – and *wanted*.

The sky is that same, gob-smacking blue, and the sound of the waves calms me immediately. It's less than twenty-four hours since I was last here, yet it feels like weeks. I've missed it so much.

Then I remember why I didn't come onto the Beach this morning and I blush. Did Danny even notice I wasn't around?

'Hey, Florrie. I'm here.'

My sister's voice is too loud, and I jam the headphones into the laptop jack, so that no one else will hear. I don't know how I'd explain *this* to a film crew and my mother.

Meggie is standing behind me, her arms crossed. 'You're a bit late.'

'Am I?' I don't want to explain about the tribute. Knowing Meggie, she'd probably write my script for me, and demand that they only use clips from the final shows, when she'd been on the Atkins to lose the half kilo she insisted showed so badly in the previous rounds. 'I thought you didn't have watches here.'

She shrugs. 'I tell the time by the shadows like a witch doctor. Anyway, I wanted to talk to you. Alone. Can we take a walk?'

I nod. What now? Maybe she's going to tell me that she's worked out I have a massive crush on Danny, or warn me to leave the poor boy alone because I'm an embarrassment. When it comes to liking people, I am almost always the last one to realise how I feel.

We walk further and further, until the chattering is a distant whisper, and the sand is completely empty. Here, Soul Beach seems less real somehow, as though whoever created this place ran out of steam or time at the last minute, and only sketched in the colours and the shapes. When I look down, the grains of sand have disappeared and the froth on the top of the waves freezes and pixellates, like a video game struggling to run on an old computer.

'Here should do it,' Meggie says.

She settles herself under a blurry palm, and I join her. 'What's this about?' Maybe it's not Danny at all. Maybe she wants to know if I've been to Greenwich and got a confession out of Tim yet.

She sighs. 'It's Triti. She's in the most awful state.'

'Triti?' I think of the last time I saw her, so utterly lonely among so much laughter. 'What's happened?'

'She keeps ... doing stuff. Like jumping off the pier head first, even though of course she never drowns. She's even started cutting herself. I mean, she bleeds, but then seconds later her skin's healed up, and she keeps trying, as though if she does it enough times, she'll succeed.'

The waves suddenly seem more like a quickening pulse than a tide. 'But she won't, will she?'

Meggie shivers. 'Nope. The trouble is, she's upsetting people. The Guests who really *did* drown, who *did* slash their wrists. It's like she's replaying what they did to themselves over and over. It's not fair.'

I hear anger in her voice. Is she cross with poor Triti, or is it more frustration at knowing that she's is in exactly the same boat herself?

'I know, Meggie.'

She stares at me, her eyes bluer and more real than anything else on the beach. 'You can help her.'

I nod. 'I want to. I *really* want to.' Though who am I to think I'm capable of helping anyone, when a stupid crush turns me into a gibbering idiot? I wouldn't trust myself to help an old lady across the road, never mind deal with life-or-death stuff.

Yet, as Danny said, maybe I'm the only person who can even attempt it.

'Well, is there any chance you could hurry it up a bit, Florrie? This is important. She needs to get off this bloody beach, not just for her sake but for ours.' Her bossy tone is the same as when she ordered me to stop biting my nails, because *'no boy will ever want to go out with a girl who gnaws away at herself!'*

'I am working on it,' I say, resolving to get back on the case the instant I log off the Beach. After all, helping Triti might help my sister too. 'I did try to find her on the web, but nothing came up. It's like she never existed.' For a moment, Meggie looks as though she's about to give me another lecture. But something worse happens: she reddens, a colour as dark as spilled blood, from her hairline to her chest. Even her eyes are scarlet.

Like last time.

'Meggie? Meggie, what is it?'

And then – it can only have been a couple of seconds, but it feels like hours – she blinks, and the colour drains away again, leaving just that flawless tan and a pale imitation of a smile.

'Sorry, Florrie. I felt like . . .'

'Like you were being buried alive?'

She stares at me, and nods. 'I . . . please don't say that. I don't want to think about it.'

'Sorry.'

'No, it's not your fault. I just . . . anyway, we were talking about Triti. I have faith in you, little sis. I know you can do it. So please keep trying. For her sake. For *all* our sakes.'

I curse myself for being distracted by trivia, when for the first time in my life, I might be able to do something worth doing. 'I'll give it everything I have, Meggie. I promise you that.'

Now I just have to work out where to begin.

45

I'm making Mr Bryant's day, I can tell, by asking his advice on my studies.

'Research is one of life's guilty pleasures, Alice. What's the project?'

I've thought carefully about this: if I tell him I want to research a girl who starved herself to death, I'll be booked in for Olavotherapy before you can say 'death fixation'. Whereas if I handle this right, the word of my new attitude will be round the staffroom in a millisecond.

'Fame and body image,' I say.

'Fame and body image,' he repeats. 'Excellent. Well, I happen to have an old uni pal who runs a small but comprehensive newspaper archive at the other end of the District line. Here,' he scribbles down an email address and a phone number.

As I leave, he's smiling to himself like a modern day Mr Chips.

I have to race to the archive straight from school on Friday because it shuts at five. The journey takes an hour, so it's seriously dark by the time I find the squat building two streets behind the tube station.

Mr Bryant's old pal isn't what you'd call welcoming. 'You've got forty minutes,' he says, showing me into a low-ceilinged, windowless room with five pods that look like sit-in driving-game consoles from an arcade.

'Microfiche readers,' he says, seeing my reaction. 'Load

your microfilm into the tray, switch on the light, and the world's your oyster.'

'I was expecting newspapers.'

'Newspapers go yellow and crumble to dust. Microfilm lasts. So, what's the publication and date range?'

'Um ... well, I'm researching body image, but specifically anorexia. I, er, got the idea from a case somewhere in London about eighteen months ago where an Indian girl starved herself to death.'

'Somewhere in London?' He scowls. 'About eighteen months ago? You do know that there are over thirty paid-for local papers in the city, with about the same number of free sheets. You're looking for a needle in a haystack.'

'Can I still try, though?'

The archivist sighs. 'If you must. OK, where shall we start? North, South, East or West?'

'Er.' I take a guess. 'North?'

'Right you are. Only thirty-five minutes left now.'

Half an hour later and I'm no longer writing the archivist off as a gloomy jobsworth.

I've skimmed just two months' worth of the *North London Gazette*, and even though there are a depressing number of teenage deaths, there's nothing unresolved about motorbike crashes or lost battles against leukaemia. Reading about so many deaths upsets me: where do *those* kids go? Another beach, or is their reward for dying blamelessly a glorious eternal sleep?

Focus, Alice. At this rate, I'll be here till Christmas and even then there's the danger that, actually, Triti's not there at all.

'That's your lot, I'm afraid,' says Mr Happy. 'Shall I leave a note of where you've got to, or are you thinking you might not come back?'

I look at my feet. 'It's harder than I thought.'

'Hmm. Yes. I've worked in archives all my life, and I hate to suggest it, but have you thought of trying Google?'

When I get home, Mum and Dad interrupt their argument for about twenty seconds to say hi and tell me there's an Indian takeaway for me in the kitchen, then go back to the rights and wrongs of this bloody TV tribute.

My curry is cold, but I'm not hungry anyway.

I take the Cinderella jewellery box onto my bed. This is where I keep my favourite things: the fuzzy, ugly Gonk key ring that Mum had herself when she was a little girl, the locket with my first curl of baby hair inside. Meggie's gold ring. And then a newer treasure: the key to Meggie's room, lying on the worn pink velvet lining. I take it out and hold it on my palm.

The questions flood through me: who killed Meggie, why is Triti on the Beach, am I in love with Danny and if so, does that mean I really have lost the plot completely?

The key was icy cold at first, but now it's hot. Red hot.

So hot that I drop it and then have to scrabble around on the carpet. I reach under the bed, grasping for the key, but I can't find it. Finally my hand closes around something else. Something I was sure I'd thrown away.

Lewis's business card, with its expensive and slightly velvety finish, and the message scrawled on the back.

Call me anytime. I know I can help.

Oh, you do, do you, Mr Geek? Well, maybe you're my last resort.

Appetite is such a trivial-sounding word, yet it rules our lives completely.

Hunger is better. Just because Meggie is not here any more, it doesn't mean I don't still hunger for her.

Perhaps I was too rash in the action I took, but at the time it felt as though I had little alternative.

Recently it occurred to me that there is a way to be happy again. Perhaps Alice was always the better sister, anyway.

More intelligent. More loyal. More . . . receptive.

After a period of famine, my own appetite has returned. If I can tame it this time, control the extremes of my urges, then maybe I can savour the final experience so much more.

46

The least Lewis could do when I call is sound surprised.

'You came round, then, Alice? Thought you might.'

'I'm that predictable, am I?'

'The way I see it, you don't have anywhere else to go.'

'Yeah, you're right that I wouldn't be in touch if I wasn't desperate.'

'We're a match made in heaven, then, because I've only agreed to help you as a favour to a mate.'

'Just so long as we're clear, then, Lewis.'

'Crystal clear, Alice.'

He comes round in the afternoon, before the TV tribute. I'm guessing his diary isn't packed with social engagements.

Mum's so excited to see me with a boy – which to her must mean I am becoming *normal* again – that she lets him come up to my room and even sends us upstairs with two different sorts of posh Belgian chocolate biscuits.

I sit on the bed and he sits on my pink chair, even though he's too tall to be comfortable. I don't know what to say next. He's smartened up a bit, for my parents' sake: he has on a different, cleaner pair of the same model of trainer he was wearing last time, and he's tried to flatten that wild hair a bit. He doesn't look any more comfortable than I do. I guess he doesn't get to spend much time in girls' bedrooms. He's probably not even interested in anything that can't run *World of Warcraft*.

'Nice kit,' he says, nodding towards my laptop. 'Good

graphics card, that model. Wouldn't have taken you for a gamer.'

Little do you know, sunshine. I love my virtual worlds so much that I've even fallen in love with a guy who can't possibly exist. 'I got it because it's got a sparkly keyboard,' I tell him.

It's a lie. Actually, I got it after researching the spec carefully, because I can have my geeky moments too, but I'm not about to tell him that.

He raises his eyebrows as if to say, girls like you shouldn't be allowed to have laptops like this. But then he says, 'You look a lot like your sister when you frown.'

The atmosphere in the room changes. It's true – Mum is always mentioning it, or she used to. But surely for Lewis to notice it too, he must have spent more time with Meggie than he's admitted to. 'You said you hardly knew her.'

'I didn't know her *that* well. But this is more like a village than real London where no one knows each other, isn't it? We were in the same year, even if we were at different schools. She dated a couple of friends of friends. And she was pretty. I mean, I know you think I'm a total geek, Alice, but even geeks notice pretty girls. They just don't do anything about it.'

I look at the floor, embarrassed that he knows I'm judging him. He doesn't deserve to be dismissed when he's trying to help. 'I don't think you're a *total* geek,' I say.

He smiles. 'I guess that's better than nothing. Now, shall we get down to business? Cara said you'd had stalkerish emails. People saying they knew where your sister was. Even actually pretending to *be* your sister. Is that right?' He takes an iPhone out of his pocket, and sets it up to record our conversation. So much for him not being geeky.

'They stopped. Just loonies.'

He nods, though his face stays sceptical. 'Lot of them about. And I guess it's not much of a surprise that some of them got obsessed with your sister. I've got a theory about why she appealed so much to nerds and losers. She was pretty, yes, but not supermodel beautiful. Girl-next-door pretty. And the fact that she went out with that Tim guy, well, every nerd and loser in the country looked at the two of them and thought, if *he* can get her, I must be in with a chance of a cute girlfriend too.'

Did you *think that, Lewis?* I want to ask, but I decide it would be too rude. 'The emails stopped, like I say.' Though I look at my watch, remembering that the TV tribute airs in two hours' time. OK, that might set the fans off again, but they can't be behind Soul Beach, can they?

Can they?

Sometimes there's so much going on in my brain that I can't think straight. I want to scream with frustration. Will any of this ever make sense?

'All right, Alice, if the emails have stopped, what do you want from me?'

I'm rubbish at lying. So much so that Meggie even tried to train me a couple of times. She called it 'an essential part of your education, especially when it comes to boys,' and explained that it's all about convincing details and looking the person you're lying to in the eye. About having your story straight, and keeping as much of the truth as possible. I always thought she only lied about the trivial stuff – where she was when she stayed out that bit too late, why she hadn't finished an assignment for college.

But what if her whole life was full of lies? Could she have got herself into some kind of trouble that led to her murder? Crazy, maybe, but is it any more crazy than the idea of Tim killing her?

'Alice?'

'Sorry, sorry. I find it hard to focus since ...' I shrug apologetically and he nods but says nothing. 'Well, I guess Cara's right, that I haven't quite been able to get over what happened to Meggie. It's a puzzle that I can't solve. Obviously more than a puzzle. A mystery. Sorry, I'm making it sound like CSI.'

'The police arrested that guy, didn't they? Her boyfriend?'

'Yeah, but ...' I shrug. 'It seems too obvious.'

'Sometimes things are obvious because they're true,' he says. 'If I'm trying to fix something, usually I have a hunch about what's wrong from the phone call, even before I remote access their systems. Ninety-nine times out of a hundred, the hunch is spot on.'

'But then there's the one in a hundred ...'

He smiles. 'Yes, those are always the bastards to fix, that's where I earn my money.'

'The thing is,' I say, taking a breath before the lying part of my story, 'it's not just Meggie any more. I keep thinking about other dead people. Dead kids. My age.' I look at him.

'*Our* age, you mean?' he asks, and I get the sense that he's taking the piss. 'I might look like a grizzled old geezer to you, Alice, but I'm only your sister's age.'

'Right,' I say, realizing that maybe I have been a bit dismissive, especially when he's trying to help. 'It's become ... maybe a bit of an obsession for me. If I can't fix what happened to my sister, then I want to know why other kids died. Kids I read about online. Kids I remember reading about. I know it sounds freaky, but I can't stop thinking about them.'

Know when to stop. That was another of Meggie's Rules of Lying. If you go on too long, you tie yourself up in stupid knots. I stop.

I wait. Is it even plausible? I struggled for ages to come up with a reason that might get him to help me. And, in terms of being believable, it's still about a million times more believable than the idea that there's a social networking site for dead teens.

He's mulling it over. Sips his beer. Looks at me. Looks at

his iPod screen. Is there a built-in lie detector app in there? 'That's a bit odd, Alice, I must say.'

'Yeah, well, my sister always said I was a bit of a freak.' That's true, too, but she meant it in an affectionate way.

He laughs. 'Join the club. Freaks anonymous ...' And I realise in that moment, in a single shared glance, that he's bought my story and he's going to help me. 'OK, Miss Freak, how exactly can I help?'

47

Lewis leaves with the sketchiest of details about Triti. He seems *more* intrigued because he's got nothing to go on, not less. 'Piece of pi ... cake,' he says as he goes.

I wish I could leave with him. Instead, I'm trying to prepare myself for the next ordeal: the tribute.

Dad was threatening to go out until he saw me give him a look that said, *I need you here too.* So we're sitting in the living room waiting for the big moment, and for the pizzas we've ordered (takeaways two nights running! Mum would never have let that happen before).

There's something eerily familiar about the whole set up. Then I realise: this is where we were this time last year, right down to the pizza order: Four Cheeses for Mum, American Hot for Dad, Mediterranean for me. The kid on the phone just now offered me the Caprese, based on previous orders.

But the Caprese was Meggie's. That night, Tim, wanting to be no trouble, said he'd have a garlic bread, and then a slice from each of ours instead of having his own.

We'd been at the recording the previous night, of course, so we knew how the show ended. But still, we were on edge waiting to see how she looked on camera. *We* thought she was wonderful, easily the best of all the contestants, but would everyone else?

Meggie had an invitation to the transmission party, but she chose to be with us. That was before she got dazzled by première and launch invitations and we saw less of her. Well, who can blame her for enjoying the attention? It was what she'd always dreamed of.

My dad catches my eye. 'Feels like she should be here, with us.'

I reckon Mum is about to bark something at him, but instead she sees this as the olive branch he intended it to be. She nods. 'Maybe she is. I feel her presence sometimes, as though she can sense when we need her.'

I say nothing, though the idea of Meggie as a kind of ultra-wet, ultra-sweet guardian angel couldn't be further from the truth.

'And now on ITV, it's time for the third season of *Sing for Your Supper*. Stay tuned for your first glimpse – and your first taste – of the stars of tomorrow.'

The sponsorship jingle appears, showing a happy family sitting in a living room not that different from ours, with trays of steaming food. The teenage boy has bangers and mash, the girl a too-bright stir-fry; Dad has a deep brown stew, and Mum is about to orgasm over an orangey chicken tikka.

Tasteful Dinners sponsor Sing for your Supper. Whatever your taste, you'll find a winner with Tasteful Dinners.

Then the gurning family fade away, and the opening music and titles fade up. I freeze. That music used to mean so much: the OTT, showbizzy theme promised that Meggie could become the star she was destined to be.

I look at my parents. Dad has taken Mum's hand, and she's gripping it back.

I wonder if Tim is watching. Or if the killer has tuned in. Or if they're one and the same.

The titles finish and the studio appears: red, black, gold, like the ugliest of nightclubs. The two presenters – a former glamour model and a middle-aged actor who used to do Shakespeare before choosing fame and wealth instead – smile brightly and read the autocue loudly with exaggerated lip movements, as though they're talking to a deaf person. Perhaps that's the only way you can talk after you've been injected with as much lip filler as they both have.

It's the usual spiel about talent and torment and tagliatelle. The 'unique selling point' of this dumb programme is that it links two viewer obsessions: talent shows and cookery shows. Each week, the kids cook for each other, eating together and making relationships that will be tested to breaking point by their ambition to win.

It's rubbish, of course. Meggie told us that no one in the house talked to each other except when the camera was running, and after they'd filmed the foodie segments, one or two of the kids would be straight to the loo to get rid of their dinner before a single calorie could be absorbed. Eating disorders never featured on the show, but they were there behind the scenes, as girls and boys fretted about every extra centimetre showing on screen and reducing their chances of making it to the final. Even Meggie went on a diet towards the end, she was made to feel so paranoid about her shape.

And that makes me think of Triti.

There's a shot of the line-up for this year's competition – fifty acts, altogether. Even this early on, as the camera pans, it's easy to spot who is there for comedy value and who will survive the brutal 'sudden death' cull at the end of this first show. Half of them will have their dreams shattered tonight. Maybe they're the lucky ones, because it seems to me that every person but one in this shot will have their heart broken for our entertainment. And some, like Meggie, could fare even worse.

They cut to close-ups of the two presenters. Uh-oh. Serious faces. Here we go . . .

'Of course, returning to your screens is a happy moment for both of us, but this year we're also aware of a very real sadness,' says the actor. 'Absolutely.' The model nods sincerely and her boobs jiggle in her slinky dress. 'I know that everyone who loves the show as we do will be thinking tonight of one of our most talented and popular contestants. The girl who won our hearts from that very first time she sang. The girl who became known across Britain, and the world, as the Songbird.'

The orchestra plays softly: the opening theme to *Amazing Grace*. The screen fills with a shot of Meggie from that first show, but they've done something to the video so that it looks softer round the edges, slightly faded. She looks as fresh and perfect as she always did – Lewis was talking crap when he said she wasn't truly beautiful – but the effect makes her seem like a starlet from the twenties or thirties. Or an icon.

'Meggie Forster was a unique talent,' the actor intones in the same voice he must have used as Hamlet. 'Taken from us tragically young. We will all be thinking of her throughout the series, but tonight in particular we wanted to mark her life and also what she did for us and our viewers on this show.'

Yeah, I think. What she did for you was double your fee. The first series was a washout. It was only when the papers started raving about the Songbird in series two that people started tuning in, from Australia to Zanzibar.

'Understandably, Meggie's parents and sister didn't feel able to join us here in the audience tonight,' the model says, her round eyes almost popping out of their sockets as she ladles on the sincerity.

'They actually asked us?' Dad says and Mum nods, raising her eyebrows.

'But Meggie's mother, Beatrice, agreed to speak to us about the six months since she lost her daughter, and how knowing she's remembered by millions helps the grieving process.'

Mum's had the soft focus effect, too. Or maybe it's the extra weight she's carrying, because she looks more like Meggie's sister than her mother as the shot widens to show her sitting in the chair that I'm now curled up on.

'From her first few weeks of life,' Mum says, 'I had this sense somehow that my little girl would end up known to millions . . .'

At the end of the tribute – which was more tastefully done than I'd expected, though the album plug by that runner-up boy band as they paid their respects was tacky as hell – the actor repeats the number for *Crimestoppers*.

As the camera switches to elsewhere in the studio, where the model is about to interview the contestants, Dad mutes the telly.

'Right. There we are then.'

'I know you didn't want me to do it, Glen, but you never know what might happen. It might make someone feel guilty enough to go to the police,' Mum says. We all know exactly which *someone* she has in mind.

'It wasn't too awful,' Dad concedes. 'What did you think, Alice?'

'Could have been worse,' I say. I wait for the moment when I can return to my bedroom and the Beach, where my sister is back in the present tense, not the tragic past.

We sit in silence. I can't guess my parents' thoughts. Maybe I don't want to. Perhaps they think the wrong daughter died . . .

Suddenly Dad stands up. 'The pizza. They haven't brought it. I'll go and chase them.'

I want to say I'm not hungry any more, but he's already gone.

'I'm off for a lie down, Mum.'

She stands up and opens her arms. 'I did do the right thing, didn't I, Alice? It was impossible to know what was right.'

I hug her, and whisper, 'Of course, Mum. You did a brilliant job.'

I release myself and go upstairs.

There are four texts on my phone.

Cara's says: **Thinking of you, chick. Why not join me and Felipe for a drink later, yeah? I bet you need it.**

Robbie's says: **Hope you're OK. Still love you, you know, as a mate. Still care. xx**

There's one from a number I don't recognise, until I remember I forgot to save Adrian's name to my phone: **Tim's been in tears tonight. He promises he'll be in touch soon. I watched it too and I still can't believe she's gone, even now. She'll always be a legend. So sorry. Ade x**

The final one is from Lewis: **I'VE GOT HER. Triti, I mean. Let me know when you can talk.**

No sympathy. No sadness. He'd probably even forgotten that the show was on.

But his is the message I've been waiting for, and the one I respond to straight away.

48

'She died in a hospital in Camden,' Lewis says, when we meet in the pub.

Oh my God. Triti exists. *Existed.*

For a moment, I can't speak. More proof that Soul Beach is real. Despite everything I've found about Danny, sometimes I still get worried that someone has set the whole thing up as a clever hoax. Or even that my imagination is somehow dredging up random stuff I've read or seen, and I really have lost it.

Yet I couldn't possibly have read about Triti. Which means Lewis might just have proved I am sane. Which means I am now pretty much his number one fan.

I find my voice. 'You're sure it's her?'

'A hundred per cent. I found her via the death certificates on one of the official registration back-ups. You don't get much more certain than that.'

'Is that public?' I ask.

Lewis smiles. 'Not really. But the security on their mirror site is unbelievably lame. Got through the encryption in under a minute.'

He reaches into his messenger bag.

I catch sight of the Gucci logo. 'Is that a real one? They're four hundred quid, aren't they?'

Lewis frowns. 'I don't care about the label, I'm not that shallow. It's just that it's more hard-wearing than the fakes.'

I happen to know the bag is *this* season's – Cara hopes her mum might buy her one for Christmas if she drops enough hints – so I wonder how he knows yet that it'll outlast the fakes. But I'm too distracted by the papers he's taken out of the bag to argue. I reach out.

'Wait, wait!' he says, determined to savour his moment of triumph. 'The weirdest thing is that the autopsy shows an Indian girl, Triti Pillai, aged sixteen and seriously malnourished. All the usual signs of eating disorders, most notably the acid damage to the back of the teeth.'

'I don't get it. Why does that suggest an eating disorder?'

'Stomach acid is evil. If you throw up all the time, your teeth rot.'

'Oh.' I think of Triti's bright white teeth and her shy smile. 'That's horrible. But why is it weird?'

He hands over the document, finally, and points to the bottom.

I read out loud: 'Cause of death: myocardial infarction, probable cause, undetected cardiac defect, of genetic origin.'

'A heart attack. But essentially natural causes. They're saying her heart just gave up because of a weakness she inherited. No mention of the anorexia or bulimia making the body less able to cope with that weakness. I mean, I'm no expert, but it's strange. Why would that be given as cause of death when she so obviously starved herself? All I can think of is that the doctors said it was natural causes so the family wouldn't have to face an inquest. Her folks were either very persuasive, or *very* influential.'

When Meggie's inquest opened, the press were everywhere. It was over in seconds, proceedings postponed until they caught the killer. Dad went alone, and the photos of him are some of the most shocking they took of him. He looks like a ghost himself.

'Surely that's a good thing though?' I say to Lewis.

'I suppose so, if your daughter dying can ever be a good thing. But what's even weirder is that *you* got to know about it. It wasn't reported. Not in the papers or the TV news. I've looked everywhere. She was just a teenager who died of supposedly natural causes. Nothing special about her. So how did you hear about it?'

He waits for me to say something.

'Perhaps ... perhaps it was in a paper that doesn't have a website,' I suggest.

Lewis doesn't smile. 'Or perhaps you're not telling me everything?'

He waits again, scrutinising me like I'm a particularly troublesome hard drive.

Well, two can stare. Nothing will persuade me to tell him how I know about Triti. I return his stare so intensely that if you were watching the two of us from the next table you'd think we were either in love, or full of loathing.

It's never occurred to me before how similar those two emotions look.

He blinks first. 'Anyway, it's only half the story. If you want the full one ...' He turns the papers over and there, scribbled in his crazy handwriting, is an address in Camden. 'How do you fancy a day trip to the wastelands of north London?'

49

I wanted to go on my own, but Lewis wouldn't let me.

'It's rough up there,' he explained. 'I feel responsible for you now.'

We take the tube, and on the way, I speculate on what might be behind Triti's death. The threat of an arranged marriage? Parental abuse? I picture a top floor flat in a grim tower block, a place where slow suicide feels preferable to a long life in shades of grey.

And then we get there, and Triti's street is about a hundred times smarter than the one where *I* live: stone semi-detached houses with German cars parked in freshly painted bays.

'You can probably leave me now, Lewis. This isn't my idea of a ghetto.' I reach into my purse, and pull out a fiver. 'Why don't you take this and let me buy you a coffee and I'll ring you when I've talked to them?'

If I get as far as talking to them.

'Put that away, silly girl. How many weeks' pocket money is that? I don't need handouts. I earn that much in ten minutes just standing here. Besides, I would really like to know what I've risked arrest over ...'

'Arrest?'

'It's not exactly *legal* to hack into government databases, Alice. Anyway, I'm dying to see how you plan to talk your way into this one.'

I don't tell him that I haven't got much idea myself.

Triti's house is well-maintained, with tubs full of winter plants stacked like sentries on the steps up to the tasteful grey-green front door. I can't see through the windows because there are blinds down, but the blinds are creamy coloured and rough textured, like hand-made paper. Everything is tasteful. I realise I've been expecting something more stereotypically Bollywood, a home that fits a girl who loves fireworks and sparkly crystal earrings.

I take a breath, then ring the bell. Maybe it would have been better if I'd had more time to prepare myself? But today's Sunday and we knew this was our best chance of catching people in.

Plus, I don't think Triti can carry on for much longer. When I saw Meggie on the Beach last night, I could hear Triti in the background, shouting and screaming. Some of the other kids had been talking about gagging her, just to shut her up.

'No answer,' I say, torn between wanting to leave before anyone sees us, and knowing that this is the only thing in my life that matters right now.

'I heard someone in the house,' Lewis replies. 'Look, Alice, don't wimp out now. I didn't give up my Sunday to fall at the first hurdle. Try again.'

Bloody hell, he's bossy.

But he also happens to be right. What would I tell Meggie or Danny if I left now? And how would I live with myself if I missed this opportunity to save Triti and get closer to the mystery of the Beach? Now is definitely *not* the time to let my nerves get the better of me.

I press the bell hard, and we can hear it this time, echoing round the house, impossible to ignore.

Through the glass panels in the door, someone moves. A slight figure approaches with the same fast but floaty quality that Triti has, and the door's open before I can take another breath.

'Yeah?'

There's no doubt that we've got the right house. This could only be Triti's brother. His face is sleek, almost cat-like. Even though he's dressed in Sunday slobbing gear – jeans and a crumpled shirt – he's so elegant.

'I'm sorry to bother you,' I begin.

'Not *again*,' he says. 'I told the last lot. We're not interested in eternal salvation, thanks. Apart from anything else, damnation sounds more fun.'

His voice is posher than his sister's, and more spiky.

'We're not trying to convert you,' says Lewis, putting his hand on the door so that it can't be slammed in our face.

I step forward. 'It's about your sister. Triti. Triti Pillai, right? She is ... she *was* a friend of mine.' Meggie's rules of lying kick in again. It is *almost* true, though the next part of my story isn't. 'I knew her from school.'

He looks at me suspiciously. 'You're younger than her.'

'Triti was two years above me,' I say. 'She was always kind to me.'

He frowns, sizing me up. 'You weren't at the memorial service.'

'I wanted to come but I was ... on holiday. Please, can we come in?'

'You *definitely* weren't at school with her, were you?' her brother says to Lewis.

'I'm Alice's boyfriend,' says Lewis, and I try not to snort. 'Look, we won't keep you long.'

The guy hesitates, but then opens the door a little wider. 'OK. But you can't stay long, my parents will be back soon and I'm not having Mum upset again.'

Lewis gives me the thumbs-up as we step into the house, which smells of vanilla air freshener. We follow Triti's brother through the wide hallway and into a conservatory at the back. It's chilly and the lighting is flat, the October clouds are so low I feel I could reach up and poke a hole in them. He gestures for us to sit down. The rattan furniture creaks under our weight.

'Lewis,' says Lewis, reaching out to shake his hand.

'Rafi.'

'I'm Alice,' I say.

'Yes. You said.' His eyes are as wary as Triti's, and I suppose I can't blame him. 'What are you doing here? Why rake it up again after all this time?'

'I . . .' God, this is a terrible idea. I want to leave, because of all people I should understand how totally devastating it is to lose a sister. Perhaps now, one year on, he's finally got some closure and then I show up, full of lies, to bring it all back.

But it's for *her* sake. I have to remember that. If I unlock why she's on the Beach, perhaps she can escape.

Perhaps my sister can, too . . .

Lewis nudges me.

'I came here because I think the same thing that happened to Triti might be happening to me.'

He looks up and down my body. Thank God I haven't felt like eating since I arrived on Soul Beach – no one would ever have believed that I could have anorexic tendencies before this.

'You've got a heart problem, have you?' There's a sneer in his voice.

'That wasn't all that killed her, was it, Rafi?'

His face closes down. He reminds me so much of his sister. Except he's more important to me, somehow: the first person I've met who proves the existence of Soul Beach. 'The doctor said it was natural causes,' he says. 'That's how we want to remember her.'

'But why was she in hospital in the first place, Rafi?' Lewis asks, just as I'm at the point of giving up.

No one says anything for ages, but then I see tears forming

in Rafi's eyes. I know how that feels. I wish I could tell him about Soul Beach, but, even if he believed me, there's little comfort in knowing his sister is suffering as much in the next life as she did in this one.

'She was only there at the end. Once it was almost over anyway. The rest of the time . . . well, you'll know this, too, but it's easy to hide stuff at boarding school. And in a girls' school, everyone's at it. Hiding food. Stealing food. I think she only started doing it to keep up with the others.'

'Hmm,' I say. *Boarding school.* I didn't know that, but I sense it could be important.

'She came home the summer she'd turned sixteen and she was so different. Thinner, and distant too. Mum noticed, Dad didn't. Well, he did in the end. Till then she'd been the typical kid sister, you know?' he asks, but he doesn't expect an answer: he doesn't even seem to be talking to us any more. He stares at the bleak garden. 'But that summer she wouldn't respond to anything I said or did. I could have pinched her and she wouldn't have squealed.' He remembers we're here. 'I didn't. Pinch her, that is. I didn't like her all the time, but I loved her. Brothers and sisters, you know.'

I nod. I know. 'So you think it was school that changed her?'

Rafi puts his head in his hands. 'Look, we were happy. Boring, but happy. I've seen how people look at us now. Mum and Dad don't get invited to dinner anywhere any more. That's the people who know. Imagine if it had hit the papers – *Indian businessman's daughter starves herself to death.* They'd have assumed the worst.'

'What do you mean?'

'The usual stuff. That she was going to be forced into some dodgy arranged marriage, or forced by me and Dad into doing all the housework instead of going to school, or something.'

I blush. I made one of those stupid assumptions too. 'I see.'

'So is it any wonder we wanted it kept quiet? It's not like it makes any difference to Triti, now, is it?'

That's where you could be wrong, I think. Maybe it's the denial of what happened to Triti that put her on the Beach. 'Did she not say anything about what was happening? What changed at school?'

'Did she say anything to you?'

I look away. 'Not exactly.'

His face hardens. 'Then, like I said before, I don't know what you're doing here. And I'd like you to go before my parents come back, please.'

Lewis touches my hand. 'We should leave, Alice.'

I stand up. There's more, I know it. But I follow them anyway, and then, as we pass through the hallway, I notice a collection of photographs on the wall. They're so ordinary: Triti and Rafi, in different school uniforms and in fancy dress, on holiday in France and Spain and, once, on an exotic shore a little like Soul Beach. At a firework display. It's everyday happiness. Triti is very slightly chubby, but only in a way that accentuates her prettiness. She's busty, too, but not nearly as extreme as she is on the Beach.

There are no pictures of her past the age of about fifteen.

'You look happy. In the pictures,' I say to Rafi as he opens the front door.

He thinks about it. 'We *were* happy. Maybe she thought she was only hurting herself, but she's not here any more. We're the ones who are still hurting.'

'Sorry to have brought it all back up again, Rafi,' I say, as we leave.

'Yeah, well, I dunno, it was kind of nice to talk about her again. We don't, as a rule. Just wish I knew what you came for. I hope you got it.'

I want to reach out to him: to say I know exactly how he feels. But instead I walk away down the steps, and he keeps watching us until we turn the corner. Lewis and I seem to have an unspoken agreement not to speak till we're back at the tube.

'That was intense,' he says.

'Yes. And pointless,' I correct him. 'All I did was upset the poor guy. And for what? I hardly know any more than I did before. I don't even know what school she went to.' I walk ahead. I want to get away from him, from any reminder of what I've done.

He catches hold of my arm. 'Look. I don't understand what it is you're trying to achieve, but I can tell one thing. And that's that this really matters to you. You're grieving, Alice, and that means you get a whole lot more slack from me when it comes to making mistakes.'

'Even if it means I'm hurting other grieving people?'

He hasn't let go of my arm. 'Maybe not. Though, despite your occasional grumpy moments, I don't think you're the kind of person who'd do that unless she thought she had a good reason. None of it makes sense to me, but if it makes sense to you, then roll with it.'

I take my arm away, but what he said makes me feel a tiny bit better. Even though nothing about the Beach – or life – is making sense to me any more.

50

I need beauty. Serenity. A clear horizon to give me a sense of perspective.

But when I arrive on the Beach, it's like Glastonbury in full swing. A dozen different melodies come at me from different directions: blues, rock, classical. I can't even see the sand for dancing bodies. The bikinis and surfer shorts have been replaced by slinky metallic dresses and crisp linen shirts, and the steaminess level is off the scale. The smoky, bloody smell of barbecues draws my eye towards the red hot coals glowing at intervals along the beach.

Immediately I know that They're trying to distract the Guests. Whoever *They* are.

I weave through the crowd towards the beach bar. Sam is inside, dreadlocks damp with sweat as she furiously chops lemons and limes for the jugs of mojito and sangria that are lined up on the bar. Guests keep coming in to help themselves.

'Busy day?'

She looks up and winces. 'Hi, mate. Yeah. It's never-ending. First I knew about it was when I spotted the kids dancing like there's no bloody tomorrow.'

I wonder where she goes between shifts. I'd ask her, but there are other, more urgent questions. 'This is all about Triti, isn't it?'

She transfers a huge handful of limes into a bowl full of sugar, and begins pounding, crushing the fruit so angrily that I can feel citrus perfume spitting up in my face. 'What makes you say that?' she demands.

'This is a massive distraction exercise. They tried good weather, now this. They want to tire them out, make them passive.'

I realise as I say it that Danny must have given me the idea; he said the same thing about manipulating the environment to manipulate the Guests. So if he's right about *that*, what else might he be right about?

Sam lifts a massive bottle of white rum, and upends it so that a clear stream of alcohol runs into the bowl. A muscle twitches in her skinny arm.

'As usual, your guess is as good as mine,' she says. 'But maybe you're right. The trouble is, it takes a lot to tire out the Guests. I'll be dead on my feet long before they are.' Finally she looks up. 'Sorry. That's not funny, is it?'

I shrug. 'If I did your job, I'd probably have a pretty dark sense of humour, too. Have you seen her?'

'Meggie?'

'No. Triti.'

'Rumour is she's gone to ground, to protect herself. Not that there are a fat lot of places to hide here on the Beach, but some of the ... well, the more thuggish elements were getting restless about her behaviour.'

'Thuggish?'

'Not everyone who died here was an angel in their old life, you know. All anyone has to go on is each Guest's own version of their story.' She adds mint to the mixture and soon the whole bar smells of a garden in high summer. Then she pours half the mixture into a massive cocktail shaker and shakes with ice, twenty, thirty, forty times.

'But they can't hurt her, can they?'

'Not physically,' she says, pouring the liquid into a jug full of more ice. 'But I'd hate to be lonely here, put it that way. If I was a Guest, the only thing more terrifying than living here for ever would be the idea of having to face that eternity alone.'

It hadn't occurred to me that bullying could exist here, as well as on earth. 'Right.'

The need to find some way of rescuing Triti is more urgent than ever. 'I'm going to find her,' I tell Sam.

'Good on you. She needs someone to look out for her. Everyone else is losing patience.'

Back on the beach, I'm about to turn right, towards the quieter shores where she must be hiding, when I see Danny.

He's in the centre of a circle of people. Two girls are holding a piece of rope outstretched, and Danny ... yes, sensitive, solitary Danny, is trying to limbo beneath it, as a couple of lads mark a rapid drumbeat on two bongos.

I think he might be drunk, judging from the way his eyes are rolling as he leans back from the waist, his body making an unnatural right-angle.

His shirt is undone, sweat darkening the fabric, and the twisted shape of his body emphasises muscles I hadn't seen before. Not quite a six-pack – I hate those vain boys who can name every single muscle in their over-worked bellies – but definitely rippled in the right places. A shadow of hair marks his skin from the belly button down towards his waistband.

I look at some of the other girls' faces and it's clear that I'm not the only one to notice that there's more to Danny than a sharp wit and a kind heart. Yes. That's definitely jealousy I'm feeling. He could be theirs by nightfall.

Whereas I can't even hold his hand.

His face has lost the cynicism and the longing, and he looks more like he does in the video I found. A sweet, funny teenager who happens to be the heir to a fortune, who kisses a girl for the camera just to avoid hurting her feelings. A guy whose life was just about to get even better before he was cheated out of everything in one last, long fall to earth.

As the beat gets faster and faster, his eyes are half-closed and he seems to twitch. Then I realise I can't hear the drums any more, but I can hear a whirring and as I watch, his body jolts and twist in impossible ways, like someone trying to right themselves while they're falling ... falling ... falling ...

At the last moment, the girl on the right winks at the girl on the left, and they lower the rope so it grazes his skin. He jumps, as though he's been knifed, and then topples over backwards with a strange, low moan and a slap against the sand that sends grains into the air like curls of smoke.

Around him, the other Guests laugh and applaud, but no one helps him up as another limbo contestant takes centre-stage.

He tries to push himself up, and looks around as though he doesn't quite know where he is any more.

'Danny?' I call out, walking fast towards him. 'You OK?'

The others can't hear me, of course, but his face breaks into the most enormous smile when he sees me. 'Alice. Cool!'

'I'd help you up, but, well ...' I hold out my hands in a gesture that makes me feel useless.

'No problem. I'll manage it soon. How hard can it be?' He tries, and fails again. 'Dizzy. From the limbo, I guess.'

'And nothing to do with Sam's mojitos?'

'OK, maybe a little to do with Sam's mojitos. She makes them too strong.' The third time, he does manage to stand straight, and then brushes away the sand that's stippling his golden skin. 'But I'd love another. Fancy coming with me?'

'I was looking for my sister. And for Triti.'

His face darkens for the first time. 'Sure. I know where they are. Have you found a way to help Triti, yet?'

'I'm working on it.'

'I knew you would be. What do you say in England? Not just a pretty face, huh?' And he looks at me so intently that

I have to look away, before I blush, or say something I'll regret.

'You're drunk.'

He's still staring. 'You know, I think you could be right.'

'I should find Triti.'

Danny's face falls. 'Not yet,' he says, his voice panicky. 'I mean,' he smiles again, 'let's get ourselves a drink, first, huh, Alice? You might need one if you're gonna try to talk to her.'

'But I can't . . .' I tail off. He seems to have forgotten that we're different: that he's a Guest and I am a Visitor. And as I walk alongside him, our footsteps falling into the same rhythm against the sand, I wish I could find a way to forget too.

51

We sit on the steps to the beach bar. Apart from the odd Guest racing in and out to fetch more jugs of drinks, the bar is empty.

'I reckon this is as quiet as it's gonna get tonight,' Danny says.

I look right, towards the wilder edges of the beach where Triti is.

He shakes his head. 'Forget her for now. Please. I want to talk about me, me, me!'

I'm about to argue, when I notice that despite his puppy dog expression, his eyes are as sharp as ever. Is he getting desperate, too? Will Danny be the next one to send me off to resolve his death, like some kind of paranormal Miss Marple?

Perhaps he knows I'd do anything for him, if he asked me nicely.

'OK. I'm here. You talk. I'm listening.'

'You're going to think I am crazy, but I'm gonna say it anyway. Tomorrow I can blame the booze.'

The sounds from the shore change and the party music becomes distant, drowned out by the waves and a kind of crackly noise, like static electricity.

'Don't. This sounds to me like a serious conversation and it's always a mistake having those when you're drunk.'

Danny smiles. 'I disagree. It's a bigger mistake not to say the things that should be said, when the timing's right. That much I'm learning from being dead a long time, Alice.'

There's not much I can say to that.

'Before you came ...' he stops. 'No, let me start at the beginning. When I first washed up here, I was so angry you wouldn't believe it. With life, with myself, with everyone. But I figured out pretty soon that anger was pointless. It wasn't going to get me anywhere.'

'I wish you could make Triti believe that too.'

'I've tried. But not everything I'm saying is about Triti.' He reaches out, but then he slaps himself on the forehead. 'If this was normal life, I would be taking your hand now, Alice. The fact I can't makes this harder to say somehow.'

'Because you're a bit pissed?'

'No, I'm not angry with you ... oh, I see. Pissed in the British sense: drunk. Yeah. But that should make it easier.' He closes his eyes, then opens them again, extra-wide. 'Back on track, back on track. So I decided to choose a new Danny to show the world. Back in real life, I made everyone see what I wanted them to see: I was easy-going, the guy with the joke and the smile for anyone.'

I know, I think, I've seen you on that video, only a few precious seconds' worth, but it was enough to understand you.

To fall for you.

'On the Beach, I decided to be different. I had to conserve my energy. Keep myself to myself. I've gone from being the life and soul of the party, to the wallflower. The observer. Well, for the foreseeable future, anyhow. I mean, right here we all have time to be a thousand different versions of ourselves and we still won't have scratched the surface of the time ahead.'

I look out at the horizon, where the sun is beginning to set. That's what it means to be here. Eternity. I shiver.

'I made a few buddies. I deliberately chose people who were different to the meatheads and the cheerleaders I'd partied with on earth: Javier, Triti, your sister. They're good people. Loyal. They understand that this is not just an endless party.'

I nod, even though I always think of my sister as a party girl. But that was the *old* Meggie. Perhaps she has had to change, too.

He continues. 'Sure, that makes them awkward to be around sometimes, but it's good not to pretend all the time. To be able to be vulnerable, now and then.

'And then you showed up,' he continues.

God, I need a drink.

'You were different.'

'Alive?' I say, then wish I hadn't because it sounds flip and sarcastic.

But he just smiles. 'Sure. But you were also different to everyone around me because you still had hope.'

'I don't feel like I do.'

'Believe me, when you're used to the Beach, then even the tiniest remainder of hope shines like a lighthouse to a shipwrecked sailor.'

'You really are drunk, aren't you?'

'Do me a favour, Alice, let me say what I want to say, huh?'

He waits till I've nodded and mimed zipping up my mouth. 'OK, so where was I? Hope. You take it for granted when you're alive but, Jeez, you miss it when you're dead. You arrived and, of course, you were beautiful, but then that's so standard here that it's boring. You were more than that. It was like someone holding up a mirror to my own face and all I could see there was hopelessness and longing.'

I nod. 'From the first time we met, I did feel you needed something you couldn't have.'

'Something? Or some*one*?'

I blush. This is getting weird.

'Jesus Christ, why can't I come out with it? I have several hundred nymphomaniac dead girls here on the Beach with nothing to do for the next few millennia except tell me how great I am, massage my ego and perfect their oral sex technique, and I'm falling in love with the one girl I cannot touch ... 'Love?' He drains the last of the cocktail. 'Let's not say love. Let's say like. Can you fall in like?' He laughs.

But he didn't say *like*. He said love.

And that's when I know.

When he looks at me again, the longing in his eyes is more powerful than ever. 'What kind of idiot dead guy falls for someone they can never have? I must be the biggest numbskull ever.'

'Two numbskulls,' I whisper.

'Huh?'

'If you're a numbskull, then so am I.'

I look into his eyes again and I wonder if the mirror he talks about is reflecting the longing I'm feeling. 'I think maybe I'm falling for you too, Danny. Love. *Like*. Whichever it is. But ... it *might* be love.'

My screen freezes. What have I done? Something against the law of the Beach? A breach of the rule book I've never been allowed to read?

I hear my own breathing, rapid and shallow, and my bedroom spins around me.

And then the picture returns, pixel by pixel. Danny is in front of me, a shocked expression on his face.

'Did something happen?' I ask.

'I thought it was just me,' he says.

'What happened just now, or ... the other thing?' I say, and then I add. 'The, well, the falling-for-me thing.'

'Both.' He's frowning, half amused, half confused.

'I've never said that to anyone before, Danny.'

'Me, either.'

The image of the girl he kissed in that news report, is in my head. 'I don't believe that,' I laugh. 'An eligible bachelor like you.'

'It's true,' he says simply. 'Never said it before. Never *felt* it before.'

'Why me?'

Danny shakes his head. 'Why anyone? Mom believed in horoscopes, despite being a Catholic. Dad believed in rationalism and working out what you wanted and then maximising the possibilities to find it. Jeez, I've wanted a few things on the Beach. A video game or two. An exit door. But a Visitor to fall in love with ... that was never going to make this better for me, was it?'

'No.' I'm suddenly aware of the distance between us. When I imagined my first love telling me how he felt, I'd pictured kisses and orchestral choruses and a tingling wonderfulness that would change everything about the world.

Yet we sit here, so close that if we were in the same plane it would take only the slightest movement from one of us for a kiss to be inevitable.

What I'd do to be on the same plane ...

'I'm sorry, Alice.'

'Don't be sorry. Be anything but sorry. I'm not sorry.'

Silence, still, except for the waves. The sun must have set completely while we were talking, and now the sky is a deep purple and the moon is so huge it looks like a hot air balloon drifting just above us.

'It's so beautiful here, isn't it? I wish I was here for real, sometimes.'

'No!' He pulls away.

'Why not? If I told you about my life in the so-called real world, you might understand that it wouldn't be the worst tragedy in the world.'

Danny stands up, his hands gripping his skull as he shakes

his head. 'NO! That's not what I want. No way. If I'd have thought for a second that you'd want to give up life for ... for a nothing like me, I'd never have said anything. *Shit.* Is there a backspace key anywhere?'

He's shouting now, and shaking his fist at the virtual heavens.

'Calm down, Danny, I didn't mean—'

He turns to me, his tanned face black-and-white in the moonlight. 'Never, ever think like that. I promise you that if you do anything, anything at all to join me here properly, I will not speak to you, I will not touch you, I will not even recognise your existence, OK? It's how it has to be. I cannot run the risk. I do not deserve you.'

My brain can't keep up. One moment we're soul-mates and the next he's turning on me.

But then I realise that what he's said is greater proof that this guy really cares for me – because he would give up everything for me, even his one chance of happiness.

'I understand,' I say.

'Do you?'

I nod. We stand, facing each other. I tingle from head to toe, and everything about this moment will stay with me for ever. The scent of mint and lime and barbecues. The sound of the sea and, only just audible beneath it, a blues melody played on a sax.

Amazing Grace ...

I will remember those eyes, no longer haunted but blazing. And those lips, that promise so much but will only ever be able to offer me words.

A long, long way off, my phone twitches with a new text.

'What was that?' he says, sensing that I'm distracted.

'Nothing important. Nothing as important as this.' But then I hear something else: a soft whimper, like an injured animal.

He looks to his left, towards the unfocused, undeveloped part of the beach. '*Triti*,' he says, and there's a question in his eyes.

'Should we go to her?' I ask.

I can tell we're both thinking that perhaps we should, but this feels like *our* moment.

'You're more help to her in your world than you are in hers,' Danny tells me.

I nod. 'I'm working on it.'

He smiles, as if he understands how tough it is for me. 'I should let you go and do that.'

'No,' I say, but he's already moving backwards.

How do you say goodbye to the boy you're falling for, but can never touch? Blowing a kiss, as I do with Meggie, seems too trivial.

Danny answers my question. He mouths *Goodnight, sweet dreams*, and then raises his hand towards his heart. Like a promise.

I do the same . . .

I stare at the screen for more than a minute after the beach fades into the mist. Then I remember the text, and open up my phone:

Don't give up on Tim, Alice, he wants to tell you the truth, I'm sure of it. I won't stop working on him till he does, trust me. Your friend, Ade.

I stare at it. Something seems off about the tone, too intimate or too intrusive. But I can't afford to alienate him, not if I'm to reach Tim and get the answers I need.

So I text back **Thanks**, and then turn the phone off so I can focus on what's just happened to me. *Love, or something like it?* Ever since my sister was murdered, happiness has seemed like something that only other people could hope to feel. I've felt like a spectator, watching a wild dance from the sidelines, unable to join in.

But in the last few minutes, it's as if someone has invited me back onto the floor.

Danny is falling for me, and I am falling for him and nothing else seems important.

52

'You're different,' Cara catches me outside the loos at break.

'Am I? How?'

Different? Different doesn't begin to describe it. Everything has changed for me.

'Well, for a start, I actually saw you smile in class, which hasn't happened for years. And you keep humming.'

'Do I?' Everything in this world looks beautiful to me now, even though Danny can never join me here. Despite the distance between us, I hear love songs in my brain because *somewhere*, there's one person who needs me more than anything, and I need him too. 'Sorry. I know how irritating it is when Mum does it.'

'Obviously, being your best friend and confidante, I'm sure you'd have told me if you'd found a bloke or something?'

I feel myself blushing. 'Me? I spend my whole life locked in my room listening to mopey music, according to you.' I smile, to show I don't mean it.

'Aha. Yes.' She grins ruefully. 'But maybe you've found yourself an equally mopey boyfriend online, then?'

'Could be.'

'Get you, Little Miss Mystery.' She looks at me closely. 'Are you coming back to us, Alice? I don't think I could stand getting my hopes up and then see you turning all bonkers again.'

I wish I could tell her what she wants to hear: that we'll be the way we were. But how can I, with everything I've seen and everything I know?

'I'm a bit better, but don't expect too much of me, Cara. It's changed me. I'd be an even weirder person if it hadn't . . .' I look away.

'Yeah.'

She goes to hug me, and I hug her back, longing to be close to her again, but knowing that the very last thing my best friend needs is to know anything about my crazy, desperate new world.

When we let go of each other, I feel sad; this is how we always were. 'Enough about me, Cara. What's the latest on Felipe?'

And she begins to rattle off tales of high drama and crazy passion and hair extensions, and all I can think is that this shouldn't be one-sided. We should be sharing our excitements and stories, like best friends do. But how can I?

She pauses for breath, and I hold up my hand. 'Sorry, I want to hear the rest, but I really do need the loo before the next lesson.'

'I'll come with you,' she says, and picks up again with details of every text, and every rumour about her Argentinian boyfriend, shouting so I can hear her over flushing toilets and running water.

When I come out, I check myself in the speckled mirror in the loos, and it's the first time I've seen myself properly in weeks.

Danny fell for *that*? The under plucked eyebrows and the ugly-bug curls and the skin that looks like it's been bleached white by so many hours in front of a screen.

He's not seeing me, though. He's seeing airbrushed-Alice, a version that could never be achieved without plastic surgery. The black rings are still under my eyes, and there's the odd spot that threatens to turn into a face-full.

For a moment, my love-fuelled high wobbles. Would handsome, loaded Danny Cross have fallen for me if we'd somehow met in real life, the way that cousin Stacie thinks soul mates are bound to?

My eyes. They're different to how they used to look. Now they're bright. Knowing. Full of longing.

Just like his . . .

I leave the toilets. The bell cuts short Cara's story just as she is confiding that he might be 'the one', and I smile because for the first time *ever*, I know how she feels. And that moment of understanding, even if I can't actually tell her, raises me right up, just for a second or two, and makes me feel close to my friend again.

Right now there's only one person I want to tell. Only one other person who can possibly know how life – and death – have a funny habit of throwing you off balance.

Meggie will understand.

'This is the nearest thing to a hangover I've had in months,' my sister says, clutching her forehead with full Meggie Melodrama, and pulling huge sunglasses down over her eyes.

'I thought you didn't get hangovers here.'

'So did I. Hope I'm the only one to be feeling this bad, or it'll really get the conspiracy theorists going. They'll say it was sent to tame us or something.'

We're in a bamboo hut, lying side by side on a red-and-white checked quilt. The hut is built without the wall that overlooks the sea, so from here all we can see is the ocean and the sky. It could be a poster in a beauty spa, except it feels three-dimensional and completely breath-taking.

Sometimes I wonder how something that's just online can mesmerise me so totally.

'Meggie?'

'That's me.'

'I think . . . I might have met someone.'

She sits bolt upright, and then winces. 'Ouch. You *think*?

Who? It can't be Robbie, not after all this time. I mean, nice boy and very cute-looking but maybe a bit dull ... So, do I know him?'

'You could say that, yes.'

'Oh, don't tell me, don't tell me, let me guess ...' she says.

'Are you trying to turn one of the most amazing things that has ever happened to me into a guessing game, Meggie?'

She gives me a wary look. 'Um ...'

And then I laugh, because actually, right now, all I want to do is giggle and gossip and count my blessings while someone teases me and makes me blush. I want to be *normal*. 'Only kidding. Anyway, you won't be able to work it out.'

She screws up her face in concentration. I know she won't guess, because, apart from Robbie and Cara, she never could remember the names of any of my friends. She just wasn't that interested.

'Who was that kid that Cara went out with when you were in Year Ten? The one who played football for Middlesex? I always thought you two would go well together.' She's stretching out again, enjoying herself.

'Not him. Like I said, you're never going to guess ...'

Suddenly I am *desperate* to tell her.

'Or that lad with the Afro, who looked like a very young Michael Jackson. He was *really* cute. Ah, my little sister in love. I never thought I'd see the day—'

'It's Danny.'

'No, I can't remember a Danny ...' But then she pushes herself up, and goes to grab my arm, which, of course, she can't. 'Danny, as in, Danny *here*?'

I nod. Once she's taken it in, I'm going to tell her why he's wonderful, why I'll never meet anyone like him again. How we're two halves of the same person. How being around him makes me feel special. She's going to tell me how she felt with

Tim. We're going to be like we were before: my big sister laughing, joking with me, telling me what's what.

I never thought I'd want to be talked down to, but right now I want to hear her poking gentle fun at me, before agreeing that he is absolutely gorgeous. I wait.

She shakes her head, although judging from the pained expression in her eyes as she does so, it's not good for her hangover. 'Hmm. Not a great idea, really, little sis.'

'We didn't mean it to happen,' I say, feeling slightly awkward now. 'I mean, you can't control it, can you? It just ... happens.'

She smiles indulgently. 'Oh, honestly, Florrie, you do make me laugh.'

'Laugh?' I wanted her to giggle, didn't I? But her voice is all wrong.

'Danny. I mean, I can see how he'd be an excellent catch in other circumstances, but, really, there's no getting around the unfortunate fact that he's, well, a tiny bit *dead*.'

'You think I'd forgotten that?'

'Don't be chippy, Florrie. It's just that ...' She takes off her sunglasses and looks at me with bloodshot eyes. 'Oh, God, you're serious, aren't you?'

'*Deadly* serious,' I say.

'How old are you?'

'Sixteen. Old enough to have sex. Old enough to leave school, and to ride a motorbike.' I know I sound childish, but I don't like her tone.

'But clearly not old enough to make any kind of sensible decision. Had you forgotten that he's not alive any more?'

'Of course not. Look, Meggie, I don't have to listen to this, you know. Should I leave until you can be happy for me?'

Her face freezes, and instantly I feel guilty for the threat. I never used to have any power over my sister, and yet now I see utter terror in her eyes.

'No. No. Sorry.' She sighs. 'Let me start again. It's not that I think you're being silly ...'

'Which means that *is* what you think.'

'Have you really thought this through, Alice?'

She must be serious, now; she's using my real name. 'I haven't thought of anything else.'

'So you're happy about the fact that you'll never be able to touch him, or be with him in any meaningful way?'

'Not happy. But there are more important things than that.'

'You think that *now*, but ... love isn't all fluffy kittens and pink hearts. Sometimes it's bloody dark, and painful and violent. And sometimes it's fatal.'

I turn to her. 'Have you remembered something? Or are you just trying to scare me?'

'No. No, of course not. But passion and hatred can be too close for comfort sometimes.'

'Was that how it was with Tim?'

Meggie looks away. 'I don't remember, Alice. I guess I'm just trying to say that the choices we make aren't always as straightforward as they seem. The idea of this pure passion with Danny is romantic, yeah, but so was Romeo and Juliet and that didn't end well.'

'I'm not stupid.' But her words are having an effect, making me feel less ecstatic, even slightly ridiculous.

'I never said you were.' Her voice is soothing now. 'But when I think how precious life is, how you have so much to look forward to, I can't bear the thought of it. You can have any man you want. There's a whole world of them out there, Florrie, don't waste your future on one of us.'

'I can't see a future in the real world. I haven't been able to believe that there's anything to look forward to. Not since you left me.'

My sister looks at me. 'We're *ghosts*, Florrie.'

'You said never to call you that.'

'Because it's too close to the truth.' She waves at the beach. Guests lie motionless, limbs blending into the sand. She frowns. 'And what does Danny say about it all?'

'He feels the same way.' I think back to the night he told me and despite the doubts Meggie has put in my mind, I tingle all over. 'We're going to take it slow. I mean, OK, we don't really have a choice *but* to take it slow, when I think about it, given that we can't even touch. But don't think that we don't understand what it means for both of us.'

Meggie sighs. 'Oh, honey. I'm sure you *think* you understand, but how could you? Try to remember, he's lonely and desperate. He'll say anything.'

'Actually, you're totally wrong. When I said how I felt, he warned me off. Said if I ever ended up here, he'd refuse to talk to me, even pretend I didn't exist.'

My sister closes her eyes. 'No. That's too awful to think about. You wouldn't, would you?'

'Of course not.' I wish I was as certain as I sound.

'My ears were burning,' a voice announces.

Danny.

He's not looking at my sister at all – he's looking at me. He's even more perfect than I remember. It was always those eyes that drew me in before – the deep green mystery of them – but now it's his soft lips that hypnotise me.

Hello beautiful he mouths.

Hello back.

'Oh, don't let me get in the way of young love,' my sister says.

Danny sighs, closing his eyes for a moment. One night, perhaps even tonight, I want to lie next to him while he sleeps, watch his eyelids flicker and try to guess his dreams.

When he opens his eyes again, he turns to Meggie. 'I know what you're thinking, but I won't let her join us. I couldn't bear to be responsible for that.'

Meggie shakes her head. 'It's dangerous. Can't you two see that? Especially you, Danny. You're older. Couldn't you just have chosen one of the other Guests? There are hundreds of cute girls here . . .'

He looks back at me. 'They're not Alice.'

My sister kicks at the sand. 'Bloody hell. I'm not ready for this. It's like being a parent.' She looks back up. 'Listen. I can't stop you, but I just hope for both your sakes that this is a crush.'

Danny and I gaze at each other, knowing that it's anything but.

'I guess you two want to be alone, but, before I go, just promise me you'll be careful?' she says, with the kind of resigned voice that makes me think she realises she's wasting her breath.

'Sure, Meggie,' says Danny.

'I promise, sis,' I say.

But in the 'real' world, my fingers are crossed.

53

Danny and I walk together, so close that if we were both alive, or both dead, we'd be skin-to-skin.

Without even discussing it, we head to the other side of the beach, as far away as possible from the huts and the bar and from the bare patch of scrubland where Triti is in self-imposed exile.

There are so few places here where we can feel truly alone. The high rocks that I thought protected the Beach from intruders, are as impregnable as prison walls.

In front of us, there's a black rock that's as tall as a giant. Behind it there's a smooth ledge with room for two.

'Like it was made for us,' I say. Danny doesn't smile but I don't mind. I could watch that face for ever, debating whether he is more beautiful when he smiles or when he frowns.

He sits down, but says nothing.

'Maybe I shouldn't have told her,' I say, 'but just because she disapproves doesn't mean she's right.'

'Except she is, isn't she?'

I'm about to argue back, but then it hits me: what if *he's* had second thoughts, not because of what Meggie said, but because now he's seen me again he doesn't find me attractive any more? 'We don't have to do this, Danny. Not if you don't want to,' I tell him.

He's not looking at me, which has to be a bad sign. *Shit*. Somehow this feels like a bigger rejection than when Robbie dumped me. 'Why? Don't *you* want to?'

'Oh, yeah!' I say sarcastically. 'That's why I risked everything by telling my sister about you. Not because I was excited, but because I'd changed my mind.'

Finally Danny turns, and when I see he's smiling I feel as though I am melting inside. 'Well, then, that's *swell*, missy. Though I guess under the circumstances, it might be a while before I can meet your folks, huh?'

I giggle. 'A while.'

How did I not recognise him the first time I saw him? It's like I've known him *always*. Those eyes, those high cheek-bones. Those lips . . .

'I wish I could kiss you, Alice. Just once.'

'Once wouldn't be enough,' I say, and then blush at my own boldness. 'I'd want it to go on for ever and ever. I don't think I'd want to do anything else.'

Danny chuckles. I notice the way the lines that appear at the edge of his eyes curve upwards, like clusters of tiny smiles. 'But I might be a terrible kisser. Slobbery.'

I giggle. 'You won't be a bad kisser, Danny. I can tell.'

'Bull. I could be all tongue. Or sucky, like an octopus.' He sucks on the back of his hand and makes a squelchy noise.

I'm laughing properly now. 'That's how we used to practise, me and Cara. In my bedroom, with the music playing so my parents wouldn't hear us having hysterics.'

'Is that where you are now, Alice? In your bedroom?'

'No, I . . . ' I drag myself away from his face, to look around me. It's a huge shock when I realise that, yes, of course I'm in my bedroom, with its flowery pop art duvet and its pink chair and the silver-sprayed radiator. 'Yes.'

Danny sighs. 'Your sister *is* right, though.'

'Don't say that. I can tell you're an eldest child, or you'd know that *your sister's right* are the most irritating words in the English language.'

'Be serious.'

'God, you really are an older brother. Lighten up, Danny Boy.'

'Which bit shall I lighten up about, Alice? The bit where I'm never even going to be able to hold your hand, or the bit where this can only end badly. Or how about the bit where love means you get to be as miserable as me?'

I feel tears prick the back of my eyes. 'Don't! Don't turn it into something awful ...'

He's about to say something even more sensible when he notices my face. 'Oh, Alice, I'm sorry.'

'S'OK.'

'I wish I could *do* something, but obviously ...' he holds out his arms in a gesture that makes me want to cry even more.

'I know.'

Then he smiles again, and it's like the sun's come out. 'Does that count as our first argument?'

I nod, laughing despite the tears that had already started.

'That's better.'

'I'll write it in my diary. Fell out with Danny. Made up with Danny.'

We gaze out to sea. We could almost be the last two people on earth.

'This could be our place, Alice. I'll come here every day and wait till you show.'

'Maybe I can just stay here till one of us falls asleep ...'

Somewhere, a phone is ringing. *My* phone.

I grope in my schoolbag for the handset. 'Hold on, Danny, I'll just get rid of this call—'

ADRIAN flashes on the screen.

Adrian ... *or Tim?*

I can't leave the Beach now.

Yet what's more important? This fantasy guy who can only ever stay just that – a fantasy? Or the sister who needs me more than ever? I need to remember what my priorities are.

'I'm sorry,' I tell Danny. 'I wouldn't go if this wasn't life or death, but . . . well, it might be. *Sweet Dreams*.' I raise my hand towards my heart, the way he did last time.

He opens his mouth but he only gets as far as *Sweet* before his face twists and his body seems to be falling and the screen cuts out.

I'm shivering as I answer the phone.

54

'Tim? Is that you?'

A sharp breath. Then: 'No. It's Adrian. It is my phone, after all.' I hear just a trace of irritation in his voice.

'Sorry.'

'But Tim is right here next to me.'

'Oh.' The shiver turns into a violent shake. Come *on*, now, Alice. You talk to the dead every day; a live person on the end of a phone line is no big deal, surely. Even a live possible murderer . . .

'Alice? Are you sure you're OK with this?'

Adrian's voice calms me a little, but the dread, the absolute panic, is still there. It's almost as though my body senses a threat, even down the phone. 'Yeah. I'd like to speak to Tim now, please.'

The microphone rustles and then I hear someone else's breathing. 'Tim?'

'Alice.' It comes out more like a sigh than a name. 'Oh, Alice, Jesus, I am so sorry. What a mess.'

Is that a confession? Does he expect me to say, *That's OK, Tim. These things happen.* 'It's a mess all right.'

'I can't talk for long. I'm being followed.' His voice is high-pitched, on the edge of hysteria. He used to speak in a rumbling whisper, like a brainy brown bear.

'Where are you now?'

'In the library. We . . . we got ourselves locked in, on purpose. They post a plain clothes guy outside when I work here. When the place closed and they realised I hadn't come out, they'll have thought I've given them the slip for a change. But they've still got triangulation. They can work out I'm here if they think I might be using Ade's phone.'

My own heart sounds deafeningly loud: it's like I'm caught up in one of the Bourne movies. 'Won't you set off the alarms?'

'We're in a storeroom. We've got torches and some food and water and something stronger to drink later, too. The library opens again tomorrow at nine and then we'll head straight for the reading rooms and no one will know.'

I picture him now. *Good* Tim. *Kind* Tim. Those bright, sincere eyes with the rings around them from staying up too late reading or talking, and the sweet, cautious smile whenever he cracked a joke.

'All this so you could talk to me?'

'Of course. Look, Alice, I know this is even harder for you than it is for me. It means a lot to me that you're even speaking to me now.'

I interrupt him. 'It doesn't mean anything one way or the other,' I say, though of course it *does*. 'I need to know what really happened that night.'

'Oh.' There's a pause. 'I didn't kill her. I don't really care what happens to me, so long as *you* believe me, Alice.' For the first time he sounds like the old Tim, not this hyped up SAS wannabe.

'You promise?'

'I couldn't kill anything, Alice. What the hell would give me the right to take life from someone?'

The answer is so precise, so *Tim*, that I want to believe it's true. Yet what about the police, and my mum, not to mention the tabloids? Oh, and Mr Bryant's statistics which show that most women are murdered by their partners?

And then there's what Meggie said herself, about passion and hatred being so close. I try to stop thinking like someone who knows him, and start thinking like the rest of the world.

I might not get another chance to interrogate him.

'Then why are the police so convinced you did it?'

'They want a quick fix. Or maybe I've been set up.'

'Oh, Tim, who would go to the trouble of setting you up?'

'The real killer. Alice, I'm the obvious person to frame, because the police always look first at the person who is closest to the victim.'

'And the last person to see her alive!' I point out.

'Second last. I swear.'

'But people in the bar saw you arguing that night.'

'There's a bloody big difference between arguing with your girlfriend and killing her!'

The ferocity in Tim's voice takes me by surprise. I've never heard that tone from him before. 'You sound angry.'

'Of course I'm angry. How would you feel if you'd lost the person who means the most to you in the world, and then everyone thought you'd killed that person? Eh? If every time you walked down the street or into a lecture theatre, people whispered and glared but never came out and said it. If the police were there every time you looked round, waiting for you to make a mistake.'

He's shouting, now, and I have to hold the phone away from my ear. I blink, and I have to remind myself that he's locked away in Greenwich, and I'm safely in my bedroom. Mild-mannered, spider-rescuing Tim has a scary side. But does that mean . . .

After a silence, he says, 'Alice, listen. I apologise. You're the last person I should be shouting at. Not like it's helping my case, either, is it?' And he tries to laugh, but it's fake.

'No.' If he can get so angry with me, then why not with my sister? Sahara said he had a temper, and Meggie can . . . could be flirty and flighty and wickedly cruel: might that have tipped him over the edge? Jealousy is potent. Until I saw Danny on that video with the girl, I didn't realise how potent. 'Do you get angry a lot?' I ask, still determined to get to the truth.

'Not before she died. I understand why you ask, but I've never been a moody person. You must remember that.'

'It's hard to remember how anything was before.'

I hear a sigh. 'I know, Alice. God, I know. I took happiness for granted. How stupid can someone be?'

It's so hard to stop myself agreeing. *Ask more questions*, I tell myself. I should have written them down. 'Why should I believe anything you say?'

'Because your sister was everything to me, Alice. She ... well, she lit up my world. Not just mine. She was like the brightest flame, and now the world feels so dark without her. Does that make sense?'

'Mmm.'

'You do believe that I loved her, don't you?'

Danny's face pops into my mind. Love. *Am I really in love with him or is it just a crush, like my sister hopes?* I know I'd protect Danny from anything and everything, if I could. That I'd never hurt him.

I avoid answering. 'If it wasn't you, who was it?' I ask Tim.

'Someone who didn't really know her, because no one who knew her could do that. But someone who thought they owned her. You know the killer spent time with her afterwards? Brushing her hair?'

I stop breathing. I *do* know that. But most people don't. Sure, Zoe told the press about a halo of hair around her, but only the police and her family knew that the halo wasn't accidental.

Correction. The police, us. *And the killer*. Or did they tell Tim too, when they were trying to break him?

'What now, Tim?'

For a long while, all I can hear is his breathing. Then, 'I don't know. Everything seems hopeless without her, and even if the police do find who really did it, then the pointing

229

and the stares won't stop. It'll never be over for me.'

I know he's right. None of us will ever be the same. Though of course it's my sister who has lost the most.

This phone call was a dreadful mistake. I don't feel better, I feel worse: more confused than ever. Tim's so believable, yet he hasn't told me anything that would put him in the clear, and my own instincts are lost in the confusion.

'We could meet, you know, Alice, if you wanted.'

Before this call, I'd have wanted that to happen, but now the thought terrifies me. 'Why would we?'

'There are things ... well, things that can't be said on the phone. But for now I should ring off. In case they're tracing *your* calls, Alice. It's not impossible.'

'I hadn't thought of that.'

'I promise I'll call again soon. Work on a way we could meet, away from prying eyes. But whether that happens or not, please forgive me for not keeping her safe.'

That's what my father always says. But how am I meant to respond? Tim isn't the man I thought he was, but does that mean he killed her?

'Just call again. Please.'

But I'm talking to dead air.

The mark of murderers is that they always 'keep themselves to themselves.'

Or at least, that is what one would believe from watching inane TV news bulletins. A neighbour of a newly convicted killer will be interviewed, or a colleague, and the same mantras are recited.

'We hardly saw them,' one will say. 'Though they kept their garden tidy.'

Another will add, 'They'd smile, but they were never part of the community, were they, Ethel?'

'No, no. Kept themselves to themselves.'

As though the desire for privacy marks out a killer.

I am not sure whether I was a loner before Meggie, but now I am, of necessity. There are times when the desire to confide, to confess all, to bare the soul, is almost as overwhelming as the instinct that prompted the act that is now hidden. But I must keep my true self to myself. All the while pretending to be normal.

To murder takes a moment's lapse.

To stay free takes a lifetime of concentration.

55

'Biscuits or Doritos? Or both? Have both if you like!'

Mum is embarrassing. All I want to do is hear Lewis's news, and I couldn't care less about snacks. But she insists on pouring corn chips into a bowl, and then filling a dish with supermarket hummus, and putting them both on a tray along with glasses of OJ and a plateful of cookies.

'I'm coming here again,' says Lewis, when we finally get upstairs.

'She thinks you're going to rescue me from my life of misery,' I explain.

'I only rescue people for ninety-five an hour plus VAT,' he says, 'but I make an exception for hacking, which I see as a hobby!'

'Tell me!'

'Ah, come on, let me do my fanfare first. Build myself up. Hero battling the system and all of that.' He sees the expression on my face. 'OK. Given the circumstances, whatever the hell they are, and even though you're not telling me the whole story, I'll tell you straight. I hacked her webmail, found her passwords and then logged into her Facebook account. And then, well . . . see for yourself.'

He takes a tiny, almost girly laptop out of his pretentious messenger bag.

'I've cached all the pages so we've got a permanent record. Actually, some of them had been messed with already, deleted or edited, but Triti had kept them all stored in her email account, so I've rebuilt the list offline so you can see it all in date order.'

OK, I'll admit I am impressed, but I'm not about to flatter his ego by gushing like a fangirl. 'Thanks,' I say, before leaning forward to read what's on the screen. Triti, according to her homepage, had 211 friends, kinda average for a kid our age, I guess. Though the Triti I know on the Beach is so withdrawn that I'm surprised she was on Facebook at all.

Her profile picture shows a girl who would be photogenic if it weren't for the fact that she looks half-starved. In the photo, she wears over the top jewellery that only emphasises the sharpness of her collarbones. Large dark eyes scrutinise the world from under hooded lids. Her nose and lips seem too large for her pinched face, as though I'm staring at her through the peephole in a door. Her skin is paler than it should be.

I click onto her photo album and it's heart-breaking to see the other pictures, which are more like the ones on the wall of her home. She was stunning when she wasn't so thin. Dewy skin, those eyes still Bambi-like in her face, but not out of proportion. In all the pictures except the profile one, she's smiling. I thought Soul Beach made kids cuter then they were before death, but Triti was far prettier and more natural in real life. Her figure is enviable, too, curvy in all the right ways without being remotely fat.

Yet the skeleton picture is the one she chose to face the world with. Because, I guess, in her distorted state of mind, that was the one she thought made her look the best.

'Start with the wall, from the bottom up,' says Lewis. 'I've highlighted the relevant bits.'

I click back to the profile and scroll down. And down, and down. He's made all her entries for the year before her death show up on the same page. I see the usual messages about parties and personality quiz results and movie star crushes.

Then the first comment Lewis has highlighted shines out in acid yellow.

TRITI IS SO FAT SHE NEEDS HER OWN POSTCODE!

It's been written by a girl called Salli Patterson, and underneath it there are comments from half a dozen other girls, all agreeing it's the funniest joke ever.

Salli strikes again three days later.

TRITI'S SO FAT SHE'S GOT MORE ROLLS THAN GREGG'S BAKERY!

Again, the stupid comment gets plenty of thumbs ups, and so it goes on: the yellow highlighter begins to take over the page. Triti is compared to a whale, a mountain, a bus. None of it is funny, or clever, and sitting here reading the so-called jokes it's easy to dismiss them as pathetic.

But to see them one after another, whenever you log in?

'I can see they're upsetting, but are you saying this is really why she might have died?' I ask Lewis.

'Now look at the private messages,' he tells me, and leans over to load a different page.

Oh, Salli has been a busy girl. The entire inbox is full of messages with single word headings: Pig and Bitch and Thicko.

'There's one every day. Sometimes more than one,' Lewis says. 'They're all like this.' He opens one.

Dear Triti,

Why don't you just give up?

I saw you in class today with your hair in that stupid plait. That's how they do pigs' tails, when they're taking them to market for slaughter. It doesn't cover up the fact you're minging. The only thing that would do that would be a big sack and even then you'd stink.

We don't want you in school. You're so thick you haven't got the message yet. But this won't stop until you do, OK?

Catch you later, dumbo.
Salli!

'What a cow,' I say. Salli's profile picture shows a pink fluffy teddy bear, so it's impossible to know whether she's fat or thin.

I click at random on some of the other messages. Some are less obviously cruel, suggesting that she can stop feeling hungry by eating cotton wool, or posting a photograph of an anorexic girl taken from the web. That one has 'Isn't she beautiful?' as its subject line.

Then there are a couple that almost read as though they could come from a genuine friend. Oh, how poor Triti must have longed for a real friend. But not one like Salli, who writes,

Almost there, now, Triti. You're going to look so gorgeous in your bikini on the beach this summer, aren't you? And then those bitches will know, the ones who called you fat. Then you'll be able to look them in the eye and feel proud of what you've done.

That last message was sent in the summer holidays, less than a month before she died.

'This Salli is evil.'

Lewis nods.

'And she must have been doing this pretty much full-time. I mean, we've all had the odd bitchy comment online but this? To drive someone . . . well, to their death.'

'It's one of the most extreme campaigns I've seen,' he says.

'So now we go get her, right?' And I think, perhaps then Triti will find peace. Perhaps she might even find the way off the Beach. Which in turn, will give me more clues about how I might, eventually, help my sister . . .

I gulp, remembering that if Meggie leaves the Beach, I will never see her again. Knowing it's what she wants should be enough, yet am I unselfish enough to deal with that?

'I don't think it's going to be that simple, unfortunately.'

'Come on, Lewis. If you can get into her Facebook account, then you can find out the address of the school. They'd still be there, wouldn't they? In sixth form. We'll confront Salli and her bloody cronies. Make them realise what they've done.'

'Sure, I know the school,' Lewis says, sounding irritated. 'It's on the south coast, and I'm happy to go down with you. But there's a bigger obstacle.'

'What?' I say, irritated and impatient myself now.

'Salli Patterson doesn't actually exist.'

After Lewis leaves, I fit in a super-fast visit to the Beach. Tonight Mum is press-ganging me into a trip to the cinema to see some mother-daughter rom com that looks sweeter than a swimming pool full of golden syrup.

I don't want fantasy worlds or face-lifted actresses who look less wrinkly than their on-screen daughters. I want to get back to the Beach, to my sister and Danny, to remind myself that some things *do* make sense, even if Triti's story gets weirder and weirder.

But while I want to see my sister, she's not exactly going out of her way to welcome me. Meggie seems to have appointed herself as my bodyguard. Whenever I log on, she's there, even though I vary my visit times, and log on twice as often, in the hope of catching Danny just once.

'This is silly, Meggie.'

She smiles at me. 'Every girl needs a chaperone.'

'Oh, yeah, because Danny and I get so many chances to misbehave when we can't actually even hold hands.' I begin walking towards the rock. *Our* rock.

She follows. 'You wouldn't even be here if it weren't for me. I feel responsible for what happens. What you do.'

'Are you sure you're not jealous?'

She stops walking and so do I. 'Don't be daft.'

'I'm not. When I told you about Danny and me, you looked like you were sucking a lemon. Are you sure this isn't about the fact you don't want me to have what you can't?'

She sinks down onto the sand, her face stricken, 'Oh, Florrie, that's an awful thing to think, I just want to protect you!'

'You can't protect me from making my own mistakes, Meggie,' I point out gently. 'Not unless I stay in my room for ever. And even then ... staying in my room is how I met Danny.'

Saying his name is like giving myself an exquisite little electric shock.

'Love sucks, Florrie. It destroys you. Look at me. Would I be where I am now if I hadn't messed around with love?'

I step towards her. 'Have you remembered something about that night?'

'It's not a memory, it's ... a feeling.'

'The being buried thing.'

She winces. 'Yeah, but ... the strangest thing is that as I struggle against the earth, I have this sense that whoever is doing it, is doing it because they love me. Or, at least, they think they do.'

'Tim?' I think of his rage on the phone at the weekend. Maybe all that stuff about being framed is just him trying to distract me.

She looks away. 'Nobody else loved me like he did.'

I feel a hot rush of fury flood over me. 'If that's his way of showing he loved you, he deserves to rot in hell'

Meggie smiles. 'Funny. I don't get angry any more about stuff I can't change. But you and Danny ... just be careful, eh? I couldn't bear to see my little sister heartbroken.'

'I ...' I open my mouth, ready to tell her that it's my heart to be broken if that's what I choose. But I don't want to hurt her. Instead, I decide to change the subject. 'I think I'm getting somewhere with Triti.'

It only occurs to me as I say that, that Triti might even disappear as soon as tonight. Lewis and I now know *why* she died – surely that counts as a kind of resolution?

She opens the other eye. 'Seriously? She needs it. She's still there,' my sister gestures to the end of the beach. 'Hiding from everyone. We've been down there once more and ... I never knew what someone in despair looked like till now.'

'Meggie, do you think she will escape? If I find out what really happened?'

She tries to smile. 'I really hope so, Florrie. Because if she can, then there's hope for us all.'

'Hope?' That was what Danny said I had given him.

Meggie looks out to sea. 'Not that I want to go anywhere,' she says. 'Not now I have my little sister back.'

I want to see Danny so badly, but how can I leave Meggie now she's said that? I turn his name over in my mind, like a precious stone. He's just two or three hundred steps away. Waiting.

'Alice ...' My mother is outside my room. 'We need to go now.'

'OK, two minutes and I'll be down.'

'*Florrie?*'

Has my sister heard my mother's voice?

'I've got to go, Meggie. But first ...' I look down the shore-line. Even if he is waiting there, I can't risk Mum coming in. I cup my hands around my lips – letting myself imagine for a moment that they're *his* lips – and then I lean right into the microphone, and call out to shore.

'DANNY CROSS!'

My voice echoes around the Beach, and it's strange to know that only four other people can hear it: my sister, Triti, Javier ... and Danny. None of the other Guests even know I exist.

'ALICE FORSTER!'

His voice comes back to me, from the direction of our rock. It sounds different when he's shouting, but he's still *my* Danny.

'I HAVE TO GO, BUT I PROMISE I'LL BE BACK TOMORROW. AND THE NEXT DAY, AND THE NEXT DAY.'

'Hmm. You know, it never does any harm to play hard to get, sis. Even with dead boyfriends,' Meggie says.

'I'LL BE HERE, ALICE. ALWAYS. THE BEACH IS NOTHING WITHOUT YOU!' Danny shouts back.

I smile so broadly that my face almost hurts.

My sister sighs. 'I guess keeping love's young dream apart is going to be tougher than I thought.'

56

Lewis has a swanky car – a show-off's convertible, in silver – and after Dad's stopped asking him questions about turbos, Lewis drives out of the close in first gear. Then puts his foot down, glancing to his left to see my reaction.

'You might impress the other geeks, but you don't impress me,' I say.

He laughs. 'Is that all you see me as, a geek? After all that I've done?'

At the roundabout, take the third exit. Then, take the motorway.

The sat nav has a low and bossy female voice – perhaps that's how a dominatrix sounds. As he obeys her instructions, I watch him and wonder why he's here. He accelerates onto the motorway, driving smoothly and not too showily, considering that the few other drivers on the road this early are giving the car admiring glances.

He's a decent guy, Lewis. I don't know why he puts up with my vagueness and my snide remarks. 'Why *are* you helping me like this?' I ask him.

'I like a mystery.'

'I don't believe you could like a mystery enough to put up with hanging round a moody teenage girl who won't tell you what's going on.'

Lewis glances at me. 'You're a mystery wrapped in an enigma, that's for sure. And very different from your sister.'

He accelerates past a lorry, into the fast lane. It's so quiet in here. If you couldn't see the world whizzing past, you'd never believe we were doing a hundred and ten.

After five hundred yards, keep right.

'How well did you know my sister?'

'Like I said before, she was in my year. Same parties, plus, you know, she went out with one of the kids from my class in Year Ten.'

'Did she?'

'For about two weeks, it was. I doubt she'd even have remembered his name, but it gave my classmate a heap more kudos. She was a catch, your sister.'

Weird to hear him talk about her in the past, when last night she was real enough to stop me seeing the love of my life. 'You never fancied your chances?'

He changes gear. 'Not my type.'

'I thought Meggie was everybody's type.'

He keeps driving.

After a few miles, he says, 'You know, I've always thought one of the hardest things about someone dying is that you can't tell the truth any more. My grandma died, my dad's mum? She was a bitch who criticised everything my mother did, thought her precious son was way too good for Mum. She didn't even come to their wedding. She was mean with money. She had no interest in me or my brother. But now, to hear everyone talk, you'd think she was a cross between Mother Teresa and a loving little old granny from a fairy story.'

'God, Lewis,' I laugh. 'I think that's the longest speech I've ever heard you make.'

He frowns into the sunlight, pulls his sunglasses down.

Leaving me thinking about all the things that Meggie was: beautiful, arrogant, funny, spiteful, passionate, cruel, outgoing, jealous, generous, controlling, intelligent, snobbish, fascinating, aggravating, selfish, egotistical . . .

'*Stop,*' I say to myself.

Lewis looks across at me. 'I didn't know your sister, Alice, but I know that what I read about her in the papers can't be the whole truth. That she can't just have been this super-sickly-sweet songbird who never put a foot wrong. After all ...' he stops.

'After all, what?' I stare at him. 'You were going to say, 'after all, someone murdered her,' weren't you?'

He shakes his head. 'No. Not like that. But I wonder whether your obsession with this anorexic girl is a way of distracting yourself from your feelings about what happened to your sister.'

'Are you a qualified psychiatrist, Lewis?'

'No, but—'

'Well, then, stop trying to psychoanalyse me. Of course I want to know who killed Meggie, I'm not a robot. But as for the rest of it, I told you at the start, I need help but not if you think it gives you the right to try to fix me.'

'I see.'

After three hundred yards, take the exit.

Lewis ignores the woman on the sat nav.

TAKE THE EXIT, she insists. Her irritation sounds very real.

This time, he does as he's told. Between me and the electronic bossy boots, he's outnumbered.

Triti's school is in a tiny, cutesy town twenty miles from Brighton. It's the kind of place parents must love and kids must hate: three pubs and three small supermarkets, so the chances of getting served alcohol under-age are almost zero.

Keyes School for Girls is an old stone house, behind a new, sharp-edged red-brick wall with a fiercely pronged gate. Lewis parks on the main road, and we get out and look through the bars.

He sniffs. 'Bit footballers' wives, isn't it?'

That's *exactly* what it is. Lush green grass that no one's ever played hockey on. A car park to the side full of solid but flashy four-by-fours. A pavilion with a glass roof that I just know will contain an overheated swimming pool.

'Ah. School's out, right on time.' Lewis nods and as we watch, girls begin to trickle out of the front and side. 'Jesus, all those hormones,' he says, and not in a way that makes me think he sees them as potential dates.

'They go to school on Saturdays?'

'Yes. *Leisure, practical and social pursuits to prepare our girls for a rounded life beyond academia,* according to their website.'

'Rounded?' I think of the messages to Triti and I shiver. Which of these girls sent them? We move back towards the car as the trickle becomes a pour. There are pretty girls, plain girls, fat, thin. Though not many fat ones, now I study them closely. Is 'Salli' at work again, spreading her poison? Not that Triti was even fat to begin with ...

'Now we wait,' Lewis says. 'See where the older ones like to hang out after school. I definitely don't want to risk getting nicked for trying to chat up schoolgirls on the premises.'

It's easy to spot the sixth-formers, as they wear their own clothes rather than the crimson school uniform. The older girls split into two posses – one heads for *Starbucks* and the other to a smaller, funkier coffee shop in the town's art gallery.

'You should go for the gallery,' I tell Lewis, 'the indie girls will go there and they're the sort that are slightly more likely to talk to a guy like you.'

'Hmm. A guy like me. Meaning?'

'Nothing. Just that you look nervous. I mean, you're welcome to the others if you prefer. They're bound to be the in-crowd. They might be a bit scarier ...'

He heads towards the gallery without any more persuasion. I stand outside Starbucks for a moment, wondering if I can really do this. I close my eyes, force myself to think of Triti and of how she must have felt every time she received another one of those evil messages, and how she must feel again now: completely alone. Then I push open the door. This is no time to be a wimp.

It's packed in here: not just schoolgirls but couples and families, too. While I queue for my gingerbread latte, I try to guess which of the half a dozen tables occupied by 'Keysies', could be my best bet. Each of the groups has its Queen Bee: could the platinum blonde be 'Salli', or is it the girl with the dark red crop whose fingers twitch like a smoker's?

A girl leaves amid lots of showy air kissing and it makes my mind up. I race towards what I think might be the only spare chair left in the place.

'Is it OK if I sit here?'

The two girls who are left give me the once-over. I'd say they're Year Thirteens. They're dressed in Abercrombie – bought, I'm guessing, on some recent girlie weekend in New York – but one has spots and the other has a brace, and I have a sudden hunch that these are not the people who hounded Triti to her death.

But I bet they know who did.

I sip my latte, and take out my notebook. Lewis said no one can ever resist sneaking a look at what someone's writing in a notebook, and as I pull a pen out of the spiral binding, I sense the girl with the brace glancing at me. I pretend to write some more, and then I chew my pen, as though I'm seeking inspiration. Finally, I look at her, as though something's just occurred to me.

'I don't suppose either of you two know anything about Keyes School, do you?'

The spotty girl smiles. 'You could say that. We've both been going there for the past six years.'

'Wow!' I say, putting my pen down. 'Wow! That's so cool. What's it like?'

'It's fun,' she says. 'Though I'd say it takes a certain kind of girl to fit in. Stylish. Smart.' She frowns. 'You hoping to come, are you?'

'How did you know?'

She shrugs. 'Just a lucky guess. What year are you?'

'Eleven. My parents think it'd be good to go into a boarding sixth form.'

Brace Girl scowls. 'Good for you or good for them?'

I laugh. 'Both, I guess. I'm ... an only child, and I think they're looking forward to having the house to themselves again.'

'Sounds familiar,' Brace Girl says. 'I'm Jade, by the way.'

'Alice.'

'Maria,' says the girl with the acne. 'So what else do you want to know?'

'Do you get to wear your own clothes? Do you get to go out? Do you get your own room?'

'Yes to the clothes, yes to going out, though there's sod all to do round here, and yes, to your own room, though new girls sometimes have to share till someone leaves,' says Jade.

'Dead girls' shoes,' Maria says. The two girls exchange a glance.

I shiver. 'Do lots of people leave?'

Maria suddenly spots something interesting in her coffee. Jade with the brace narrows her eyes. 'Like Maria says, it's not for everybody. People who don't like it, don't always stick it out.'

'Is there bullying?'

She stares at me. For a moment, I think I've gone too far. 'Schools are no different from anywhere else. You need to fit in. That's not bullying. More a case of ... natural selection.' She smiles a closed-mouth smile, to keep her braces out of view.

'Ignore Jade. She's a biologist,' says Maria.

If I really was considering this school, that idea of natural

245

selection would be enough to make me think twice. But knowing what I know about Triti makes her words sound even more sinister.

'There was a girl from round our way who came here,' I begin, realising that if I don't strike soon, they'll get bored and freeze me out. 'Her name was ...'

But then I hear a rush of air as the door to the café is flung open. Lewis stands there. People stare. Especially the Keyes girls. Maybe I've misjudged him, and actually he is more attractive than the average computer guru.

Or maybe it's the thunderous expression on his face that's making everyone look. I'm surprised at how angry he seems, on behalf of a girl he never even knew. Maybe it's that sense of injustice that makes him willing to do so much for me.

It's the weirdest moment: a break in time, where this small-town Starbucks suddenly seems to have transformed into a saloon in a spaghetti western.

'I'm looking for Demi,' Lewis announces. 'I was told I could find her in here.'

57

A lot of things happen, one after another. A baby cries, which breaks the High Noon moment. Pressurised steam shoots out of the coffee machine. And a dozen schoolgirls look towards the window, where a girl in a too-tight V-neck black sweater is staring at Lewis.

It can only be a second or two, but it feels like years, before she stands up.

'I'm Demi.'

She has a gruff voice, like Cara's when she's thrown an all-nighter. She wears jeans that strain across her thighs, and her stubby nails are painted coral-pink. I didn't even notice her when I came in. She's too ordinary to be the spiteful but smart Salli, surely?

Lewis gestures towards the door and steps out into the street. Demi hesitates, but I see curiosity in her plump face, and I know she's going to follow him. As she steps out of the café, three of her mates are behind her. Her gang.

I stand up, too, leaving my coffee on the table. 'My brother,' I say to Jade and Maria, who are struggling to make the connection between this avenger, and their first assessment of me as a slightly dim potential pupil.

In the street, Lewis and Demi face each other, with the posse behind her like backing singers in a teen musical. He waits for me to get close enough to hear.

'I want to talk to you about Triti Pillai.'

I watch her face, see the flicker of panic that disappears almost instantly, to be replaced by a slappable blandness. Her mates aren't quite so quick – one looks scared, one grumpy, one clueless. The three monkeys.

'Who?' asks Demi. 'The name rings a bell.'

'I'll bet it does,' says Lewis. 'Because you bullied her to death.'

Two of the girls gasp, but Demi just pouts. 'Eh? You're nuts.'

'You know what, I might well be,' he says, with a smile that suggests unpredictable mood swings. 'But that doesn't mean you're *not* responsible for a girl's death.'

Demi's sulky pout wavers. 'Come on,' she says to the others, and she begins to walk back towards school.

Lewis walks alongside her. 'Don't mind if we tag along, do you? Actually, we'd quite like to have a chat with the teachers, too, because surely after Triti's death they want to avoid future scandals, am I right?'

Demi stops. 'Who the hell *are* you?'

'Friends of Triti and her family,' he says.

'What did she ever do to you?' I ask.

Demi takes a sharp left, into an alleyway, then begins to run. Lewis chases and corners her, before I've even gone a few metres.

He doesn't need to touch her. He just stands in front of her, and the message is clear. 'All yours, I think,' he says to me.

'There's definitely no mistake?' I ask.

'No. A girl in the other café told me they all thought they knew who it was, but no one could prove it. Well, so they reckoned.' He takes his iPhone out of his pocket. 'Actually, took me about four seconds to match her mobile IP address with the imaginary Salli's.'

Demi scowls at the name. I stand close to her and she turns her face away from me. Behind me, I sense the other girls getting closer.

'Boo!' Lewis shouts in her other ear, and Demi jumps and turns back. Her face has lost its bravado.

'Triti is ... was my friend,' I say. 'She was a good person. What made you do it?'

'I don't know what you're on about,' she says, but she no longer sounds so cocky.

'Fine,' Lewis says. 'I've got enough now to take to the school, or maybe the police. I don't know what the going sentence is for bullying someone to death. What do you think, Alice? A year? Two? Having been to boarding school, I bet Demi will fit in just fine in a young offenders' institution. Full of girls like you, eh, Demi? Though I bet they could still teach you a thing or two about bullying.'

I'm not sure if what he's saying is true, but I don't think Demi is either.

'What do you want?' she demands, and there's a choking sound in her throat, as though she's trying not to cry.

'Tell us what you did and why you did it,' I reply.

There's a sound behind me. Two of her friends are still here: Grumpy, and Dopey. The scared looking one has gone already. I wait for them to lash out or defend her, but instead they just stand there, watching.

'Do they know about you?' I ask Demi, gesturing towards her friends. 'Do they know what you did? Did they join in?'

They keep gawping. And then it occurs to me. *Perhaps she bullies them too ...*

'I'm not known for my patience,' says Lewis, cracking his knuckles. He seems to be enjoying his new role as a well-spoken psychopath a little too much, though to me he seems about as scary as a pantomime dame.

Lewis turns on his iPhone and begins to read: '*You're going to look so gorgeous in your bikini on the beach this summer, aren't you? And then those bitches will know, the ones who called you fat.* Sound familiar?'

Demi stares straight ahead.

Dopey takes a step forward. 'Can I see?'

Lewis looks slightly nervous at the idea of handing over his precious phone, but I nod. The girl reads. After a while, she hands the phone to the second girl, who reads very slowly, her finger against the text.

'You never said you were sending actual personal messages,' Dopey says to Demi. 'You said it was just a laugh. Jokes. A way of making her less smug.'

'It's a hoax,' says Demi. 'They've typed the messages themselves.'

Grumpy is shaking her head. 'No. Because you *were* Salli. We all knew that. And we all said you'd gone too far with the stuff on the wall. But *this* ...'

'Why her, Demi?' I ask. 'Why pick on Triti?'

Demi says nothing. Maybe she was pretty once, before hate made her eyes go sour and her lips tight.

Grumpy hands the phone back to Lewis, then slaps her hands together as though she's trying to remove invisible dirt. 'It *was* you.' She looks at Demi, and I think I see the moment when she realises that she has the power to decide what happens next. Her expression changes to something like triumph. She knows she's top dog for the first time in her twisted little life.

She steps right up to Demi and spits the words into her face. 'You killed Triti.'

And then she turns around without waiting for Demi's response, and walks back up the alleyway. Dopey hesitates as Demi's eyes lock onto hers. Is the power still there?

Dopey breaks the gaze.

Demi calls after her, 'Please,' and that's when we all know she's lost everything.

Lewis waits until the sound of the girls' footsteps has

receded as they turn back onto the high street. 'Where were we, then, Demi?'

She whimpers. She really believes he might hurt her, even though he hasn't laid a finger on her. 'I didn't expect . . .' Demi stops. Shakes her head.

'Yes?' I say.

'It was a joke. She was a stupid little Daddy's girl. Thought she could have anything – and anyone – she wanted. I just wanted to teach her a bit of a lesson. Never expected she'd take it so seriously.'

'So it *was* you?'

She nods.

'Say it out loud, Demi. Say that you drove Triti to starve herself to death.'

She swallows several times. We're so close that I can smell stale coffee on her breath, and hear her throat rasping as she tries to clear it.

'I drove Triti Pillai to starve herself to death.'

58

In the distance, I hear a crash.

Thunder.

The sky has darkened so that what little light there was in the alleyway has gone. Fat raindrops fall thickly and loudly onto the cobbles and our heads.

Within fifteen seconds, we're soaked. But Lewis doesn't move away from Demi, even as water runs down her face, and his. Her carefully styled hair lists like a ship, then clumps together in thick, gluey strands. Mascara runs down her slightly mottled cheeks like tears of regret, though I am pretty sure the only person she feels sorry for right now is herself.

'Why did you do it?' I ask her. 'What did Triti ever do to you?'

'She ... she bloody loved herself, didn't she?'

'Not by the time you'd finished with her. I'd say that by then, she hated herself.'

'I was only messing. I did it to some of the other girls who were full of themselves, but they never took it that seriously.'

'Er, if you think that's going to help justify what you did, Demi, then you're even madder than I thought,' Lewis says.

'She floated round school like she was better than the rest of us. Her dad even bought her her own room, ahead of people on the waiting list. Well, she wasn't better, was she? She was weak.'

I look at her twisted face and I think of Triti in her family photographs, beaming at the camera and at life. 'But why would that make you do what you did? Go to all that trouble because someone else was happy? Or over a *room?'* Demi stares back at me, like she doesn't understand the question. But I have to keep asking, don't I? I don't know what resolution is, or whether it really will offer Triti her way out, but I have to try to get all the answers to questions I haven't even thought of yet.

I try to imagine what Danny would ask. *He'd* find out the truth.

'Were you jealous of her?'

I see contempt in her eyes. 'No way.'

'Was there a boy involved?'

Demi looks away.

'Tell me,' I say.

'All the boys *loved* Triti. But she wasn't allowed boyfriends. Which made them love her even more.'

I think about it. 'Including a boy you liked, maybe, Demi?'

She shrugs. 'Can't remember.'

Lewis looks at me, shakes his head very slightly. 'You know what, Alice. I think Demi's too stupid to work out why she did it. She taunted a girl to death and she *can't remember*. People like her make me sick.'

Demi scowls. 'I am *here.*'

'Don't worry, sweetie, we haven't forgotten you,' says Lewis, leaning in closer to her. 'What shall we do with her, Alice?'

'Are you going to tell school?' Demi asks nervously.

He laughs. 'Not so brave now, are we? Brave enough to torture a girl anonymously but scared to face the music, eh, Demi? Worried you're going to get into big twouble? Did-dums!'

I ignore him, though it strikes me we've fallen into a weird good cop/bad cop routine. 'Did you not realise it had gone too far?' I ask. 'Did you never see her fading away and think, this is wrong? I mean, she was *dying in front of you.* It took months and yet you kept going right until she went over the edge.'

'She was mad. That's not my fault.' Demi's eyes are defiant, but scarily blank. It's as though she's dead herself, or deadened to the effect she has on people. Maybe she wasn't always like this. Maybe what she did to Triti killed off what little humanity she had.

I shiver, then look down at myself. I am dripping wet. We all are. 'I think we've heard enough,' I say. Though, of course, I can't be certain till I'm back on the Beach.

Lewis looks reluctant to let her leave. 'Really? You sure you've got everything you need?'

I hear fast footsteps behind me, and as I turn a woman's voice calls out, 'What in God's name do you think you are doing to her? Stop!'

'Miss Jacobs?' Demi cries out. 'Miss Jacobs, they're robbing me!'

We look around to see a middle-aged woman in a Mac rushing towards us. Behind, the third girl, the one we thought we'd scared off, is standing in the shadows. She must have run to fetch a teacher.

How much did the teacher hear? Enough?

Lewis moves back, and Demi slumps against the wall, then he grabs my sleeve. 'Let's go.'

I do as I'm told, but as he passes the teacher, who looks too gob-smacked to try to stop us, he presses the mobile phone into her open hand. 'This is what you need. This is what Demi did. Read it all, listen to the audio recording I've just made of her confession, and then make sure it never happens again.'

The teacher just stares, and then I feel the pull on my arm again, and we march away, our trainers squelching and throwing out water. I hear sobbing behind me, and maybe it's not nice of me, but I feel bloody glad that Demi might finally have realised what she's done.

Even though I suspect she's not crying for Triti.

We wait for almost an hour in a park before daring to go back to the school to pick up the car. After all, we couldn't get any more soaked. When we reach Keyes again, there's a police car on the drive.

'For us, or for her, do you think?' I ask Lewis, when we're finally back on the road.

'With any luck, for her. If they've bothered to read the data.'

'Can't believe you sacrificed your phone. That was your good deed for the day.'

He smiles at me. 'Oh, no, that's not my phone. I'd prepped an old fake Smartphone with the emails etc., and cleaned off all my own data so I could hand it over to someone once she'd confessed while I was recording.'

'Ah. You thought of everything.'

'Couldn't let her get away with it, could we? Not after we went to so much trouble. Plus there was no way I was taking my pride and joy on such a dangerous mission. Demi wasn't worth risking my iPhone.'

Lewis continues to amaze me. 'You're a genius,' I tell him. 'I'm going to call you Mastermind from now on.'

He smiles. Then silence takes over and I feel relieved and do nothing but watch the outside world. The sky doesn't clear as we drive back. The rain clouds just get darker and dusk comes and goes, and then it's night.

'Did it help *you*, Alice? What we did?' he asks me, when we're back on the motorway.

'I don't know yet.' I shrink down in my seat. The knowledge of what happened to Triti – and of the petty envy, or whatever tiny dispute triggered Demi's hate campaign – feels like a burden now. 'Do you think we should tell Rafi, and the rest of her family?'

Lewis sighs. 'If I had a sister, I wouldn't want to know how she suffered if there was nothing I could do to change it.'

'I guess not ...' Except I might just have changed every-thing. Is Triti's ordeal over now?

Red brake lights blur in front of us as the car picks up speed, and the wheels cut through deep puddles on the carriageway.

'... but in the future, maybe, you know you can tell me. If it'll help.'

I suddenly realise Lewis is still talking to me and I haven't been listening. 'Sorry. I was miles away.' I think of Javier's joke. *Light years away*. Where my sister is. Where Danny is waiting for me.

'I was just saying, Alice, that I hope you know by now that I wouldn't pry. But if you do want to share what's troubling you, any time, I promise I'll listen and I won't judge.'

I turn my face away. It's dark enough that we can't see each other properly anyway, only the black-orange-black-orange flicker of the motorway lights.

He deserves to know the truth after all he's done, but I am trapped. '*I won't judge*.' Hmm. I bet that if I did tell him the truth, he'd be running in the opposite direction as fast as those dirty trainers could carry him.

'Thanks. Maybe I will, one day soon,' I say, but we both know it's a snub. Sometimes I feel really, really alone.

When I dare to look at him, the light darts across his face and I see coldness there.

The second time it lights up I realise it isn't coldness. It's hurt.

'Sorry, Lewis. I know I seem like an ungrateful cow but really, I'm not. I feel incredibly lucky that you've helped me. You're amazingly kind and maybe I will be able to tell you, one day. If I can ever tell anyone, it'll be you. I ... well, I trust you.'

'Thanks. I think.'

'You're welcome.'

As he drives, I sneak glimpses of his face. I think of the other men I trust in my life: my dad, Danny.

Tim . . .

Could Lewis possibly help me solve that mystery too? I take out my phone, switch it back on. There's a new text from Adrian: he's sending several a day, now, since the conversation with Tim.

Still making plans for a face-to-face meeting, Alice. Expect to have more news soon. Your friend, Ade

'New boyfriend?' asks Lewis, with a smile.

I tut. 'Not interested. Boys are so shallow.'

The motorway skirts London. Forty five minutes till I can go back on the Beach. *Where Danny is waiting for me.* I stare up at the dense, black heavens above us and try to imagine the cloudless blue.

A bright pink light flashes across the sky. Then orange. Then green.

'Oh my God, *fireworks*,' I whisper, thinking of Triti. Could that be a supernatural sign that she's gone?

'Well, yes,' says Lewis. 'You do remember the date, don't you?'

I blink, and try to remember. October? Or November? Isn't asking the date one of the tests they use on accident victims and old people when they want to work out if they've still got all their marbles?

No. It's no use. Some days I don't notice if it's summer or winter.

'It's Bonfire Night,' Lewis tells me.

Another firework rips into the sky, then cascades. A white chrysanthemum. Isn't that the flower of death?

The memories are fading, like old photographs, and what's left is loneliness.

Every day that passes, Meggie becomes less real to me. There was something so precious about her last moments, because they were just mine and hers. For so many months, she'd been public property, pawed over and fawned over, and worse, by millions of so-called fans.

And then, suddenly, we were completely alone.

But sharing a perfect memory with a dead girl is not as good as I'd imagined it might be. For one cannot reminisce with the dead, and the details soon blur at the edges. Once or twice, I have even resorted to doing what the stupid do, and watching the videos of her on the internet. They repulsed me.

I don't want to be alone any more. I crave company. Someone to understand me, as she did. Someone to love.

I've tried to fight it, but that same name, that same face, appears in my day dreams and my night dreams.

Alice.

It ought to be enough just to see her, hear her voice.

But I fear a time is coming when the battle against myself will be lost.

59

I sit in front of the screen, trying to summon up the courage to go on the Beach.

All it takes is half a dozen clicks of the mouse.

'I'm afraid, Meggie,' I whisper, even though she can't hear me yet.

Afraid that I've changed nothing, or that I've changed everything. Over the last few months, the Beach has been a safe haven. A place I cannot change, or influence, because I am only a Visitor. I might be able to cheer my sister up now and then, and I might have made Danny think there's a reason for his living death, but there's been no connection between my world and theirs.

Until now.

The snap, crackle, pop of our local, crappy fireworks display has started outside. The air will be full of damp smoke and the pub car park full of terrified babies and disappointed kids and desperate parents trying to get excited about sparklers that snuff out before you've written a single letter of your name in the air.

Meggie didn't like fireworks. Dad used to joke that she couldn't stand anything else being the centre of attention, even dynamite.

Not much of a joke any more.

Get on with it, Alice, I say to myself. I stand up, pace the floor, then catch sight of myself in the wardrobe mirror. I look a bit of a state after all today's dramas. OK, so on the Beach, everyone is beautiful, but would it do any harm to give my webcam a bit of help along the way?'

As I pick up my hairbrush and make-up mirror, I know this is probably just another way of putting off the moment when I find out, but if it makes me feel more confident, then maybe I can justify it.

The brush struggles through the tangles at first, but I keep going, holding onto the knots so they don't pull at the roots, just as Meggie always used to when she styled my hair for me when I was little. Slowly, surely, it begins to look glossy again. All right, maybe not glossy, but at least I don't look as though I've been living rough for the last month.

But now my eyes look tired. I find my neglected make-up bag in the bedside drawer, and apply a coat of mascara. *Bloody hell*, I actually look awake again. I empty the lipsticks and pencils out onto the desk, remembering how my sister showed me what they can do. 'You've got such gorgeous lips, Florrie. If you use this rosy shade of gloss, it'll make all the boys want to kiss you!'

I smile to myself. I don't want all the boys. I want one who'll never be able to kiss me. But at least today there's a chance I might make him proud of me.

Enough time wasting. I have to get this over with. I reach under the bed, pull out the box with Meggie's room key in it. I don't know what I expect – for it to sing me a song, or glow in the dark – but it's just a key.

Click, click.

Not half a dozen clicks at all. Two. The distinction between real life and the Beach has been getting thinner and thinner until it barely exists.

Mist. Breeze. The smell of coconut. I guess it seems more intense right now because of the day I've had, and because of the contrast with the night air outside, full of sodden firewood and slippery, rotting leaves.

I blink, hard, because the screen won't clear. Something

has changed, but I don't know what. The site is slower to react on screen, but the smells, the sounds of the waves seem even more intense.

'Alice!'

'Over here, over here!'

'Florrie . . .'

Danny, Javier and Meggie are calling out to me, but I can't see them. Their voices circle me.

Yet when the mist finally clears, I am sitting in the beach bar at the table nearest the ocean, just me and Sam. She looks different. I see lines and dry skin around her eyes and nicotine stains on her teeth.

Sam smiles. 'You did it, mate.'

'Triti?'

'Gone.'

I feel dizzy. 'It was definitely me? What I did?'

'I don't even know what it was you did, Alice, but what or who else could it have been?'

Is that sweat I can smell when she leans towards me?

Everything is so much clearer now. It's as though I was looking through grubby glasses before, and now someone's given them a good clean. And I can feel the rush seat of my chair scratching against my bare legs, even though, of course, I am in thick, November-proof jeans on a pink velour office chair in my bedroom.

'When did she go?'

'There was a storm. At first we could still hear her howling like a banshee, but then her voice changed. It was like she was calling out to someone she knew. Someone she loved. To tell you the truth, Alice, I almost didn't recognise her voice because she sounded . . . well, happy. For the first time since the fireworks. And then when the storm had blown itself out, there was nothing. No howling. No calling out. Just the sound of the waves.'

I close my eyes and I see Triti's face: not the skeletal mask but the round-cheeked, beautiful girl she was, smiling. I feel tears pricking at my eyes but then she mouths, *thank you* and then is gone.

It's so bizarre to think I have made that happen. I'm sixteen: I can't drive, I can't vote, I can't have a credit card, and yet I have that *power*.

And it's not just the power to help Triti. Now I know that Danny's theory was right, I can push on to solve Meggie's murder too. Even though freedom for her will mean I lose her for ever, and I'm not sure I'm ready for that.

But, whatever it takes, I'll put Meggie first. I know that helping Triti is just the first step, that I've only just begun. But right here, right now, it's enough to have achieved something so life-changing – or should that be *after*life-changing?

'Alice? Are you with me?'

'Sorry, I'm just ... surprised it worked.'

'The thing is,' Sam says gently, 'I brought you in here to warn you that it might not be all that's changed. As far as I know, we've never had any Visitor intervene like this, but now you have, there will be ... rewards.'

'What rewards?' Making Triti happy is enough.

'Better for you to find out for yourself. I just didn't want it to be too much of a shock.' Sam smiles at me. 'You don't want to hang around with me for longer than you need to. Go see for yourself.'

I stand up. Beyond the bar, there's the ocean. And standing on the wet sand, the waves lapping back and forth over her feet, is my sister.

Every step I take now feels more real. It's a bit like when Dad replaced our old telly with an HD set. Under the soles of my feet, a thousand grains of sand shift and prickle.

My sister waves. She's beaming. 'You're a star, Alice, you really are. Everything's different here. Not just because we know Triti isn't suffering, but also . . . there are changes. You'll find out for yourself.'

I nod.

'But that's not the main thing. What really makes things better is that now we know that any of us might be able to escape one day. It makes all this,' she gestures at the Beach, 'well, I guess it makes paradise bearable. Even somewhere we can enjoy while it lasts.'

'I can't believe it,' I say.

'Thank you so much, Florrie. I think you might just have saved all of us from a fate worse than death.'

Her hair is blowing behind her in the breeze and her eyes match the water: clear, blue, alive.

I'm ecstatic that I've made my sister so happy. For a split second, I forget we're on the Beach, and I step forward to hug her. But I stop myself before she notices: I can't bear to spoil the moment by reminding us both that however close we feel, we are really light years apart.

'It was nothing,' I say.

'You and I both know that's not true. What you've done is . . . well, it's almost a miracle.'

I feel myself blushing. I want to stay with her, and yet I also want someone else to know what I've done. 'Meggie?'

'Mmm?' she looks up and then her face changes as she senses what's coming. 'You still feel that way about him?'

'I do. I feel even more strongly that he . . . well, he might be the One.'

She stares at me: now she has her back to the sea, it's almost as though she's translucent and the seawater and sky are shining through, giving her light.

'Go to him, Florrie.'

'What?'

'Go on. If there's ever a time when you deserve not to get a lecture from me on being silly, I think it might be now.'

60

I run towards our rock. The slap of my feet against the sand is painful, and although I know it's not possible, I swear that some of the Guests are turning round, hearing my steps.

Even seeing me too?

They're smiling at me.

But I don't care about them. I care about the boy I can see in the distance, his back to me as he stares out to sea. His head bobs as he follows the path of a group of seabirds swooping through the sky.

Sea birds? There are no animals on Soul Beach, surely.

I want to call out to him, but instead I decide to tiptoe the last few metres, to surprise him.

Then, right at the very last moment, I am afraid. What if waiting has changed his mind? What if, when I catch him unawares, I'll see in his face that he doesn't feel what I want him to feel? That he's just been playing with me, to pass the time in eternity?

I have to keep going, but just before I reach him, he turns around.

'ALICE!' He calls out, even though we're close enough now to whisper.

'Danny.' Speaking his name is like reciting the world's shortest, most beautiful piece of poetry.

'You did it, didn't you? You helped Triti escape.'

I nod. He looks so wonderful, now, at least a thousand times better than I remembered. Almost real ...

'You look different,' he murmurs. 'Just as perfect, but, well, almost real.'

'So do you,' I tell him.

We stand so close that in the real world a sigh or a breath or a word would be enough to bring us together physically. If only . . .

'Alice, I—'

I jump back, as though I've been electrocuted. His eyes widen, as though he has been, too.

'Was that . . . ?'

'It can't have been,' he says, his voice high-pitched.

Our hands rise at the same moment – my right hand, his left – as though we're looking in the mirror at ourselves. It's not true. It can't be.

Sam's words echo in my head. *There will be . . . rewards.*

Danny and I watch each other's hands as they move, so slowly, so tentatively, wanting to prolong the delicious possibility for as long as we can, to postpone the inevitable disappointment. His palm is smooth, white, the hand of a boy who was on the edge of becoming a man. A long, softly curving lifeline stretches from his chunky wrist up around to the wide space between thumb and forefinger.

He shouldn't be dead yet. Even though, if he was alive, we would never have met.

Somewhere, in another universe, my mobile's ringing. But it could be the Queen or the President of the United States and I still wouldn't answer right now.

'Ready?' he asks.

'Ready.'

The gap between our hands closes, millimetre by millimetre. At the last moment, I close my eyes, so that I won't have to see the exact moment when our bodies miss each other, light years apart.

Now . . . or now . . . or . . .

I feel warmth. *Touch.*

My eyes spring open. His mouth is curved in a perfect, shocked circle. Now we push our hands together, thumb to thumb, fingers against fingers.

How can one person's hand against mine feel like a miracle? The warmth floods my body, and it's like I've been frozen ever since my sister died, and this is the first time I've thawed.

Our hands stay together as we stare at each other over the tops of our fingers.

'Does that mean ...?' I say, but I don't dare finish my sentence.

'I think it might,' he replies.

And then he leans forward, and I taste his breath – fresh, green, alive – and even before our lips touch, I know *this* is going to be the kiss of my life.

Don't miss the second gripping book of the trilogy

SOUL FIRE

Available July 2012

It's getting hotter on the Beach

Read on for a sneak preview . . .

Another death is coming, I can feel it.

Maybe I gained a sixth sense when I decided I would be the last person to hold Meggie Forster. The last person to touch her skin. The last to brush her hair.

It wasn't murder. I was protecting her from the others, the ones who wanted to exploit her face, her name, her soul.

Yet the news headlines talked of slaughter. No! She left the world so gently, under that feather pillow. I made sure of that.

Those unjust stories make me burn with rage, though I try to stay calm. Alice calms me. She is every bit as radiant as her elder sister, but unlike Meggie, Alice doesn't see how special she is. Which, of course, makes her even more precious.

But her obsession with truth endangers us both. An innocent like Alice doesn't realise that in this ugly world, there are a billion versions of the truth. If she cannot accept my version, then another death is inevitable.

1

Happiness is simple. All you need are the people you love.

After Meggie died, I thought I'd never be happy again. Yet here I am on the Beach, where life is absolute heaven. I can hear my sister humming softly as she draws patterns in the sand. I feel the warmth of the sun on my skin, and the touch of Danny's body against mine, and the sway of the hammock as the sea breeze rocks us.

How many people get a second chance like this?

'Are you daydreaming again, Alice?'

I hesitate before I open my eyes, because there's always the fear that one day this could all disappear.

But Danny's still there, his face so close to mine that I can't decide whether to kiss him or just admire him: eyes as green as a tropical lagoon, blond hair that's curly after swimming (he hates that, I love it), lips that fit mine so well it'd be a crime not to kiss them again . . .

'Why would I need to daydream?' I whisper. 'Everything I want is within reach.' And to prove it, I reach out to take his hand.

'Right answer.' He leans in to kiss me.

'Come on! Guys! Can you not leave each other alone for a minute? I will have to throw a bucket of water over you, like they do with dogs!'

Javier is the grit in the pearl of paradise: sarcastic, occasionally cruel. But I can't imagine Soul Beach without him. Every group needs a comedian. Some of his jokes are on the dark side, but he *is* dead. That could give anyone a strange sense of humour.

Danny and I smile at each other. Maybe we should make an effort to be more sociable.

We whisper, 'Three, two, one . . .' then tumble out of the hammock onto the soft bed of pillows below. However hard we try to do it gracefully, it never works. Maybe it's because we can't resist hanging onto each other till the last possible moment.

'Such elegance!' Javier scoffs, and my sister giggles. Beach life seems to suit her more and more. Her hair is blonder, her million-dollar smile now worth at least a billion. When she was alive, the TV production people kept telling her to lose weight – 'the camera adds five kilos and the audience only votes for thin girls' – but now she's happy in herself and has the perfect figure again.

Danny and I check out Meggie's drawing. It's a bird-of-paradise flower, with spiky petals sprouting like wings. 'You've got hidden talents, big sis.'

She laughs. 'I'm inspired by how beautiful the Beach is now, thanks to a certain Very Important Person.'

I blush. When I first arrived here, it was beautiful but barren. There were no exotic flowers springing up from the sand, no jewelled birds swooping across the blue sky, or diving towards the ocean where metallic fish ripple through the warm water.

Then I helped a desperate girl called Triti to escape, and the Beach became more bewitching for those left behind – almost like I'd unlocked a new level of experiences by doing the right thing.

And since then . . . I can't get used to the hushed tones the Guests on Soul Beach use when they talk about me. Especially not the way *Meggie* talks about me. When she was alive, she was the star: the prettier, smarter, more talented sister.

But now I'm the one who stands out. Everyone wants a Visitor, but I'm the only one anyone can remember. In my real life, I'm just sixteen. I can't even drive.

Here, I can change lives – and afterlives, too. Sure, the Beach seems like paradise, but there's no way out. Unless I can solve the mystery of a Guest's death, as I did with Triti. *Then* they can find peace. Or at least, disappear. No one knows where they go from here.

It's my sister's death that brought me here, of course. Her killer's still out there, and finding who murdered Meggie is my top priority. Even though if I do that, I'm terrified I might lose her for good, and the Beach too.

'You're the best, Alice Florence Forster. You know that?' Meggie says. 'Don't you dare leave me, right? Not ever?'

I smile at her, but I don't say anything, because I can't promise her that, and she knows I can't. Anything could happen.

Out in the bay, some Guests are wading out to neck height, catching fish. There's talk of barbecuing the catch later, when the sun's gone down. I'll probably leave, then, because the one thing I can't do here is taste. Sometimes I forget, and reach out for a slice of mango, or an ice-cold beer, and as I raise it to my lips, it tastes of nothing ...

Or worse. Of *ashes*, or reality. And that breaks the spell of the Beach, and brings me back to earth in my dingy bedroom, where I'm hunched over my laptop. And that starts the doubts off again: is soulbeach.org a hoax, or even some kind of mirage I've invented because I can't bear the thought of Meggie being dead?

But her hugs and Danny's kisses and even Javier's insults seem so much more real than homework, chores and bitter April gales.

'You daydreaming again?'

I blink. 'I told you, I'm not day—'

But then I realise I *must* have been, because something's changed. Meggie and Javier have disappeared, and the Guests are rushing towards the water's edge and in the far distance there's a single figure, the head only just above the waves.

The swimmer seems to be struggling, even though it's impossible to drown off Soul Beach. You can't die twice.

'It's someone new,' Danny says.

I turn towards him. 'A new Guest?'

He tries to smile. 'Must be. Poor bastard. This is how we all arrive, as a castaway. I still remember washing up here, coughing, blinking. None of it made sense. Where was I? Was I alive? Who were all these people?' He shivers, then stands up. 'Come on. You want to understand the Beach? Then you'd better see how it all begins.'

2

The walk towards the water's edge takes effort, our feet sinking into the hot, dry sand. Ahead of us, more Guests than I've ever seen appear from nowhere. A hundred, maybe more. The chatter gets louder, *shriller*.

'It's a guy.'

'Are you sure?'

'I can't see him. Is he cute?'

'Is that all you girls ever think about?' Javier's voice rises above the hubbub. 'The guy's just died. He's about to discover the so-called gift of eternal life. Show some humanity, please.'

It *is* a man, tripping and staggering as the waves sweep him ashore. He struggles to stay upright, arms held up, reaching out for something or someone to steady him.

My lungs won't work. I gasp for air but nothing comes. I feel his *terror*. His breathlessness. The sensation of Danny's hand gripping mine becomes more distant, and I'm floating above everyone and everything.

Is this what *dying* feels like?

'Alice. What's up?'

Danny's voice is so far away, soft above the uglier sound of Guests gossiping.

'Where do you think he's from? He has auburn hair. Quite Celtic looking.'

'Ugh, but he's too short. When are they going to send someone taller? Plus, he's a mess.'

'Be fair on the guy. I bet you didn't look so hot when you'd just died, did you?'

I lean against Danny. My vision is blurred, my breath short. 'I'm ... OK. But this feels so intrusive.'

No one else seems to care. I'm shivering. What's that phrase? It's like someone walking over my grave. Even though I'm the only one on the Beach who doesn't *have* a grave.

Danny nods towards the bar, which is deserted. 'Now could be a good time for a drink.'

I'm about to agree when something makes me stop. 'Where's my sister? We should find her first.'

I scan the faces, looking for Meggie. I hate the idea that she's alone in the crowd. In spite of the fierce sunshine and the azure sky, the Beach feels a dark, raw place right now.

Then I see her. She's almost at the water's edge, her long hair blowing in the breeze. I'm about to call out to her, beg her to stay away because it's bound to remind her of her own first hours on the Beach ...

But then I see *him* and I can't call out. Can't even breathe.

My eyes lock onto the shipwrecked man.

No.

Impossible.

It can't be.

But even as my mind fights it, my heart knows it *is* him. Red-gold curls, freckles, that bewildered expression. It's a face I haven't seen for eleven months, yet I could draw it from memory.

It's Tim.

The first – the only – boy my sister's ever fallen in love with.

And the chief suspect in her murder.